N

THE FAT MAN'S DAUGHTER

Copyright © 2005 by Caroline Petit

Published by
Soho Press, Inc.
853 Broadway
New York, N.Y. 10003

Library of Congress Cataloging in Publication Data

Petit, Caroline.
The fat man's daughter / Caroline Petit.
p. cm.
Includes bibliographical references.
ISBN 1-56947-387-0 (alk. paper)
1. Art, Chinese—Appreciation—Fiction.
2. Hong Kong (China)—Fiction. 3. Fathers—Death—Fiction.
4. Antique dealers—Fiction. 5. Smugglers—Fiction.
6. Orphans—Fiction. I. Title.

PR9619.4.P47F38 2005
813'.6—dc22
2004058932

10 9 8 7 6 5 4 3 2 1

CAROLINE PETIT

THE FAT MAN'S DAUGHTER

SOHO

FOR
MICHAEL

ACKNOWLEDGMENT

I AM GRATEFUL for the support and guidance of The Varuna Writers' Centre in Katoomba, New South Wales, Australia. Thank you.

A Sigh From a Staircase of Jade

Her jade-white staircase is cold with dew;
Her silk soles are wet, she lingered there so long. . . .
Behind her closed casement, why is she still waiting,
Watching through its crystal pane the glow of the autumn
    moon?

                            —Li Bai (701–762 A.D.)

I am all the daughters of my father's house,
And all the brothers too.

      —William Shakespeare, *Twelfth Night*, Act ii, Scene 4.

CONTENTS

PART I

HONG KONG,
AUTUMN 1937

1

REQUIEM
OF INSECTS

THEO KOLBE WANTED to teach his daughter Leah everything. Now he taught her death. Leah watched her father's head appear. His wisps of hair no longer concealed his bald patch. His dear face, sickly grey, was pockmarked with insect bites. She moaned softly.

The morgue attendant bobbed his head in acknowledgment of her dry anguish. "It was a squeeze to put him in. It would take three or four of your average Chinee to equal your father. I know, it's hard—"

"Don't," said Leah, flinching and turning away to hide her face.

He shut the drawer, and then led her back through the labyrinth of passages underneath the hospital. Occasionally he glanced sideways to reassure himself that she was following. She was so young, so pretty. He had liked the openness of her face. Even in her grief-shocked state, she had been able to look. He had seen grown men suddenly faint or throw up. Once, a well-dressed European woman had hit him repeatedly with her handbag and yelled at him, as if he had been to blame for her husband's heart attack at his Chinese mistress's house, and for the body having been dumped at the hospital with the trouser flies still undone. There was no call to attack *him;* he was as white as them and doing a job no Chinese would do. He had nearly quit over the incident. But he liked the work and had developed a good rapport with the dead. They asked for so little.

Leah ignored the attendant's glances. Pity, sympathy, she could do without. What she wanted was answers.

DR. Welbury Mitton, Public Health Surgeon, gawked at Leah as he tried to reconcile obese old Kolbe with this lovely slim young woman with grey eyes set wide in her face, an expressive mouth and blunt high cheekbones. She glowed with intensity and the need to know. For a moment, he considered simply handing her the report and watching as she read his medical notes. But that would be an act of cowardice—and, in all likelihood, she would not understand his scrawl or the clinical words.

He held up the report and kept his eyes on the page as he intoned, "Mr. Kolbe died of heat paroxysm caused by his corpulent body's inability to cool itself during a walk in the gardens of Victoria Heights." He rustled the dry papers as if to prove his point.

"No," said Leah. "My father never strolled in the heat of the day. He much preferred to take a rickshaw and see a skinny man sweat for them both."

She pictured Theo in his flapping suit, red-faced, his hair slick with oil. How could he have left her? Already the tentacles of an approaching migraine were reaching out. She shut her mouth and stared back at Mitton, trying to will the creeping pain away.

Annoyed, Mitton frowned, drawing his craggy eyebrows together. "I'm not going to record our conversation." He rushed on as he saw Leah open her mouth to protest. He waggled his head severely. "No point."

"Please, I—"

"No," he said more kindly. "Take it from me, it's better this way. You really don't want to go through the rigmarole of an autopsy. There's no need, spare yourself, spare your father." Her stare of outraged disbelief was so disconcerting that he felt compelled to add, "What if we did hold an inquest? How would that help? Hong Kong inquests are notoriously left open. It just muddies the waters. Those who are left behind are unhappier still, unable to get on with their lives. No, my girl, a man like your father, excessively overweight and living here as he did, well, anything could have killed him. Let him go with a little dignity."

He patted her shoulder. He believed it was always best to tell the truth. He had never dealt directly with Kolbe, but he had heard the rumours. His antiquities business just skated the edge of the law. Smarmy Theo had been an awful man: a liar, a cheat, and, probably, a thief. Besides, he was American. He didn't belong in Hong Kong. How the hell had he produced such a beautiful daughter? It had to be chalked up to the vagaries of genetics and evolution. But the girl would have to face facts. Kolbe was dead, and no one was much interested in why.

"I wish you all the best, my dear. My office will release the body later this afternoon. You'll need to make arrangements."

Dr. Mitton rose and bowed from the waist.

Leah nodded curtly, then walked out of the office, her head pounding with indignation and disgust.

Mitton's door closed with a firm click. In a little while his clerk would bring him his afternoon tea.

EYES shut, Leah sprawled in a steamer chair in the hot garden as she recounted in a monotone to her old amah, An-li, what Mitton had said. The afternoon's events already seemed far away, hazy. She wished they had happened to someone else.

An-li nodded. "You must arrange the funeral."

Leah didn't respond, focused on the rill of sweat that had formed between her breasts in the thick heat that pinned her to the chair. A mosquito landed on her bare leg. As An-li raised her hand to shoo it away, the mosquito bit. Leah gave a heavy resounding slap, glad to be feeling something.

"Please, Leah, the funeral. Think about it."

"I can't, An-li. I know I must, but I can't. You do it," said Leah, opening her eyes to look at the small neat figure in her silk long-sleeved white tunic, black trousers, and soft slippers. An-li seemed smudged around the edges, greying and disconcertedly frail. When had she grown so old? Leah closed her eyes.

Helpless in front of Leah's shuttered mourning, An-li said, "Very well, if that's what you want."

Leah heard An-li's quick shuffle over the dry grass and the opening and shutting of the conservatory door.

The last of the late afternoon heat built up. More insects swooped. Leah savoured their stings, rubbed at the bites. She longed for the bugs to mark her body like the sacred scarring of African women she had seen in magazines. She considered smearing her body with honey to attract more insects. Behind her eyelids she saw clouds of flies, swarming and buzzing over Theo's body abandoned in the gardens of Victoria Heights: a requiem of insects.

What were the last words they had spoken that morning as he had reached for his Panama hat, a lifetime ago? Theo had smiled that secret knowing smile of his and winked. She had said "Tell me," and he had shaken his head. Then she'd said "Be careful," and he had blown her a kiss and said "I can take care of myself." Now he was gone.

Leah shivered in the heat and opened her eyes to the garden with its covered walkways, its pond and artfully placed stones and willow trees. Already the Victoria Peak house appeared to be grieving. The house was massive. Originally designed to imitate an English country house, Theo had transformed it over twenty years into a Chinese scholar's paradise: the conservatory's sash windows had become moon windows to frame his oriental garden, gates had been built out the front to ward off ghosts, and the roof line had been altered to curve upward to show vitality of spirit. Inside, the house groaned with hand-carved rosewood furniture, ancient scrolls of exquisite calligraphy, and priceless antiques. From its perch high in the misty green hills of the Peak, the mansion peered down onto Hong Kong Harbour as if boasting that here lived money to which due respect must be paid.

Even as a child, she had felt the house contract when empty of Theo's fat reassuring presence. In her dreams, she had sensed when Theo wasn't home, was perhaps with Mr. Everston and his pretty assortment of *singsong* girls at a grownup party. She would wake with a start to stare into the dark. Missing him, she would have to get out of bed and touch five things she liked, starting with her baby jade and her blue hair ribbons and ending in her wardrobe with her favourite silk-embroidered party dress. Often these familiar things soothed her, though once she had felt compelled to take the party dress into her bed. In the morning, An-li had scolded her for scrunching it into a ball.

The touching hadn't always worked. The dark might still hold Chinese ghosts, wanting to snatch her away. To escape them, she would run down the hall to An-li's room. There, she'd creep to An-li's low bed, fit herself into the tiny remaining space and place her hand lightly on An-li's worn nightshift. Usually, An-li slept on, while Leah had sniffed her fresh-laundered scents and wrinkled her nose at the astringent witch hazel An-li used to clean and whiten her skin. Asleep, Leah had sometimes dreamed that An-li kissed her.

Another insect bit, hard and vicious. Fat tears wet Leah's cheeks.

LEAH felt An-li's hand on her shoulder, shaking her awake in the soft dusk. On the table was a tray with cups, an iron teapot containing, no doubt, a concoction of herbs and teas meant to soothe and heal, and piles of gold paper and silver papers.

"The funeral, it's arranged—the European way. The funeral people are putting a notice in *The South China Post*. The reception will be in the conservatory. They told me it's what people do," said An-li, not bothering to mention the hour-long telephone conversation she'd had with the rude Englishman. He'd said, "Are you certain you are able to speak for the family? It's most unusual." Then he'd quoted her an outrageous amount of money for the casket. Theo would need a very large coffin. When An-li agreed, he became nicer and explained the finer points of Occidental funerals.

An-li poured the tea and said, "It's not enough. Mr. Theo won't like it. We must do it the Chinese way, too." She studied Leah's face, expecting her to object, but Leah had retreated to some mournful place and was barely listening. "Leah," she said sharply, "Wasn't I like First Mother to you?"

Leah nodded mutely and sipped her tea.

"You can't become your father's ghost. You must put his spirit to rest. At nineteen, you have your own life to live."

The tea warmed Leah. The aroma was strangely spicy, prickly. She set the empty cup down. Her fingers played with the rattan of the chair. Nuggetty pieces came off in her bite-ridden hand, round o's. O is for orphan. She sounded the word slowly aloud: "Or-phan." In the same thin, childlike voice, she continued, "I was so little. I used to think my mother had disappeared behind Theo or retreated to some cool corner of the house instead of dying, and now—"

"Enough. Too much grief and his soul won't leave. You have to provide for his journey."

Had they ever discussed death, or what might come next? Yes, they had watched Chinese families burning joss sticks at their ancestors' graves, witnessed funeral processions with their hired Chinese bands sometimes playing catchy Western songs like *Sunshine,* or marching tunes. But she was pretty sure Theo had not wasted a minute of his time thinking about the afterlife. He was too much of a pragmatist. Sweet Theo was only interested in the relics of death: century-old funeral urns, long-buried terracotta warriors entombed by dead emperors, and immortal jade pieces that had been used to seal the body's orifices and keep it pure.

"Theo—" she began, then corrected herself, "My father had no beliefs. He devoted his life to antiquities and me."

She would miss his touch. He took great pride in his hands. His fingers were long and tapered, remarkable in such a fat man. Vain about his hands, he had weekly manicures. The pads of his fingers were soft and pink. He loved caressing beautiful things. Often, instead of a kiss goodnight, he traced his fingers over the planes of her face, the prominent bones of her cheeks, her broad mouth. It was such a loving gesture. "Touch," he said, "it never lets you down; it reveals perfections and imperfections, everything."

An-li believed her employer's ruthless pursuit of the next beautiful thing had caused his death. If he had his things with him, he might depart and leave Leah in peace. To Leah, she said, "He loved China. Let him have one small Chinese cere-mony. Let him take his treasures, to help him on his travels. I brought the paper." She held up the gold and the silver sheets. They fluttered in the wind.

Leah had a sudden vision of a ghostly Theo, a jade figurine clutched precariously against his mountain of a belly. She creased the paper and made a fold, transforming one sheet into an ingot, another into a crude vase. When these replicas were burnt, he could take them with him on his final journey. She was glad Theo would not be going empty-handed.

An-li left the garden, returning with a terracotta pot. She blew on each offering, then dropped it in. Leah stood, straightening her sundress, but didn't bother with her discarded sandals. She had read somewhere that to be barefoot was a penance.

An-li hoisted the pot over her head. Leah followed behind, her feet cool on the smooth tiles. The procession ended in Theo's study. An-li placed the pot in front of Leah. They knelt on the floor. An-li pulled out a box of kitchen matches. Leah struck a match, hesitated as the flame grew, then in one swift motion set the gold and the silver objects on fire. They erupted into blue flame, burnt rapidly into curling ash. Smoke rose and circled round the room. An-li opened the louvres. The smoke eddied out into the night.

Leah tried to recall the last thing she had said to Theo. Was it "Be careful," or had she been the one to say, after all, "I can take care of myself"?

2

THE STRANGER
AT THE FUNERAL

THE CONSERVATORY WAS noisy and hot. The
servants had carried the rosewood table in from the
dining room and heaped it with cold meats, salad, and
Chinese delicacies. The salad was wilting in the heat. Chinese
businessmen and a small contingent of their gold-adorned wives
devoured the shark-fin soup and an assortment of dim sum. Five
black-gowned mandarins clumped together to murmur softly
about Theo's vast knowledge of everything Chinese.

Horace Cuthbert, thin-faced, with an ingrained alcoholic
flush, stared at Leah as she returned the mandarins' compliments in fluent Cantonese. He shook his head and said to his
wife, "No good will come to that girl. You can't trust them
once they speak the lingo. It affects their brains, makes them
go soft in the head."

Cuthbert's wife half-nodded and added, "Like father, like daughter." She had forced her husband and her daughter, Hope, to attend. Mrs. Cuthbert waved in Hope's direction. Hope continued talking gaily to a group of young people, ignoring her mother's jaunty gesture.

"I was so afraid no one would turn up to mourn the old devil. It's at times like this that the Colony must rally round." She cast a disapproving eye at the mixed bag of people who filled the room. There was that awful White Russian woman, Sonia Rubstov, a female Rasputin, who wore the most revealing dresses despite her age; a pot-bellied Chinese man whom she was certain was the same person whose picture she had seen in the newspaper, indicted for swindling poor refugees; and several Chinese women (tarts to her way of thinking) who were certainly not married to the sleazy European men who had brought them. Mrs. Cuthbert plucked at her husband's arm. They had stayed a decent amount of time.

Leah bowed her head to let Mrs. Cuthbert give her a perfunctory kiss on her cheek before they left. Hope mumbled her condolences. Leah was pleased to see that Hope was going to turn into the same sort of horse-faced woman as her mother. She hadn't seen Hope since they had been at school together, was glad Hope and her parents were leaving early. She always felt that Mrs. Cuthbert, in particular, was grading her. Leah doubted she had passed. Still, it was kind of them to be here today.

"Hope," said Leah, "thank you for coming. It's been so long."

"Yes," said Hope, annoyed that she had done the right thing and worn black, despite the way black made her complexion sallow, while Leah, dressed in demure white, the Chinese colour for mourning, looked luminous in her grief. "We must get together after this. . . ." Hope fluttered her hands as if the funeral gathering was an unimportant party.

They shook hands. Hope looked away first and followed in the wake of her parents, who were already bustling down the hall.

Leah resumed acting the gracious hostess, accepting bland condolences and patiently listening to little reminiscences. Only Sonia Rubstov, the one old family friend, her mother's confidante, seemed deeply affected.

With tears in her eyes, Sonia hugged Leah to her scrawny chest, bracelets jangling. "I'll miss him so."

Leah nodded and squeezed Sonia's ring-laden hands. Without meaning to, Sonia's gaze gravitated to the buffet. She couldn't help it. Food was a reassuring presence in her life, even if she only ever nibbled at it, part of her Russian-refugee legacy that Leah knew from Sonia's storytelling. The stories all revolved around a beautiful young countess forced to flee her Russian homeland, leaving behind a glittering life, to starve on the plains of China. Dryly, Theo would say "Please, Sonia, a little less drama," and Sonia would snap "Theo, you don't know the half of it," and look soulful.

"Please do eat, Sonia," said Leah, leading Sonia to the food. Sonia heaped her plate.

Leah drifted to a quiet corner, away from the chattering gloved and hatted wives of the Colonial public servants. Snatches of conversation reached her: "Tom's tennis is improving." "Do join us for a swim and a moonlight picnic at Deep Water Bay. It will be such fun." "We let the houseboy go.

He was so unhygienic. He used his own toothbrush to clean the silver. It's an uphill battle to make them understand the need to wash their hands." There was a loud peal of laughter from a rotund little woman in a fussy hat.

Leah turned to gaze out the moon window to the calming garden. She wished she were alone in her steamer chair, the reception over. When she turned around, a Chinese man in a Western suit stood before her. He was tall for a Chinese, had a thin face, a precise nose, and a good haircut. He held out his hand.

In English, he said, "I extend to you all my sorrows, Miss Kolbe."

She shook his hand and was struck by how callused and rough it was for a man in such a well-cut suit. "Thank you," she said with genuine warmth.

"It's a pleasure to meet Mr. Kolbe's much-admired daughter. Mr. Kolbe was an astute judge of Oriental antiquities and people."

His voice was harsh, at odds with his generous words. His gaze was disconcertingly direct. His eyes had almost no pupils. Leah didn't think he was a client or a middleman: his approach was too plainspoken. Why had Theo never mentioned this man? A flash of resentment coursed through her. Theo and his secrets.

The man continued: "Now is not the time, but later I would like to discuss a matter of business. Shall we say six o'clock Thursday, here?" He bowed his head and gave a sad smile.

His eyes remained hard pinpricks of blackness. His clove breath was strong. "Mr. —?" she asked.

Before he could reply, Theo's lawyer and friend, Richard

Everston, tapped Leah on the back. Leah wheeled around with a start. Everston looked terrible. His eyes were red-rimmed and his skin, a faded pale white, resembled a suit of clothes that had gone baggy at the knees, as if it belonged to someone else. Everston gave a loud bronchial cough.

Over Everston's shoulder, Leah caught sight of the tall Chinese man gliding in between the disparate groups of people dawdling in conversations. No one waved or nodded to him, though Leah was almost certain Sonia had recognised him: she had stopped chewing.

"I am so sorry. I had no idea. It beggars belief," said Everston.

Leah didn't know if Everston meant he had only just heard about Theo's death, or if he referred to the manner of his death. It was odd, though. Everston was a precise man when it came to words. Theo had a high regard for his canny talents.

"It was shock to everyone," she said.

Everston looked as if he might cry.

3

SECRETS
AND LIES

LEAH STOOD AT the door of Theo's study. She had put off sorting his things, but she felt his reproach whenever she passed by the closed door. She inhaled deeply, trying to detect if Theo's smell lingered in the room. No, there was no hint of his cigar or the sweet French cologne mixed with his sour sweat.

She walked to his desk. When she was small, she would do a little tap-dance across the parquet floor. Theo would stand and applaud, his loud claps resounding through the room. Then, as he levered himself back down, she would hear the chair groan and cry. Sometimes she felt sorry for the chair and petted it when Theo was away. Now she ran her hand over the chair's cracked brown leather seat. There was a deep sag in the middle and the stuffing had grown lumpy from use. Rubbing her cheek along the worn blackwood surface of his desk, she traced her finger over the scratch marks made by his pen. She wished she had kept every scribbled note, made a collection of his disused pen nibs and recorded the exact timbre of his throaty voice on the telephone. He wasn't a *funny* fat man. He was imposing and had such a vast compendium of knowledge that she feared she could never catch up.

As a child, perched on his knee, she watched and learned. Skinny Chinese farmers brought him relics discovered when their hoes hit forgotten burial chambers. Theo heaped praise on them: what cunning, what foresight they had. He kept their secrets, he had waiting buyers for their rich finds. He asked no questions of the businessmen who presented him with an endless supply of someone else's heirlooms. She could tell how valuable and rare a piece was by how Theo's hands tightened around her waist. Sometimes he squeezed until she was dizzy and light-headed, while he lied about imperfections in the glaze or declared the porcelain cup was from a much later T'ang period, which naturally affected the price he was willing to pay. Discreet mistresses offered their former lover's valuable trinkets in return for cash. Everything had a price; everything could be bought and sold.

He had bought her the best education. She recalled her last prize day at school. Theo had entered late, as Miss Kemp, the headmistress, was giving the closing speech. Manoeuvring down the middle aisle, he had stood alone, a Colossus of Rhodes bridging the gap until scowling Mr. Crawford appeared holding a chair aloft, wading through the polite parents to place it in the vacant space. Miss Kemp glared at him. Theo waved his fingers as if delighted by the recognition. Miss

Kemp fumbled, had to restart her sentence. At the end of her speech, Theo billowed to the bottom of the steps of the stage and pumped Miss Kemp's hand. He called out in his booming American voice, "Well worth the fees, well worth the fees." Miss Kemp smiled weakly and tried to extract her aching fingers from his grasp.

Hope Cuthbert had dug her elbow into Leah's side and rolled her eyes. Incensed, Leah turned to Hope and said, "Don't be naïve. The school's reputation wouldn't be half as good if it were cheap." Her own reputation was bad. Her teachers disliked and mistrusted her because she spoke Cantonese, which they regarded as beneath them.

Now at her father's desk, she fiddled with the gilt-framed picture of Theo at about fourteen. It was the only family memento he had possessed. Once she had prised the frame off and seen, on the back of the photograph, the stamped signature "Kalinsky's Photographic Studio, New York City." She had never been able to piece together how exactly he had ended up in Hong Kong.

Leah stared into Theo's hooded adolescent eyes. He stood alone in the photographer's studio against a dark curtain, his feet planted wide apart, his hands clasped behind his back. He wore a tight-fitting suit with a restrictive white starched collar. His expression was difficult to decipher. Bravado, perhaps. The large boy pretending to be a big man.

Theo had always pushed her to do more. He wasn't interested in failure, hated mediocrity. Every year she'd won the school prize, which had dwindled under Miss Kemp's resigned gaze to a dreary uplifting book. The last had been a slim volume of minor Victorian poetry, venerating a long-dead English

past and winter days. When Theo took her to dinner to cele-
brate her release from school forever, he read the inscription.
"It's the same," he said, "always the same."

"Yes," she had said, "I expect when I die, my tombstone will
read 'In recognition of your achievements.' Only Miss Kemp
won't be there to sign it."

Theo had laughed and watched amused as Leah spent the
time between dinner courses tearing up the pages of the book.
His lessons had been much more important than Miss Kemp's.

Leah had learnt early that polite Colonial society was built
on what you didn't say. People pretended they had come to
Hong Kong for noble reasons, but Theo knew better. He'd
told her, "It's one of the last places on earth where the white
man does almost nothing and lets the Chinese middle men—
those wily compradors—do all the real work while the for-
eigners drink gin at the club and make money, lots of money."
He was good at that, seeing through pretension.

Living with Theo was an education in itself. Together they
had collected the rarest and finest Chinese art: the carved ivory
scroll-shaped armrest with its rising-sun motif; the rhinoceros-
horn cup incised with dragons; the silver kettle with an
engraved horse drinking from a cup; the late-tenth-century
porcelain ewer; the fourteenth-century copy of the masterly
Song Dynasty hand scrolls, and horses with the perfect *sancai*
glaze, the vivid green, brown, and yellow colours created by
adding copper oxide and iron to the glaze base.

He had schooled her relentlessly at the rosewood dining
table. It began with a red inkstick on her twelfth birthday. He
recounted how Li T'ing-kui of the Southern T'ang dynasty
made his inksticks from one bushel of gold paste, three ounces

of pearls, and an ounce of jade clippings stirred ten thousand times.

"Even now these scripts can be read. The writing is clear and hard as if just completed," he said, holding up a deep red inkstick incised with the words "red jade" in Chinese characters. He let her touch it, weigh it in her hand. It was truly a wondrous thing.

"Sell it to me," he said.

He pushed back his chair from the table, crossed his hands over his belly and waited. The silence grew. His eyes narrowed to slits, his breathing was heavier.

No words came to her. Her stomach growled. This was her birthday. It wasn't fair.

He drummed his fingers on the table. "Now. Remember, business first."

She spoke of the importance of words and writers to the Chinese. His drumming had stopped, but he still frowned and looked sullen. She stumbled and mixed up her words. What did he want? Ah, the negotiations to begin. Triumphant now, she said, "It's priceless."

His hand slammed the table. The rice bowls trembled. Her chopsticks clattered to the floor.

"Everything has a price. Again."

"There was once a Chinese prince," she said. "He had three grades of brushes, distinguished by their stems, to reward writers who gave him pleasure. The mottled bamboo was for the most capable writers, the silver to reward virtuous conduct, and lastly gold for the loyal and filial." She looked hard at him, "Which one are you, Theo?" It was the first time she had dared called him Theo. She trembled when she finished.

He clapped his hands, "Bravo. Now the buyer must set a price that won't embarrass himself in your eyes. We are partners now. So you may call me Theo."

As a reward, she was allowed to eat her birthday cake first. Halfway through dinner she threw up. An-li barged in and scolded Theo for making his daughter sick, teaching her bad things. Theo ignored her.

When Leah left school, she had expected to be a full partner in Theo's antiquities trade. Theo had different ideas. There were so many intricate twists to his business. Things were to go on much as they had. She must still watch and learn. She had offered to act as his secretary, take over his correspondence, do the accounts. At the word accounts, his face had paled. He kept his accounts in his head. It was safer that way. As to correspondence, Theo always wanted to know what was happening first. He'd snatch the post out of her hand, read the names and addresses, and tear at the envelopes from important clients—wealthy Europeans and Americans seeking to extend their collections, or new museums on the lookout for artefacts or paintings that would make scholars take them seriously. Exasperated, she argued that he should let her take over newly wealthy Chinese clients desperate to put their peasant past behind them.

"But, Leah," he wheedled, "they are often our best sources. They know whose business is thriving or going under. I need this intelligence."

She found herself relegated to a decorative role, a meeter and greeter, another ornament in Theo's collection. True, he usually asked her opinion, invited her to sit in on most of his meetings, but occasionally he was distant and cagey. He would fob her off with the caution that these negotiations were "delicate," meet his contacts in places he did not want her to go. Now there was no choice; she would have to carry on the business on her own. That would be her future. What else could she do?

Her hands itched to dig through his correspondence, to understand exactly where the business stood financially, to discover what treasured antiques and artefacts he had been pursuing. She opened his desk drawer and pulled out a pile of manila folders stuffed with yellow foolscap notepaper. It was a shock to see his thick, bold writing again.

A disapproving An-li appeared at the study door. Behind her was the stranger from the funeral.

"He said he had an appointment," said An-li.

The tall Chinese man bowed to An-li and walked around her to stand in front of the desk.

"Oh," said Leah, "I forgot."

"Time," he said, "takes on a different dimension when one is grieving."

"Yes," said Leah as An-li shut the door and left. Leah was certain An-li was listening on the other side.

The man pulled out a cigarette case and offered it to her. She shook her head, and studied him as he lit a cigarette with a gold lighter. The scent of cloves filled the air. He wore round spectacles now. They made him look slightly bookish, like a mature-aged student.

She smiled and said, "Please sit down. I'm at a disadvantage. I don't know your name."

"I am Mr. Chang."

"Well, Mr. Chang, you knew my father?"

She had expected flowery pleasantries, an exchange of compliments. What she got was: "What do you know about China, Miss Kolbe?" She cast around for an impressive response. She settled for saying, in Cantonese, "I know a great deal, but I am always learning." Then she bowed her head, looking up at him modestly through the fawn fringe of her bobbed hair.

Behind his glasses, his eyelids twitched in acknowledgment. He switched to Cantonese and spoke in low tones full of feeling. "China can be a great power again. We are one country. Manchuria is part of China. It will never be Manchukuo." His voice tightened. He glared at her as if she was threatening to come to Japan's defence. "'Manchukuo' is an abomination supported by the West."

How to respond? That the West had nothing to do with it? It was all the fault of the Japanese? Japan had tricked the world. By stealth they had wormed their way into every facet of Manchurian life. Then had come the Mukden incident. According to the Japanese, they had bravely and courageously fought the marauding Chinese army in retaliation for blowing up a Japanese goods train. Only the heavy Japanese train had defied gravity to hurdle over the 31-inch gap left by the explosion and return to Mukden station unscathed. Or, if there had been an explosion, it happened after the train was safely back at the station—there were eyewitnesses who swore to it. As to the bitter fighting, the Japanese army attacked a Chinese barracks. Hundreds of Chinese soldiers died, but only two Japanese soldiers were killed in the "battle." Everything had been stage-managed by the Japanese to gain a foothold in China. In the interest of order, peace, and protection, the Japanese proclaimed Manchuria was now theirs, renaming it Manchukuo.

The Chinese had appealed to the League of Nations. Two years of investigations, claims, and counterclaims. A thick report was published. No one believed the Japanese. The newspapers wrote boring articles about the commission's findings.

Lowering the paper at the breakfast table, Theo had winked and dismissed the uproar. "The Japs are no different from the Europeans. They all want a cut of China. We all want what we know we shouldn't have," and he had smiled a conspirator's smile. She had smiled back.

To Mr. Chang she said, "Manchukuo is a rogue state."

He continued, "A puppet state with a puppet emperor, Pu Yi."

"Yes," said Leah, recalling the newspaper photographs she had seen of Pu Yi, the last emperor of China, the boy-king who had abdicated in 1912, only to become a hapless, gullible playboy who had been enticed by the Japanese to sit on Manchukuo's throne. "Though I always thought he looked like a praying mantis."

Mr. Chang looked blank.

"The stick insect that camouflages itself to look like a green leaf or a twig."

Leah had used the same words to Theo, that Pu Yi looked like a bug. Theo had laughed, but said, "Don't underestimate him. He is dangerous because he is stupid."

Mr. Chang was not stupid. He had not come to discuss politics. He said, "There is a job that needs doing in Manchuria. We think you can do it."

"Oh, yes," she replied, noncommittal.

"Don't be modest. We are aware of your education, your ability to speak Cantonese and Mandarin. But," he leaned forward over the desk and gazed into her face, "what most appeals is your youth and beauty. Those stumpy dwarf men will not suspect that someone like you would work for someone like me." His eyes, magnified behind his glasses, were cold and penetrating. She tried not to blink.

"Pu Yi has stolen many jewels and treasures from us. They are our heritage." He gave a thin smile, took one last puff of his clove cigarette and stubbed it out. Its scent hung in the air.

Trying to keep her voice even, Leah said, "I am not a thief. My father and I ran a respectable antiquities business." Why hadn't Theo told her about Mr. Chang? If she knew what was going on, she'd be able to play his game better. She attempted to return his hard smile. "I intend to take over my father's business," she said.

"Your father was an admirable businessman. We hope his daughter will be too. We want you to go to Manchuria's new capital, Hsingking. Pu Yi is a fool for the study of ants. It is his one interest. We have arranged for British experts to ask to study insects in Manchukuo. Your job will be to arrange for this, ah, study tour. Set up accommodation, laboratories, or whatever these professors want. And, more importantly, make contact with Chief Eunuch Quan under the nose of Pu Yi. Quan has agreed to help us. For you, it will be a *very profitable* arrangement."

He rose and started to inspect Theo's collection. He stopped before the exquisite owl-shaped *tsun*, a cast-bronze wine vessel. Its bird head formed a removable lid. On its chest were intricate carvings: a cicada insect head combined with two small dragons, and the fine *lei-wen* thunder pattern had been incised on its wings. Theo had been beside himself with joy and self-congratulation when he acquired it. He had hired a photographer to take pictures of it against black velvet to show off his find. Academics scoffed "It's not ancient," but Theo had proved them wrong when a similar owl was unearthed in the tomb of Lady Hao. Beyond a doubt, twelfth century B.C., the Shang Dynasty. When the British Museum wanted to buy it, he refused, saying, "The impression it makes on private collectors makes it twice as precious." Really, Theo simply couldn't bear to part with it.

She had to think. She had no intention of accepting Chang's terrible offer and wasn't even sure how much of his story she believed. Go to Manchuria? The job would be time-consuming and dangerous. Meanwhile her business would suffer. But it was not possible to refuse his offer pointblank. Such discourtesy would be unforgiveable.

Leah said, "There is my father's estate to settle." She held up the bulging manila folders. "And the business to re-establish. I would like to help, but . . ." She gave him her most appealing smile as he wheeled around with the *tsun* in his hands. She bit her lip to stop crying out "Don't touch, the oil from your fingers will damage it."

"Have you heard about the new antiquities board in Peking? It is very concerned about so many valuable antiques leaving the country. We Chinese are very attached to our history. The Hong Kong Government has pledged its help to stop such trafficking. People will gossip over who has what artefacts and their worth. All lies, of course, Miss Kolbe." He gently put the *tsun* down.

"I can't leave Hong Kong at this time. I am not the right person for this commission. I am so sorry."

He nodded gravely. "We'll talk again. I'll see myself out."

He bowed to her and opened the door. An-li was rearranging a scroll on the wall next to it. He followed her up the hall.

Leah laid her head on the desk. Later, when she raised it again, she saw Chang's greasy thumbprint on the *tsun's* wing.

4

PAPER
TRANSACTIONS

LEAH WOUND HER way through the busy streets of the Central District, down Pottinger Street with its endless stairs and stalls. A cobbler hunkered down on a step, industriously mending a child's shoe while the mother screamed at the child to be still. The cobbler's wife had spread out a sheet, upon which were displayed a vast assortment of embroidered shoes. She tried to interest Leah in a pair of ridiculously small slippers. "Good for dancing," the old woman cackled. Leah shook her head.

Today the harbour sparkled in the sun, and the faint smell of sewage and salt was barely detectable. The port was jammed. Sampans cut risky paths between the larger junks and the big ships. With Theo's sweaty hand in hers, she had often wondered if she could hopscotch from one sampan to another until she was so far out that she could look up to Victoria Peak and see her house gazing down on her kingdom.

She passed the newly erected Hong Kong and Shanghai Bank headquarters that now dominated the waterfront. Its two halves bore down to squeeze and dwarf the once-imposing statue of Queen Victoria. It was such a grand architectural gesture, as if the bankers were declaring that they knew who held the power in Hong Kong and were thumbing their noses at the queen.

The office of Everston, Hallawick & Deebs, Solicitors (Offices in Hong Kong and Bombay), was discreetly tucked into a nearby building. She wished old Mr. Everston was handling Theo's will. He had understood Theo and Hong Kong. Everston liked *singsong* girls, the younger the better, but he was always the gentleman when he came on business. Both men would retreat to Theo's study. Passing by, she would smell their good cigars and hear their complicit laughter. Sometimes Everston had attended Theo's very private cocktail parties and brought with him one of his charming young ladies. Then he was avuncular, exchanging witty insights with Leah about Hong Kong society, while his pretty companion nodded her head.

An anonymous clerk had left word with An-li that Everston had taken a turn for the worse after Theo's funeral. It was rumoured that he was dying of pneumonia. However, Jonathan Hawatyne, the bright son of an old friend from England, had been hired to take over his partnership. When Miss Kolbe was ready, she should make an appointment to see Mr. Hawatyne about Mr. Kolbe's will.

She was ready.

Leah entered the lawyers' rooms. In Cantonese, she said to the clerk behind a high desk, "Please, I'd like to see Mr. Hawatyne. I'm Miss Kolbe."

The Chinese clerk sat stunned for a moment. He forgot to ask if she had an appointment as he hopped off his stool and hurried down the hall. She heard returning footsteps, turned and looked into a young Englishman's pink, smooth face and suppressed a stare of doubt. Hawatyne was a male ingénue. She pictured him in tennis whites, jumping over the net and saying "Good show," while pushing his fair hair off his forehead. Could she take him seriously? Theo would have relished the irony, his conspiratorial existence and complicated affairs to be pored over and resolved by this choirboy.

Hawatyne's abrupt, formal bow was unexpected. She was struck by his unease.

"Miss Kolbe, I am so pleased to meet you." He cleared his throat. "Though an appointment might have given us more time. I have a luncheon engagement."

His flush had receded, and now he seemed hesitant. She smiled sweetly and said, "The Chinese have a saying, *A chance meeting is a greater pleasure than one by formal invitation.* Here one forgets English customs."

Hawatyne said, too loudly, "Please, follow me."

He led her down the passageway to his office. For Hong Kong, the day was cool, relatively dry; still his room was stuffy. She made no comment about the weather, but it was obvious he was unaccustomed to the heat. He tugged at his jacket as if he wanted to remove it.

She sat in the visitor's chair, comfortable in her lemon silk dress, and was struck by his inability to begin the proceedings.

He smiled as if expecting her to break the ice, to commence the meeting.

In the silence, she studied his public-school face and his desk stacked with files, his desk set, a pen and crystal pot of ink, placed square in the middle of the leather blotter. Finally, Hawatyne picked up a sheaf of papers and ruffled through them, as if trying to locate a document.

His glance reluctantly returned to her face. He hadn't been expecting such a face. He had imagined a podgy woman with little piggy eyes who would be nasty, but resigned, when he told her. He should not have been thrown in at the deep end like this. He would figure as the villain of the piece forever, and none of it had been his doing.

"Mr. Hawatyne, you have your desk in the wrong position," she said.

Beads of perspiration broke out on his clear forehead. He smiled. "I get the morning light behind me as I read. I like it."

"Bad feng shui, Mr. Hawatyne."

"You can't *believe* that mumbo-jumbo."

"Perhaps not," she said, crossing her slim ankles, convent-style, against the legs of the chair. "But the Chinese do."

A token nod and a dry clearing of his throat replaced his frown. He played for time as he mouthed stilted phrases of condolence.

She looked at him stony-eyed. He hadn't known Theo.

He picked up the folder again and flicked the edges of the thick wad of papers with his thumb. It was an insistent sound. "Miss Kolbe, there have been some developments in regard to Mr. Kolbe's last will and testament. . . Mr. Everston, as you know, was Mr. Kolbe's solicitor and adviser. Mr. Everston arranged certain transactions for Mr. Kolbe, offshore. They agreed that the assets would be placed in a holding company. For reasons I am still trying to determine—"

He stopped. When he had pored over Everston's handwritten notes, they had been indecipherable, full of obscure references. But scattered throughout Everston's incomprehensible notes were block letters stating "Mr. Kolbe agrees." He had also found a scrawled power of attorney, with what Jonathan assumed, and fervently prayed, was Kolbe's true and accurate signature. The power of attorney allowed Everston to manipulate the holding company.

Everston had borrowed heavily against the assets of the company. The loans had been for very short terms, at high interest rates. When Kolbe died, the Portuguese bank—not the Macau branch—had called in the loans. The bank had taken the cash assets, over £60,000, to repay the outstanding loan balances.

Jonathan had gone to see the Macau bank manager, who was apologetic but said the matter was out of his hands. Then Jonathan cabled the Portuguese bank, seeking the holding company's records and assets. The Lisbon director, in a very correct reply, had said the matter was confidential. Legally, they could only deal with the signatory, Mr. Everston. Everston, damn him, was delirious and dying, and his wife, on doctor's orders, forbade visitors.

Jonathan wet his lips and stood to demonstrate he was in charge. Slowly and painfully, he explained most of what he had found out, smoothing over the questionable nature of the transactions in the telling, concentrating on the holding company, the legalities of loan instruments.

Leah listened, hearing the words, trying to make connections. She knew nothing about a holding company. Theo hadn't believed in financial instruments. He had kept well away from banks. The idea of other people, bloodsuckers, using his money infuriated him. "What are you trying to tell me, Mr. Hawatyne?" she finally asked.

"Mr. Kolbe's estate no longer contains any liquid assets. The money is gone."

She clasped her hands together and said, "Let me see this power of attorney."

He riffled through the papers and handed it over.

She studied Theo's signature, held it up to the light. She wasn't sure, but then neither was Hawatyne. "It's not his handwriting," she asserted.

He offered a small ingratiating smile and ran his hand over his cheek as if, by rubbing it, the right words would magically appear. Slowly and deliberately, he replied, "I think Mr. Kolbe's signature would hold up in court."

Leah saw the smoky plume of Theo's gold and silver funeral offerings dissolving into the ether.

Hawatyne changed his tone. He said, "The good news is that the house on Victoria Peak and its contents are yours. There aren't any liens on it."

The cheek, the gall. First they rob you, then they congratulate you for keeping what was yours in the first place. She reached for Theo's file and threw Everston's self-serving scrawled papers at Hawatyne's head. "How am I to live? I'll sue the lot of you."

He let the papers rain down on him. He deserved it. She was right. Everston was a scoundrel, but he couldn't say so. It would mean his job, his career. He'd go back to London with his tail between his legs, the only Englishman ever not to make money in the Orient. People would point at him in the street. Anyway, it wouldn't do her any good to sue in the Colony. Everyone would rush to Everston's defence.

She stood, seething.

Dryly he said, "I don't think you want to take this matter to court. You would lose."

Behind her anger, she knew Hawatyne was right. Theo had been tolerated in the Colony, but he hadn't had social standing. They thought him a slippery character, made snide comments behind his back. Yet now it seemed that it had been Everston, with his plummy tones and right connections, who was the outright swindler. "I hope Everston dies slowly. Maybe I'll get his latest *singsong* girl to send his wife a sympathy note. Or maybe one of them will turn up with a bastard baby in tow. It would be very touching."

He could see she was capable of that and probably more. She would be deadly in the witness box, pleading poverty, an innocent orphan, done over by a corrupt bank and a crooked lawyer. "Please," he said, "I am truly sorry about your predicament. It must be awful to deal with this while you're still grieving." He looked at Leah. She was calmer. He took it as a good sign that she sat down again. He wished they hadn't met like this. He collected the strewn papers.

She didn't offer to help. It was such a lawyer's apology, careful, deliberate, essentially meaningless. Hidden behind an enormous fern, she spotted an earthenware court lady—once a gift from Theo to Everston, she guessed. Its back was toward her, but she appreciated its charm and gracefulness. This must have been Everston's office. There were traces of black paint in the tomb figure's hair and powder-green in its flowing robes. If she turned it around and saw its mellow face, she could make certain it was from the T'ang dynasty, probably the first half of the eighth century.

She walked over to the foot-and-a-half-high statue. It was a valuable piece. She picked it up, cradling it her arms. "I'm taking this. It belonged to Theo. Consider it a down payment on what you owe me," she said.

She marched to the door, fiddling awkwardly with the doorknob, afraid she would drop the clay woman.

Hawatyne opened the door wordlessly.

Leah ducked under his arm as she made her encumbered way through the doorway.

Hawatyne placed a hand on her shoulder. "I'll be in touch." He said the words wistfully.

His tone surprised her. She nodded.

He watched her march down the hall, back straight, head up, covering ground rapidly. Over her shoulder, the enigmatic smile of the court lady held him transfixed.

5

THE FAMILY
FRIEND

OUT ON THE hot pavement of Queen Street, she staggered under the weight of the statue and was jostled by the lunchtime crowd: hawkers; labourers nearly doubled under their heavy loads; women in print dresses, hats, and gloves, scurrying to meet their friends; office workers. The air was laden with the overpowering smell of rice and soy. A woman struggled with containers of food slung from a bamboo pole. She careened into Leah, nearly decapitating the court lady. Leah brushed her effusive apologies aside.

It didn't make sense. Theo always said, "Trust no one. Advisers are for fools." How could he have been duped? She hoped when the two of them met in the underworld, Theo would strangle Everston.

An-li greeted Leah at the door.

"I don't want to talk about it," said Leah. Desolate, she made her way into the living room, still clasping the court lady. She set the terracotta statue down, kicked off her shoes and flopped onto the couch, burying her face in a cushion.

The door chime sounded.

Leah heard Sonia's contralto voice echo down the hall, "Is Leah in, An-li?"

"She doesn't—"

"In the living room," called Leah. Sonia would take the wretched court lady. Leah didn't want it. It would become a stinking albatross around her neck. She'd say it was a legacy from Theo. Sonia loved presents. She would purr and say soothing things about Theo.

Sonia lived an airless existence. During the day, in her ornate Mid-levels flat, the windows were invariably closed and the curtains drawn. "To keep the cool air in," she said. But even at night, she never opened a window. She lived in the half-light with her dead-eyed icons. She burned incense too, a heavy smell that lingered on your clothes long after leaving. The place was crammed, a grab-bag of uncomfortable Victorian sofas, bare-breasted art deco maidens holding up lamps and large ashtrays, and the occasional painted Chinese cabinet. Theo had hated the place. He'd said, "It's a cross between a bordello and a spirit medium's parlour." The tomb maiden statue would fit right in.

So Leah said, "Theo wanted you to have it," placing the court lady at Sonia's feet.

Sonia peered at the statue's face, its welcoming arms and the folds of the gown. "I'm sure I've seen this statue before, but not here."

Offhand, Leah said, "It's a generic type, though each artist varies the form, the head, the placement of the arms, the drape of the dress, the expression of welcoming sadness. It's what gives the figures life and charm."

"She's lovely. Theo loved beauty, like your mother's. Vestna was exquisite." Sonia lit a cheroot and continued to stare at the serene face of the figurine. It bothered her.

"Sometimes I think I remember her smell, a mixture of musky perfume and strong cigarettes. But maybe I heard that from Theo."

But Theo had never talked about Vestna, who'd died when Leah was two. To Leah, Vestna was a shadow hovering just out of sight, perhaps frightened off by the ghost gates Theo had built. Intently, Leah had studied her own face over the years, working out which features she had inherited from Theo and which from Vestna. Her wide lips were Theo's but she was certain her cheekbones and Slav-grey eyes were her Russian mother's. Once she had screwed up the courage to ask Theo what Vestna had looked like. He had gone so silent, his features frozen, that Leah had covered her mouth, as if to take back the question. Finally, Theo had simply said, "Beautiful. You get your beauty from your mother. She moved like music," and he began to waltz in a light-footed way, holding out his arms as if to embrace a partner so fleeting and graceful, his long fingers curled around the air. Then abruptly he stopped, his eyes full of despair, and Leah asked no more questions.

"Theo," Sonia said, "was in love with the romance of the fallen White Russian aristocrat."

Sonia's bracelets jangled. When Leah was little, Sonia allowed her to wear her precious jade bracelets, pushing them up her arm and listening to them clack against each other. Leah focused on the smoke rings Sonia was blowing.

Sonia scanned Leah's noncommittal face. Something was going on. It wasn't grief. The girl would tell her eventually. She continued: "Theo's need to grasp history in his hands passed. It couldn't be 1917 forever." Her voice became tight and hard. "Vestna didn't realise opium is a commodity here, a business. She wouldn't listen. We did what we needed to do. . ."

Sonia segued into old hardship stories: no work, no money, crawling to the Chinese to find a job, unable to leave Hong Kong because White Russians were stateless people. The things they did to get by. She relished the details of who had been a prostitute, made a fortune, or worked for Chinese gangsters. At the end, she said, "Of course, it leaves one with plenty of contacts." She looked knowingly at Leah, waiting for her to respond.

Leah frowned. She had been re-running her meeting with Hawatyne in her head. What would she do now for ready money? Chang's face pushed its way into her thoughts.

"Do you think Theo was a clever man, Sonia?"

With triumph in her voice, Sonia said, "Got it. Theo gave this statue to his lawyer. Is Everston dead too?"

"Not yet," Leah said grimly. "How would you describe Theo?" she persisted.

Sonia picked threads of tobacco off her tongue. What could she say? Sometimes she hated him. Vestna had used opium to escape him; he couldn't follow her into her dreams. But she admired the way he coped, made a life for himself. When her own gambling debts mounted, he bailed her out. He introduced her to men who helped, too. And then, she told Theo their secrets. It was a useful arrangement. True, when she saw him salivating over a rare find like the court lady—she had been there the day it had been delivered to him—it made her queasy. His hands had trembled when he lifted the statue out of the wood shavings. He kept licking those large lips of his as if he might kiss it. He wouldn't, of course; it would ruin the patina. She was surprised when he told her he was giving it to Everston. He wasn't a generous man. Always blunt, she'd asked why. But Theo had only smiled that superior smile of his and said, "Ask me no questions, I'll tell you no lies."

"Your father," said Sonia, "was a man who knew what he wanted." She gave Leah a long appraising look. It was true, Leah had the same phenomenal beauty as Vestna, but she was too self-contained, not flamboyant like Vestna or at least the Vestna Sonia remembered. But what was Leah without her shell of respectability, beneath the cool exterior that stupid school had imposed on her? Even now she sat ramrod-straight, her ankles crossed demurely; butter wouldn't melt in her mouth. How much of her was pure scheming Theo, and how much was poor gullible Vestna?

So many rumours had swirled around Theo's sudden end. Personally, Sonia hadn't believed any of them, though she was surprised when Chang had come to see her on the evening of Theo's death. A coincidence? Young Chang was so much taller than his father. She had dismissed him as a fervent political type—Nationalist, Kuomintang. Whereas Old Chang had been a considerate lover who never mixed business with pleasure, right away Young Chang had started probing about her Russian connections in Manchuria. He'd known about her friend Vasiliev, who had assisted Old Chang with his investment in the

South Manchurian Railroad, and who had links to Pu Yi's puppet regime and to the real power behind the throne, the Japanese.

Young Chang had informed her of his plan to finance the Chinese war effort. He had heard that Kolbe's daughter was a connoisseur of all things Chinese. The Japanese would never suspect someone like that. He'd said that Sonia would have to accompany Miss Kolbe to Manchuria, to provide a steady hand in these uncertain times—a watcher, a minder. His eyes had narrowed to black points.

At first Sonia had been reluctant, but he'd agreed to settle her gambling debts and promised her a large reward on her return. She didn't want to end up some sad-eyed crone at the *chemin de fer* table, wheedling Hong Kong dollars from lucky winners who felt sorry for her. Leah had to grow up sometime. Kolbe had kept the girl hidden away, sheltered, for long enough.

She stubbed out her cheroot and squeezed Leah's hand. "Are things difficult for you now, Leah?" she said.

Leah let her hand rest in Sonia's dry one. The gesture of comfort moved her, but she couldn't betray Theo by admitting to Everston's swindle. "Theo's affairs are complicated."

"Ah," said Sonia, "he was always robbing Peter to pay Paul." She loved those English expressions, so telling if you dropped them into the conversation. "To get his hands on another treasure."

Leah withdrew her hand.

Sonia lit another cheroot. "I know about Manchukuo, Leah." She told Leah about Chang's son's visit and flattered her about her language skills and curator's knowledge.

Leah listened quietly. She longed for Theo to be there in a dim corner of the room, his hands laced over his belly, giving her a sly nod as if saying "All is not lost, we'll get the bastards. There's a way out of this." Offhand, she couldn't think of one.

"Don't look like that, Leah," said Sonia. "It's a very *fluid* situation. Theo taught you well. It's your chance now. We'll be a team."

Some team, some chance. Already Leah had learnt partnerships were dangerous and trust led to betrayal. She called a servant to carry the tomb lady to Sonia's. Sonia placed a goodbye kiss on Leah's cheek; Leah kissed the air. Sonia badgered the young boy as she walked, jangling and clattering, up the passageway.

Left alone, Leah contemplated her next move. Sonia was dependent on her. Once they were in Manchukuo, she would be in charge. The success of the venture rested with her. She was young, clever. Things would work out. The business would sustain her, after all. Why shouldn't she view it as an adventure? Life was risk. This one gamble, then she would have a stake and her future would fall into place.

6

THE NIGHT
VISITOR

EXHAUSTED, LEAH COULD barely lift her head off the couch to sip the soothing tea An-li poured. She didn't want to talk. It was too difficult to make sense of her day.

She wanted to retreat to her room, like a schoolgirl. Much of her adolescence had been spent naked in the heat, dozing spread-eagled on her bed, waiting for time to pass until she was grown-up. During the hot afternoons following school, she drank the lemon water An-li left for her as an antidote to the barbs the girls slung her way during the day, especially at lunch when she left untouched the slimy puddings the other girls wolfed down.

"It's not Chink food, so you don't like it," Hope had taunted her. "You'd better watch out, Leah, your eyes are beginning to slant." Hope had pulled the skin of her eyes tight.

A glob of pudding had clung to Hope's thin upper lip. Leah flicked it off with her finger and, smiling, called Hope a whore in Cantonese.

"You dirty girl, Leah. You no speakee English." The other girls laughed.

Leah upset her pudding onto Hope's lap.

Miss Kemp threatened her with expulsion but settled for excluding Leah from games.

Leah hated games, pointless winning and losing that changed nothing. This wasn't a game. It was real life.

An-li rose to draw the curtains against the night, then sat and began to sew. Leah liked to watch An-li's hands at work. Her knuckles were enlarged now. The veins on her hands stood out as she pulled the thread through the fine silk. Once or twice Leah thought An-li was going to question her, but she just pursed her lips and stabbed the material again.

Leah turned on the radio. It took a while for the tubes to warm up. She fiddled with the knobs until she found dance music. Every now and then, the music was interrupted by the clipped enunciation of the announcer repeating a song title and the band's name. She slid down into the pillowed depths of the sofa and slept.

In her dream, people surrounded her, dancing. She wore her lucky red dress. Attached to her wrist by a gold string was a thick white card. She smiled at the men who seemed to be a long way off and never asked her for a dance. Girls were sashaying about, holding the hems of their long gowns, weaving a circle around her. Their faces changed: one was Everston's *singsong* girl, another became a tall dark woman. There was someone in the shadows whom she struggled to catch a glimpse of through the women's bobbing heads.

Far off, the gong of the doorbell sounded, then she heard muted voices. She fought to emerge from her dream and sat up. The houseboy knocked on the living room door. A visitor, a Mr. Chang, was here. An-li looked as if she was going to say something, but Leah ignored her and nodded.

Chang stood just inside the living room. He busied himself with lighting a clove cigarette.

Leah said, "Please go now, An-li." An-li took a long time to collect her sewing things and cast a dark look at Chang as she left the room.

Uninvited, Chang sat on the couch, crowding her. She had to turn at an awkward angle to speak.

"I heard that Mr. Kolbe's estate has now been settled," he said.

Her mouth went dry. She clasped her hands tight. "You have good information."

He blew a smoke ring.

The clove smell pricked her nose. She gave a slight cough.

"Oh," he said, "we pride ourselves on having good information." He offered her a cigarette.

She shook her head.

"It's an acquired taste."

She didn't like his tone but said, "I expect so."

"Miss Kolbe, we think you should begin preparations for your journey at once. You will need the approval of the Japanese Government to travel to Manchukuo. Mr. Hawatyne is being courted by the Japanese Consul."

She recalled the blushing Chinese clerk at Hawatyne's office. The clerk, no doubt, had a family. A family "friend" asks a few questions. Why not supply the information? He would have been well rewarded. It was strictly business.

Chang continued: "The Consul tries so hard to make friends amongst you Colonists. He will be delighted to help a young woman like yourself."

His unpleasant eyes roamed her body as he leaned in close, but he didn't touch her.

She wanted to cover her breasts with her arms, but instead said, "And if I can't get a visa? Or I decide not to apply for one?"

"Have you heard? There was a big fire at the Lucky Eight Restaurant. It was such a lively place and the owner so hard-working. It is thought he may recover from his burns. Such an unlucky man." He wore an expression of sadness briefly.

She tried to keep her face neutral, but she could not help looking at the unblistered skin of her arms. A nearly imperceptible smile crossed Chang's face.

"Our joint venture, Miss Kolbe, will be profitable for you, too. We will want you to sell the jewels and artefacts you bring back through your contacts. In return, we will pay you a five-percent commission."

She saw Theo's stern face urging her on. "There's a lot of risk. Surely the job is worth more than that to you."

"But, Miss Kolbe," he said, "you will bring back the finest collection of antiquities in the Orient. Five percent of the sales price will be a small fortune. Your business will grow and profit."

"I see," she said. No more words came into her head. She watched him stand and walk to the large onyx ashtray on a side table. His back was toward her as he ashed his cigarette.

"And, of course, we want the eunuch Quan," he told her.

She had a sudden vision of a soft man with a fleshy face disguised as her female servant sitting next to her in the train, leaking fear as the plains of China lumbered by. Her voice was strained as she said, "Will I be paid a commission for that, too?"

He turned around, a hard, amused look on his face. "Very good, Miss Kolbe. Let's just say he is part of the package of goods. Your commission will be calculated on the value of what you transport from Manchuria to Hong Kong. Quan will provide us with a list."

"I can't guarantee success. Things beyond my control may happen."

"Miss Rubstov has a number of contacts. They will ensure that all goes smoothly."

She understood that this meant Sonia was part spy and part helper. "But—"

"*Failure* is a very unhappy word," he said and blew a thin line of smoke out his nose.

"Yes," she agreed, determined not to let her voice falter or to turn her face away as he went on to explain the reasons why China would beat the Japanese and win back Manchuria.

It was a one-sided argument, full of airy rhetoric and patriotic phrases. Her mouth was dry and her dress sweat-soaked. She was surprised the dance music was still playing. It sounded odd as a background to Chang's harsh voice.

"China must reassert herself as a world power," he concluded.

Idly, she wondered if she would be dead by then.

"But I am haranguing you, Miss Kolbe. So impolite, as we are business partners now. I must go."

She wasn't sure she could see him out; if she tried to rise, her knees might give way. There was a tap at the door. An-li peeked in.

With relief, Leah said, "An-li, please see Mr. Chang out. We have concluded our business."

He bowed. "To success, Miss Kolbe," he said before following An-li.

Leah heard their footsteps grow fainter. She was shaking. She calmed herself by repeating, in a hoarse whisper, "I can do this, I can do this." She hoped Theo was listening.

LEAH woke in pain. She struggled to sit up and focus her eyes. A steel band of agony, a vise, was tightening around her skull. Months would go by without a migraine attack; then, without warning, it would strike, forcing her to lie in the dark and sip An-li's special teas until the flashing lights and strange aromas receded. Theo would tiptoe in and sit by her bed. He comforted her as he smoothed her hair. Then, he would kiss his fingers and gently brush them against her cheek. She would murmur "Daddy," and he'd answer, "Sleep, my darling Leah, sleep. It will pass." She'd nestle into the cool cotton sheets and fall back to sleep before he'd closed her door.

She struggled into her dressing gown now and made her fumbling way to An-li's room. She covered her eyes with her hand as she switched on the light, calling softly, "An-li, please, I have another sick headache."

Roused, An-li said, "Sit here," and patted the bed. She put out the light and began massaging Leah's head, pushing hard on the pressure point in her palm that led to the pain.

The odd smells disappeared. Leah sat in the dark with her eyes open, waiting for An-li to return with herbal tea.

"Drink, drink," said An-li as she poured the tea from the steaming iron pot.

Leah cupped her hand around the teacup and drank.

An-li stared at Leah. When she was certain the pain had retreated, she said, "I'm coming with you to Manchuria."

Of course she had eavesdropped. "Please, An-li, not now," said Leah.

"No, I'm coming with you."

An-li had been spying; she ought to fire her. An-li could join the ranks of laid-off elderly amahs one sometimes saw on Nathan Street, hand out, begging. Instead, Leah said, "It's too dangerous. I need someone here I can trust."

"Who can you trust in Manchuria? The Russian will play her own game," she said darkly. "Mr. Chang . . . only wants money."

"No," said Leah. "You can't come." But really, it was only a matter of time. An-li would wear down her resistance. And, she conceded, An-li did melt into the background. She could be useful.

7

SQUEEZE

BEHIND HAND-PAINTED screens, separating them from the rest of the Pearl of the East Restaurant diners, Hawatyne and Leah explored their menus.

"It's so damn confusing, Miss Kolbe. You order, otherwise I'll have to ask the waitress to choose."

Leah motioned to a waitress in a brocaded cheongsam who flitted about, flirting with a table of six loud drunken men. The waitress fluttered over and beamed at Hawatyne. In Cantonese, Leah castigated the waitress for simpering. She ordered fifteen expensive dishes that in all probability Hawatyne would not like. Cowed, the waitress bowed her head and skittered off.

"Can you use chopsticks, Mr. Hawatyne?"

He shook his head.

She noted his tight smile as he brushed wisps of blond hair off his forehead. He was rattled. Good. She demonstrated how to rest one chopstick between the second and third fingers and manoeuvre the other stick between the first and second fingers.

"It's easy. Even a child can do it."

He fiddled with the chopsticks. Hopeless, the only way he would be able to eat would be to stab his food with the damn things. He decided not to touch the rice. It would end up down his shirt or stuck to his tie. It was not how he had imagined their first dinner together. He'd been so happy when Leah had invited him. In more intimate surroundings, he felt he would be able to distance himself from the shameful Everston business, show himself off in a better light. Sheepishly, he asked the waitress for a fork when the chicken feet arrived. He made polite noises of satisfaction as his teeth crunched on them.

"Unusual," he said. "Exotic, it's what I came for."

"Chicken feet?"

"No. I mean I wanted to see the world. Bit of an Orientalist."

"Do you see much of Asia, working at your law office?"

"Well, no. But I like living here, walking the little streets, hearing the clatter of bamboo and ivory mahjong tiles being slammed down, the shout of the sidewalk players blaring out their moves and the hawkers yelling. There is such energy here. No men in bowler hats and umbrellas."

Surprised, she rewarded him with a wide smile.

The waitress brought a steaming platter of prawns and a spicy sauce.

Leah dangled a prawn from her chopsticks, dipped it into the sauce and offered it to him.

He opened his mouth obediently.

She placed the prawn on his tongue.

A whoosh of heat and chili pepper overcame him. Tears came to his eyes. His tongue burned. He wondered if it would swell and blister as he gulped hot Chinese tea. He gasped and coughed.

"I am sorry, Mr. Hawatyne. It's an acquired taste."

He managed to speak. "Please call me Jonathan, Leah."

"Jonathan," she said, "I need your help."

Savouring the moment—the taste of chili peppering her mouth, his eagerness to please—Leah spun him an almost true story. She had a client. No, she couldn't give him a name. "I have to respect my client's wish for confidentiality, Jonathan," she said. "My client trusts me and I deserve his faith." She saw a glimmer of remorse pass over his face. "He is Manchu and had to leave behind him valuable family heirlooms. A friend of his is a professor of entomology, in England. This man and his colleagues want to study insects in Manchuria. As it was explained to me, it's an important public health issue to do with crops and the outbreak of disease. Anyway, they want me to go to Manchuria; it's the only way to deal with the red tape. They want me to help them, to make arrangements for their field studies, and also to see if I can retrieve my client's heirlooms. I thought you could get the visas for An-li, an old family friend, and me. There's a mountain of paperwork entailed. I don't know where to begin." She smiled, helpless and appealing.

Jonathan stared in astonishment. He had heard such rumours about her father. Most he had put down to spiteful gossip. People didn't like it when outsiders did better than they. Now, here was this vulnerable—he checked Leah's face—yes, vulnerable, impressionable girl, about to set out down the same shadowy path. Reluctantly, he shook his head.

"Don't you think your law firm should provide assistance to a distressed client, *Jonathan*?"

He let out a small sigh. "Don't do it. Don't put yourself in danger. From what I hear, no one is in control up there. It's a war zone. Not just the Japs, but rival Chinese warlords and the regular Chinese army are all vying for power." He lowered his voice. "There are even rumours that the Soviets have taken a hand, playing both ends against the middle. You can't trust any of them: not the Japs, the Chinese, or the Reds."

She knew what he said was true. Everyone plotted and deceived. Look at Sonia, conspiring behind her back.

Jonathan captured Leah's hand. It was soft and warm.

She let her hand rest in his. "The English still trade with the Japs," she said.

Stung, he released her hand. Maybe he should appear to consent. It might take a long time to get the visas. The Japanese were bureaucratic. He could forget to sign something. It would be the perfect excuse to keep seeing her.

"Promise it's not political and I'll do it. The firm can't be seen to be mixed up in anything political."

"No, fraud must take up a great deal of the firm's time. A thriving business, it must keep you busy." She had him now. "You'll pay the squeeze?"

"The squeeze, Leah?"

"Hong Kong runs on squeeze." She mimed handing out dollar bills for the bribe. She smiled.

He nodded.

Squeeze worked on so many levels, thought Leah. "It's a business deal, Jonathan. I have to provide for myself *now*."

He winced.

That's another for me, she silently acknowledged and wondered if Theo was watching and keeping score. For the rest of the evening, she flirted with Hawatyne, teasing him with anecdotes about Colonial society.

He watched her talk and daydreamed about kissing her. He punctuated the conversation with loud laughs during her pauses. She asked him questions about his life in England. He told her funny stories about his growing up. How his second-rate public school practically starved them and forced them to write glowing letters home. He had become adept at pinching food from the kitchen after hours and sharing it around. She could believe it. With his cherubic looks, no one would have suspected him.

In response, she told him about her brush with school religion. Once a year, the notice board filled with grainy photographs of the mission and a hand-drawn map showing its approximate location in the Chinese hinterlands. Badly typed captions were attached to photos. Invariably, there would be the smiling cook and masses of small children bundled up against the cold sitting in a barren classroom, a large picture of Jesus pinned up over the blackboard. The leaving-form girls were made to attend the Reverend Bostock's lecture, "Our Work Amongst the Heathen." Afterward, the Reverend would serve tea and biscuits and sidle up to the bored girls.

Jonathan nodded. He remembered his icy feet as the local vicar had droned on in school chapel.

"They had me, Jonathan. I couldn't make my escape. The headmistress, Miss Kemp, guarded the door and the Reverend cornered me. He asked me all these questions: was I a believer, did I want to improve the lot of the poor and heathen. I said no. Miss Kemp glared. The Reverend said, 'Doubting Thomases make the best converts. Miss Kemp tells me you speak Chinese. A remarkable talent.' Miss Kemp said I was a clever girl who knew so much about the Chinese—only she didn't call them the Chinese, she said 'our yellow friends.'

"Can you see me as a missionary, Jonathan, wearing a frowsy dress, my face pious, eating gruel, then reading aloud passages from a tatty Bible?"

He laughed. "You are definitely not the missionary type, Leah. Beautiful and exotic, yes; missionary, no."

Leah coloured. She hadn't expected this from him.

She asked to be taken home. Jonathan insisted on hiring a rickshaw. She agreed, but only if the driver pulled them as far as the Peak Tram and took the side streets. "I'll show you the sights," she promised.

As they passed the Tai Wong Temple, she urged him to consider having his fortune told. Under the lamplight by the low temple wall, there were the usual battered tables containing ink drawings of bland faces partitioned into sections, and the same ragtag fortune tellers. Jonathan was in the midst of refusing when Leah noticed Sonia standing beneath a tall palm talking to a man obscured by half a dozen cigarette-smoking companions. They looked Russian. Sonia was not getting her fortune read. She was stabbing the air with her cheroot.

Leah caught the words "You wouldn't dare—" as the puller turned into Tai Wong Street East.

What was Sonia up to? Who were the men she was talking to? In an excited voice, Leah insisted, "Jonathan, you absolutely must get your fortune read."

The puller obligingly turned the rickshaw around and headed back to the Temple.

Sonia was gone. Leah thought she caught sight of the backs of two of the Russian-looking men, but they mingled with the crowd and disappeared.

Jonathan stood patiently by a toothless woman who studied his face and demanded to know his birth date and the time of his birth, then examined the palm of his right hand. Leah translated his fortune. He would live a long life, but his earlobes distressed the fortune teller.

"She doesn't think you'll be wealthy, Jonathan. Your earlobes are too small."

"I can live with that," said Jonathan, pulling at his ears.

Oh, you fool, thought Leah.

8

TRAVEL
ARRANGEMENTS

THE JAPANESE CONSUL, Mr. Okari, oozed amiability as he shook Leah's hand in the Western style. "I'm so delighted, Miss Kolbe, that you could attend this little gathering." The reception room was crammed with people drinking generous shots of whisky and black-clad waiters offering delicacies on silver platters.

Leah thanked him. She forced herself not to bend her knees, to stand straight and not to talk to him as if he were a child. Some child. It was rumoured that Mr. Okari or his consular staff had a network of spies operating throughout Hong Kong. They listened hard to who was making anti-Japanese statements or slurring the good name of the Emperor. They made lists. Sometimes people were killed.

Okari and Leah walked around the room. He lingered in front of the display of samurai swords locked inside glass cases.

"We have a code of chivalry older than the West. Even today, we are the courtiers of the old school, bringing our civilisation to our fellow Asians. The Orient looks to us for leadership."

Leah bowed to his superior culture. She told him she longed to understand this new Japan based so firmly on ancient traditions.

Flattered, he told her about his nation's Manchukuo experiment. In a confidential whisper, he said, "The Manchus who live in Manchukuo are not of Chinese origin. They are a sub-Japanese race. That is why they have welcomed us."

She nodded. "I think it must be wonderful to see the dawn of a new country. Exciting."

Mr. Okari looked pleased.

She hurried on, telling him Mr. Chang's false story about the entomology expedition, how she had been asked to set up accommodations, to make arrangements for the scholars' visit.

His face brightened as he thought about the snippet he would add to his monthly report to Tokyo, describing how he had assisted with the advancement of scientific studies in Manchukuo. "How interesting, Miss Kolbe. If I can be of help. . ." he offered modestly.

Leah said, "I hate to take advantage of this informal meeting but, Mr. Okari, if you could assist me to obtain the necessary visas, I would be very grateful. Such things can take time; delay would be unfortunate. When I return, I will have firsthand knowledge of how well things are progressing in the new country of Manchukuo. I shall tell all my friends in Hong Kong how this newest Asian country is developing. I would almost be like an ambassadress." She gave a modest becoming laugh.

The consul smiled. "Miss Kolbe, thank you for entrusting your request to me. I will see what can be done." He sighed. "Still, there are forms that must be filled out, certain procedures to be followed. . ." He moved closer.

She stepped back and felt Jonathan's hand on her bare shoulder.

"Oh, here you are," said Jonathan. "Your drink, Leah."

Leah sipped the gin and said, "Mr. Okari has graciously agreed to help me get the visas I need for Manchukuo."

Jonathan bowed to Mr. Okari.

Okari nodded. "Now, sadly, I must leave you and Miss Kolbe and speak to my other guests."

Leah and Jonathan watched Okari slip away in his patent leather shoes, a beady magpie in his dinner suit, looking for another victim to peck.

Leah laughed and said "Thank you, Jonathan. Your timing was superb."

She gave Jonathan a kiss on the cheek. He reached out with his free arm to hold her closer. She wiggled free.

"Okari will check out your story, Leah. It may take him a long time. The Japs are masters at obfuscation."

She knew her cover would be watertight. Mr. Chang was not the kind of man to make mistakes. She drank slowly to steady her nerves. "It won't take very long," she said, a convincing smile on her lips.

LEAH rehearsed expressions in front of her bronze mirror. Theo had given it to her on her fifteenth birthday. He had been so pleased at his insight: she was undoubtedly feeling excluded, a figure of fun among her well-connected classmates and an ungainly tall Westerner amongst the diminutive Chinese women. He never asked her "How was school?" He had seen her strained face and guessed the rest.

She would let out a small groan of relief and march straight to her room to pull off the disgusting sticky uniform with its navy blue serge underpants that gave her a pimply rash underneath the confining elastic. She would walk naked around her room, flapping her arms or standing beneath the fan blades, the thick air puffing against her back, her armpits, her breasts, over her feet.

Theo had revealed the power of the bronze mirror when he presented it to her. "Examine the carved back, Leah. See," he'd said, "the hare is preparing the elixir of immortality." She had turned it over to see, engraved in its centre, petals radiating around a hare pounding an herb with a pestle in a mortar. He had pressed his fingers to the engraving, then to her face, as if smearing the contents of the mortar on her. In this mirror she had practiced expressions that would hide what she really felt.

Now she stared into its polished surface, willing Theo to appear behind her. She waved to the empty space. It was a trick of the light, but for an instant her face seemed to thicken, her features spread. She closed her eyes. When she opened them, she saw her cabinet of ivory figurines, glowing in the lamplight. Theo had given them to her, one by one, as she passed his dinner-table tests, buying low and selling high his antique masterpieces. Each time she passed a test, Theo had presented her with an ivory figurine. The first was cheap and nasty, a creature of the curio shop. As she progressed, the age and workmanship of the statues improved. He did not allow her to throw any away. "You must learn to live with your mistakes."

Eleven figurines stood enclosed in a glass-fronted rosewood case: mementos of family time. Now she lined them up on her dressing table, making two rows of five, and placed her last and most valuable acquisition, a foot-high fifteenth-century warrior, in the vanguard of her white brigade. She ran her fingers over the intricate carving of its black wooden pedestal, and was surprised to find a groove. She pushed on the groove. With a faint click, the back opened, revealing a silk-wrapped package. Inside was a nickel-plated derringer. Had Theo hidden it there? Was this his final present?

It was comfortable in her hand. She pointed it around the room, at the other figurines, the window and then at the doorway through which An-li was just then walking, with the tea.

The lacquered tray slipped out of An-li's grasp. The cup and teapot fell. Tea splashed the front of An-li's tunic and dribbled onto her trousers. An-li waved Leah away and picked up the splintered remains.

"I'll need bullets."

"So it begins," said An-li. She slammed the door as she left.

Before she went to bed, Leah surveyed her clothes. It would be cold up north. An-li had made her a peasant costume, a quilted jacket, thick trousers. It might be necessary. But for travelling, for meeting the Japanese, she needed to look businesslike. She dressed and undressed, took up various stances. She hoped it would be like the movies where everything turned out all right in the end. Theo hated movies. He couldn't follow the plots, resented sitting in the dark waiting for things to happen.

She sat on the bed sewing late into the night. When she had finished, every skirt and jacket had a secret pocket. She slipped the little gun into one and posed in front of the mirror. She could detect no telltale bump or ridge. Her precaution was probably unnecessary, but why take chances?

9

A PLEASURE
TRIP TO MACAU

A MONTH OF edgy waiting to hear from the Japanese Consul had sapped Leah's confidence. Secretly, she had begun to hope her request would be refused. Then Chang would have to find someone else to play his nasty game. He was keeping an eye on her, though; Sonia came around constantly with invitations to go shopping together, have lunch, go to the races at Happy Valley.

"Leah, come with me to Macau. Portuguese men are delightful, and the casinos, if you have the luck." Sonia paused and gave a fatalistic shrug, "Well, you can win a lot of money." She held up one of her jade bangles. "It all helps."

"Why not?" At least it would take her mind off the endless waiting. And her worry: if her request for a visa was refused, then what would she do?

ↄ

OPPOSITE the Star Ferry landing were rows and rows of Chinese gambling houses strung with coloured electric lights glowing dimly in the still daylight of waning autumn. Each gaming house proclaimed it was the finest casino in Macau.

"Don't be fooled," said Sonia. "These are for the nobodies. You have to know someone to be admitted to the places I go to."

"I expect so," said Leah dryly. Perhaps she should not have come. But Sonia said her Russian connection, Vasiliev, might be there.

"Vasiliev takes his vacations here," said Sonia. "What a joke. The Soviets pay a comrade in Manchuria to come to Macau where everything is for sale."

Sonia was acting as Leah's guide. They strolled around, arm in arm, like Portuguese girls on parade. Sonia was vague about how she had come to know Macau so well. Leah thought it must be from her own gambling. Or perhaps Sonia had once been the mistress of a rich Macanese merchant.

Leah was entranced. Macau presented a picture-postcard image of the Mediterranean, but with a Chinese flavour: pastel houses, curlicued wrought-iron gates, graceful squares with decaying fountains at their centres. Portuguese men with dark eyes and women with alabaster skin glided up narrow cobbled streets to wooden-shuttered stucco houses, or crossed themselves as they passed the mellow rose-coloured churches. Leah read the blue-tiled name of the narrow street, Rua de Felicidade.

"Don't let the gracious name fool you," said Sonia as a young man in a linen suit and silk tie tipped his hat at them. "This is the street of happiness for men."

They heard lute music. It came from a two-story grey building engraved with astrological signs.

"The lute girls, the *pei-pas chais,* live here. See, there's one now," said Sonia, inclining her head toward a heavily made-up girl in a skin-tight cheongsam of peacock blue on the arm of a silver-haired, pot-bellied Portuguese.

Leah attempted a cool, non-judgmental glance.

"But the real treasures are the golden lilies, the girls with four-inch feet," said Sonia. She laughed and looked at her own large feet encased in open-toed sandals. She had painted her toenails plum red. She shrugged. "Other men have other tastes. I have a catholic taste in men. You know what I mean, Leah?"

Leah blotted out an image of Sonia naked and blowing smoke at a man in a stained undershirt sitting on a rumpled bed. They stopped in front of a trickling fountain. Sonia dipped her hand in the rusty water and cooled her neck with it. Leah didn't want to think about an ageing Sonia consorting with men. Disgusting, middle-aged desire; it made her feel slightly ill, like the incident at the silk merchant, buying dress material with Theo. Together they had chosen the Nile green—it would bring out the grey of her eyes—from a sales assistant who wore white cotton gloves to prevent the silk snagging. Then, arm in arm, they were walking down the cramped street, chatting and laughing, when Theo started. She saw a pleasant round-faced Chinese woman in a beige silk two-piece skirt and jacket. Neither Theo nor the woman acknowledged each other.

Walking on, Leah asked, "Do you know her?"

"Yes, she is my mistress. It's nothing to do with you."

They never spoke of the woman again. Several times, Leah retraced her steps to the silk merchant, prowling the steep laneways, hoping to catch a glimpse of the woman. Later she experimented with pinning her hair up in the style the woman had worn, but it didn't suit her and the pins kept falling out.

Leah had ceased listening to Sonia; she was wondering if she would try once more to locate the woman.

"Well, do you, Leah?" said Sonia.

"Do I what?"

"Your taste in men."

"Oh, that." She had been groped at dances and leered at during cocktail parties by enough men to know what they wanted. But the question was, what did she want? Jonathan had blushed when she kissed him lightly on the cheek. On dates, he was polite, reserved, though he breathed heavily in taxis and held her hand tightly. She didn't want to be revered. To be honest, she hadn't met anyone who excited her.

Sonia appraised Leah. "This isn't child's play here. We are not going to the Hotel Central casino. That's for tourists. This is for real. We are going to a private club. The Sam Hop Wui owns it. You *do* know what that means."

Leah knew. It was Triad-owned.

"Watch and learn, Leah. Watch and learn."

IT was difficult to see inside the club through the smoky haze. The noise rose and fell in deafening waves. Men sat at mahogany tables in hunched attention watching the cards, the dice. Pretty girls carrying drinks on lacquered trays tottered around in deeply split cheongsams. Even in the feeble light, the men's white shirts were tinged indelibly with deep brown sweat marks. The few suited men had thin grey creases down the back of their rucked-up jackets. The air was stale and hot. Shouts from the fan-tan room cut off normal conversation.

"I am going to scout around for Vasiliev," said Sonia, grabbing a whisky from one of the girls. "Enjoy yourself." She sailed off, squeezing in between the gaming tables.

Leah scanned the room, determined to look as if she belonged. She was damned if she was going to stumble along in Sonia's wake. She spotted the teller's cage, which held a skinny man with an abacus. In Cantonese, Leah asked for twenty thousand Hong Kong dollars in chips. The man grinned, revealing his four teeth. Through the bars he took the wad of crumpled notes, put a greasy rubber cap on his finger and counted them. Carefully, he formed the coloured wooden chips into stacks. When they were straight, he undid the catch at the bottom of the grill to hand them through. Leah pulled a velvet pouch from her handbag and swept the chips into it.

She ducked into a still-warm seat at the blackjack table. The squat Chinese croupier, his fat fingers squeezed into gold rings, grunted. The gamblers didn't lift their eyes from the table. The round started. She won a little and stayed for another round. She looked around for Sonia, but the smoke hung low over the table, obscuring her vision. Leah left a ten-dollar tip for the croupier at her empty place and gravitated toward the bar.

She ordered and waited as the black-jacketed bartender splashed a generous serving of gin into a glass. A slim Eurasian man smiled at her. He was tall and confident and wore his dinner jacket open as if he had just dashed out of a high-class party and was likely to return any moment. He looked good, smooth and intriguing. His brown eyes and long eyelashes stood out in his creamy face.

"Having fun?" he asked.

She took the cold glass from the bartender, sipped, and said, "Yes. I won a little."

"Don't win too much. It will upset the owners."

She laughed.

"Cezar da Silva, pleased to meet you." He held out his hand.

"Leah, just Leah, for now," she said.

He kissed her hand and his eyes ran up and down her body, pausing briefly at the curve of her breasts and finishing with a stare of approval at her face. His approach was so direct that Leah smiled.

With a liquid easy grin, da Silva said, "Well, Leah-for-now, want to try your luck again?"

He led her toward the quietest table, a baccarat table where the men sat unblinking before stacks of fifty- and hundred-dollar chips.

She was relieved to see there were no empty chairs amongst the gimlet-eyed gamblers. "Shall we watch?" she said.

Da Silva shook his head. "Oh, no. I can tell it's your lucky night." He stood behind one of the seated gamblers. The man's shirt had a succession of worn yellow stains mixed with new damp ones. Around each chair leg was a conical pile of cigarette butts. Da Silva rocked on his heels. The man turned, then scowled and picked up his remaining chips.

"A place for you," said da Silva. Leah sat down and he pushed her chair in. He rested one hand on her shoulder as she arranged her chips.

The baccarat dealer shuffled eight decks of cards and placed each deck in the "shoe," a black teak box. The player next to her controlled the shoe. He had a large stack of chips. The dealer's bank hand kept winning as the bets mounted.

When it was her turn to bid, she called her bet in Cantonese. The dealer dealt one card face-down to the shoe man and one for the bank hand. As the bids went around the table, Cezar squeezed her shoulder. A test, thought Leah, and bet the bank's hand. A small thick-lidded man who reminded her of a lizard in a creased suit stared at the dealer who turned over a nine in the player's hand. The banker's card was an eight. The dealer shuffled the cards. The shoe passed to the thick-lidded gambler. He called out a HK $5,000 minimum bid. Several men nodded and threw in the required chips; two bolstered their dwindling chips with bank notes. Under the weight of Cezar's hand, Leah matched them.

Everyone studied the two hands, counting cards, calculating the odds to get to nine, the winning score. Now and again, one of the gamblers shifted his gaze from the table to stare at da Silva. What expression was playing across Cezar's face.

At the last call, she was the highest bidder for the bank; the previous winner was the highest bidder on the player's hand. The dealer turned over the player's card, a jack, which counted for zero, and a three. She stroked her face for luck and stared as the dealer revealed an ace; one point for me, she thought. Her breath slowed, and a queen, worth nothing, and a two appeared. The player's hand was entitled to another card. In aggressive growls, the men called out their bets. She spilled all her chips onto the table. The dealer revealed the player's card, a five. Her heart raced; the bank still had a chance. The dealer spat, took a drag from his cigarette, and placed the card face down on the table. The lizard man turned it over, the six of spades. A winner! She breathed out. The dealer raked in the chips of those who had bet the player's hand.

Cezar whispered into her ear, "Well done. Let's go."

As she swept her hands across the table to gather up her winnings, the lizard man looked as if he were going to object. His gaze shifted to da Silva; he stuck a cigarette into his protesting mouth.

Cezar's arm encircled her waist. He pulled her close as he guided her toward the cage to exchange chips for cash. His lime scent was strong. Mesmerised, she was dimly aware of all the money she had won as she stashed it into her bulging purse. Cezar's breath was on her neck.

"Shall we go?" Cezar asked again.

"I came with a friend, a female friend," said Leah, scanning the room.

"There are other rooms, more private rooms," he said watching her face.

She felt her face reddening. "No, it wasn't like that."

"Perhaps you want to try the opium room?" He said it softly as if it were an everyday word.

Leah's hands trembled. She couldn't quite get the words out. She shook her head. Once Theo had introduced her to a young French-educated Russian-Chinese man. Tong was to be their connection to French dealers. He was so beautiful, elegant in his couture suit. She was fifteen and overcome when he kissed her hand and bowed from the waist, saying "*Enchanté,* mademoiselle." All through dinner, she watched Tong as he spoke knowledgeably about avant-garde painters who were incorporating Chinese elements into their paintings and the vibrant market for porcelain, ivory carvings, anything one could claim had belonged to the old Empress. He relayed salacious gossip about rich families; he had visited important collections in Europe and North America. Theo quizzed him about the families he knew in Paris, what he thought of the dealer Monsieur Frederic Martin, if they should open a shop near *Sacré Coeur* or simply have engraved cards and have private, discreet viewings.

Tong opted for the private audience. "These are one-of-a-kind pieces. Exclusivity deserves a higher price," he said.

Theo exchanged knowing looks with her, and she pictured more delightful dinners with Tong.

On his next visit, he wore a Mandarin's black silk robe. Leah was even more fascinated as he mixed more French into his conversation, called himself the *Asiatique,* talked about the *fantastique* dreams of the Orient. Theo nodded less, stared more at Tong's face. He let the young man talk on and on. When dinner was over, Theo made no move to offer cigars and cognac. Tong giggled, "I'm expected at Monsieur Morrison's house. Do you know it?"

Theo ignored the question and opened the door to the dining room. One of the servants walked Mr. Tong to the front door.

"How could you?" said Leah.

Theo mopped his face with his napkin, muttered something as he blotted his perspiring face.

"How could you be so rude?" she demanded.

He took the damp cloth from his face and met her eyes. "Opium," he said. "I recognise the signs. His pupils were dilated. He had no appetite, his complexion was muddy."

She didn't know where to look, whether to give him a con-
soling hug or stay still and ask the questions she had been sav-
ing for years about her mother, since the day she been out
walking with An-li and An-li had whisked her away from the
begging, stick-thin European man with black teeth. An-li
kept repeating, "He's sick, bad man," and the final insulting
"Opium eater," said with such venom that at first Leah could-
n't make out the words, "Like your mother." Then An-li
shook her hard, making her promise she wouldn't tell Theo
about the bad man and what she had said about her mother.

Theo had been pale beneath his flushed face as he pushed
his chair away from the dining table. The capillaries on his
nose had swollen. His face had taken on a lumpy, ugly look as
he shut his eyes. Coward, thought Leah. He won't tell me, will
pretend that Vestna contracted a mysterious illness and wasted away despite the best of care. Even now he was busy dissembling, putting a gloss on Vestna's addiction, unable to con-
front the possibility that Vestna had hated him and her baby
daughter. Fed up, Leah said, "She didn't love either of us. Isn't
that the plain, simple truth?"

Theo opened his eyes. "It's not that simple," he'd said quietly.
"People don't do the things they do to spite us. Opium has its
own allure. She told me she was bad at loving. I was never
loveable."

She had jumped out of her chair and flung her arms around
her father's neck. Absently, Theo had patted her arms, mut-
tering, "There, there. There, there. We are what we are."

Now Cezar asked, "Are you all right, Leah? I think you
could use some air. Your friend will find her own way home."

"Yes," Leah agreed and followed Cezar out into the Macau night.

Outside, the fresh air was a comfort. He put his arm around her shoulders. She relaxed a little.

"Come," he said, "I'll show you Macau, the nightlife."

"I'd rather just walk around the streets and squares." She wasn't in the mood for noisy bars and drunken men with their painted, painfully young Chinese girls.

They stood in front of the ruined façade of the Church of Saint Paul. It had a ghostly glow and a ravaged beauty; its intricate portals, statues, and engravings moved her.

"We live on our crumbling history here," said Cezar.

He made small talk about the cunning Macanese and told sly jokes about the Chinese. She wondered what group he thought he belonged to. She decided it was impolite to ask.

He stopped and turned to her. "You're beautiful, Leah-for-now," he said, kissing her.

She kissed him back. He tasted lovely with his heady lime scent. They kissed some more, then wandered around with their arms around each other. She knew she had decided even before they reached a small two-story hotel, *Pousado Portuguese,* facing an intimate square that held a trickling fountain in its centre.

Under a streetlight, he looked into her eyes and hugged her tight. He whispered into her ear, "Stay with me." He gestured toward the hotel. "It will be more private here."

She didn't know if she should be insulted. She kissed him and held his hand as he led the way to the hotel.

Inside, she stood beside a potted plant and pretended she wasn't interested as Cezar talked to the desk clerk. If the clerk turns this way and leers or if he gives me an appraising glance, she thought, I'm going to lose my nerve. But the clerk was only annoyed at being roused from sleep and didn't bother to look at her. She followed Cezar up the stairs to their room.

There wasn't much to see: a double bed covered in a maroon chenille spread, a wooden chair with two white towels on the seat, and a threadbare murky pink carpet on the floor. There was no wardrobe.

Cezar locked the door, leaving the key in the lock. "Okay, Leah?"

She smiled a little and stood at the end of the bed, her arms hanging by her side, waiting. Instead of crushing her in his arms as she half expected, Cezar opened the window. He spent several minutes looking down at the quiet square. Silence filled the well-used room. Awkward, she surveyed his back and kicked off her high heels. They made a slight thumping noise. Cezar continued to stare out the window. She didn't know whether to be grateful for his inattention or annoyed that he didn't think he needed to make an effort to seduce her. Then she thought, *I* want to do this. Whatever happens, I made this choice of my own free will. She unhooked her dress.

When he turned around, she was naked. A faint line of perspiration ran between her breasts. She looked right at him, observing him observing her. He swept her up in his arms. In between their touching and kissing, he wriggled out of his clothes. They laughed together and fell back on the bed.

His entry hurt more than she had expected, but she clung to him. He pulled out at the last moment and came on her stomach. Oozy and wet, they lay together. He licked her ear.

"Pleased?" she said.

"Pleased," he said and fell asleep, fast asleep, on top of her. She eased him off and he stirred. They made love again. The second time was better. She snuggled into the crook of his arm, sniffing his skin, his hair, touching his body, licking his salty shoulder. Later, she dozed as he turned away to sleep.

She awoke in the grey light. Noiselessly, she got out of bed and tiptoed to her clothes.

Through half-shut eyes Cezar watched.

She dressed in a hurry and carried her shoes in her hands. Easing the key in the lock, she opened the door. She looked at Cezar, whose eyes were closed, and sighed. He looked so good, so out-of-place, in this dreary hotel room. If things had been different, she would have kissed him awake, laughed, then spent the day in bed, making up for all that useless time when she had felt compelled to protect her virginity. She kissed her fingertips, blew him the kiss, and eased the door shut.

10
LOVE ME

LEAH OPENED THE door to her house to find An-li asleep in a chair.

An-li jerked awake. "Where have you been?"

"Out with Sonia."

An-li observed Leah's dishevelled hair and wrinkled clothes. "No, you haven't."

"Stop prying, An-li."

"All night I wait for you."

"I'm fine. Wonderful, in fact." She twirled around An-li, then dragged her into a reluctant quick two-step. An-li sniffed Leah's clothes, neck, hair. A knowing expression passed over her face as she hastily disengaged from Leah's exuberant embrace.

Leah blushed. Why should she have to explain?

"It's a hold over you."

"He doesn't even know my name—"

"Aha, I knew it."

"Go to bed, An-li. That's enough."

"That Russian woman, she's a whore. She has done this to you."

Leah raised her hand. An-li, red-faced with fury, ducked.

"Stop it, An-li. I'm grown up now. I make my own decisions." She ran down the hall to her bedroom and slammed the door.

An-li wrenched the door open.

Leah shielded her naked body with her slip.

An-li stood in the doorway, her hands crossed over her chest, glowering. "I'm going to Manchuria. Mr. Jonathan got the visas. One for me, too."

An-li banged the door closed.

LEAH entered Jonathan's club to whirring fans that blew the stale smoke, alcoholic fumes, and the heavy scent of hair cream around the cluttered room with its rattan chairs, hunting pictures, and photographs of cheerful cricket teams.

Jonathan's back was to her. He was propped against the bar, a foot on the brass rung that ran around the base, staring into a large gin gimlet that he clasped in both hands. A thin line of pink skin showed at his hairline. The new haircut was for her.

Slowly, she walked toward him. Men stopped their conversation, smiled, and moved out of her path. They watched her press her hands against Jonathan's eyes but couldn't hear her murmur "Guess who?" Several of the men sighed.

Jonathan let her hands remain covering his eyes, enjoying her closeness, her breath in his ear. He put his drink down, took her hands in his. "I've been waiting for you." He pulled her toward him and landed a kiss on her cheek.

She twisted free. "I'll have a gimlet too."

"The visas have arrived. I need you to sign for them." His voice was calm. He was doing well, pretending it was just business when right now, what he wanted was to put his arm around her, draw her close and say, "Let's go back to my place, Leah." Instead, he said, "They are at my office. I thought we'd have dinner first, then go there to collect them."

She gave him a cousinly kiss and let him rest his arm around her waist.

Over dinner, he watched her eat, her hands sawing delicately at the meat and popping in each morsel between her soft red lips and white teeth. He tried to keep up his end of the conversation. She said, "When I come back," and he interrupted and said, "Don't go." For a moment, he thought she was going to agree but she shook her head and said "I have no choice. I will leave tomorrow." Then he wasn't hungry anymore. He blamed himself for being party to the firm's fraud. Could he quit and sue the firm on her behalf? But nothing he could do now would deter her; somehow her trip to Manchuria seemed destined.

Leah reached across the table to take his hand, "I do appreciate what you have done, Jonathan."

"Do you think you could love me, Leah?"

"I don't . . . there is . . . it's not the right time, Jonathan."

"Marry me. We could live in England. You wouldn't have to go to Manchuria. You'd be safe."

"It's not what I want."

"Stay the night with me."

"No, Jonathan."

ᕗ

AN army of ragged refugees camped outside Hung Hom train station.

Leah and An-li picked their way through the beggars, children, wizened women, whole families with their hands out.

"More refugees from the Japs," said An-li.

Leah nearly tripped over a toddler being chased by his older sister.

"They may bring disease," said An-li. "Cover your mouth."

The children's mother sat sunken amid her washed-out bundles. She yelled at her children, then bared her breast to feed an infant.

"Where will they go?"

"Where they all go, to the back streets, to Tai Ping Shan. It's very bad there. No place to live."

"Ask them how it is in China. We may learn something."

An-li shook her head. "No, too many Japanese spies. It's best not to ask of strangers."

The toddler tugged Leah's skirt. For luck, Leah handed the boy five Hong Kong dollars. The sister bobbed her thanks and scarpered off. The mother shot her a yellowed-toothed grin.

Railing at the porter to hold her luggage higher, out of the reach of dirty hands, Sonia burst through the crowd. "My God, can you believe this madhouse? I'm sure all these people should be quarantined." She pulled out an embroidered handkerchief and held it to her nose.

On the platform Leah spied their suitcases, guarded by one of her servants, and Jonathan, lugging a wooden box. He looked sheepish.

"I hope you don't mind, Leah," he said as he set down the box. "I brought fruit for your trip. It was the only useful present I could think of."

It was kind. Jonathan was a brick. Even when they had gone to his office and she had signed for the visas, he hadn't brought up the topic of marriage again. Now they sat on a bench in the waiting room and discussed his offer to check on her house and servants from time to time. She had authorised him to pay her bills while she was away. With what? The irony of this was not lost on either of them. He told her he would miss her.

Jonathan pushed the luggage trolley to the first-class section of the train. He supervised the stowing of the luggage, then ran off to buy magazines no one wanted. Sonia smirked at Jonathan's officiousness. Leah avoided Sonia's raised eyebrows when Jonathan returned laden with magazines. An-li sat quietly watching them all as if she were at the motion pictures.

"Don't, for God's sake, leave the train, even if there are delays," advised Jonathan. "Inside China, I am told, the train can take off at any bloody time. Make sure An-li buys only cooked food or, if you must, wash all the fresh fruit and vegetables well. Drink only bottled water. There have been terrible reports of disease outbreaks in a number of cities along the way." He knew he was running on and sounding like a public health inspector. He didn't care.

"Mr. Hawatyne," said Sonia, "we will follow your instructions to the letter, of course."

Jonathan snapped, "It's for your own good."

"I appreciate your good advice," said Leah. "I'll try to keep in touch. I'll cable you."

The gong sounded. A conductor made his way down the aisle calling out, in English and Cantonese, "Visitors must leave."

Gravely, Jonathan shook An-li's hand, then Sonia's. Leah jumped up and kissed him hard on the lips.

His face a map of confusion, Jonathan rushed off the train, then reappeared on the platform outside their compartment window. As the train pulled away, he ran alongside waving and mouthing "Goodbye, good luck" and just before Leah lost sight of him, she was certain he said, "I love you."

Sonia arched her eyebrows and said, "Your Mr. Hawatyne, Leah, has seen too many films. It puts very strange ideas into Englishmen's heads, robs them of their reserve. Then what will they have left?"

"Oh, do be quiet, Sonia."

An-li nodded in agreement. At the last minute she had packed a special tea. The Russian was a cruel, stupid woman. The tea would give the old sow a lot of bad stomach. An-li smiled to herself as she settled into the comfortable first-class seat and closed her eyes.

Leah watched Sonia, engrossed in reading one of Jonathan's magazines. She hadn't spoken at length to Sonia since their trip to Macau. Macau: she let her thoughts drift and replayed meeting Cezar; wandering the streets with Cezar; in bed with Cezar. What was he doing now, right this minute? Had he been surprised, or relieved, that she wasn't there in the morning? She couldn't imagine Cezar in a day job, going to an office. Perhaps he worked at the club. Yet this didn't seem likely. She wished she were going away with him, a trip into China, just the two of them, for delicious times together.

Sonia leaned over. "Leah, do you think this evening dress would suit me?"

She pointed to a photograph of a young woman with crimped blonde hair, draped over a balcony. The model's midriff was bare; the tight satin skirt clung to her nonexistent hips. On scrawny, aging Sonia, such an outfit would look macabre.

"I don't think we'll need evening clothes where we are going," said Leah warily.

Sonia nodded and returned to her reading.

What was Sonia planning? Everyone was spying. It was reported in the press: "Barber caught selling British army defence secrets to Japs," "Japanese businessman bribed prostitute to get information from civil servants." A few times, Leah had sensed a nondescript man studying her as she went shopping or to the bank or to see Jonathan. To attempt a disguise would be stupid. Theo hadn't believed in them. "I am a big white man who stands head, shoulders, and belly above the crowd. How can I hide? In Hong Kong, people who want you always know where to find you."

The train passed through the tunnel under Lion Rock, emerging in the Sha Tin Valley. Out the window, Leah saw workers in the rice paddies. The train cut over to the coast to Tai Po and went onto Fanling, a military town. There were a great many jeeps and trucks around. Soldiers milled about in large groups waiting for something to happen.

The train crossed into China at Lo Wu Bridge over the

River Sham Chun. Self-important guards with grim faces made all the passengers get off the train and walk to the Customs Office.

Leah gave their papers to An-li. Sonia and Leah stood passively behind her as the young official inspected their visas and tickets.

The official stared at Leah a long time. He said to An-li in bad Cantonese, "It's not a good time for foreign devil ladies to be travelling."

An-li shrugged.

The man stamped their passports.

The women boarded the older, shabbier Chinese train and made their way to their compartment.

PART II

CHINA,
WINTER 1937–1938

11

THE
CHINESE TRAIN

THE ATMOSPHERE ON this train felt different to Leah. It was in the air, a certain brittleness, as if one had to step warily. The other passengers stared guardedly, then lowered their voices as the three women squeezed down the passageway, a porter in tow. The porter piled their luggage precariously above their seats. The women stood and watched, taking in the compartment's cracked leather seats, yellowing linen headrests, and black-spotted mirror.

An-li took a seat facing forward. Sonia humped herself into the opposite seat and blew smoke rings. The rings hung in the air. An-li flicked them away. Sonia gave a pleased smile. An-li pulled down Jonathan's crate of fruit. She took out an orange and peeled it using her fingernails. A squirt of juice landed on Sonia's hand-tailored taupe skirt.

"You did that on purpose, you dirty—"

Leah sprang out of her seat. "Don't, Sonia, it was an accident."

An-li pulled down a thermos of water and mopped at the stain, turning Sonia's skirt into a watery mess.

"Stop it," said Sonia, slapping at An-li's hands.

"It will dry," said An-li. "You won't notice once it dries."

"You have no idea," said Sonia.

"I'm going to the dining car," said Leah and pushed open the door with a bang. Sonia let out an exasperated breath as Leah passed, then closed her eyes, feigning sleep.

The restaurant car was nearly empty except for a morose old couple sipping tea. Leah stared at the menu, not hungry, glad to be alone. The dining car door opened, and a thirty-something European man in a creased suit entered. He had a bullet-shaped head, a receding hairline, thick eyebrows, and a questioning look on his face. He quickly scanned the diners and headed for Leah. Leah buried her head in the menu, willing the man to go away. He stood next to her table and said, hurriedly, "May I?" as he pulled out a chair and sat down. "Benjamin Eldersen," he said, extending his hand across the table and waited. Leah stared.

"You're supposed to say 'Pleased to meet you, Mr. Eldersen. My name is Miss So-and-So, I'm a missionary,' or you might say 'I'm Miss So-and-So, and I'm a teacher.' Or you might say 'I'm *Mrs.* So-and-So;' then I would be disappointed."

She laughed and said, "Leah Kolbe, and none of the above."

"Thank God for that. What do you recommend? . . . Oh, damn. Please, Miss Kolbe, look happy, let me hold your hand, he's coming. Don't look around."

A breeze from the opened carriage door preceded a bulky pale-faced man with faded blue eyes. He stopped at their table and inclined his head. Eldersen stood up and said in an emphatic voice, "This is my good friend Leah Kolbe. We just happened to bump into each other. Extraordinary coincidence, don't you think, Pastor Heinslater?"

The pastor nodded solemnly and gazed heavenward. "You must have a lot of catching up to do. I'll just sit over at that table and converse with *my* friend." The pastor held up his black tattered Bible. Leah smiled sweetly.

When the pastor had gone, Eldersen whispered, "Thank you. I have the misfortune of sharing a compartment with the pastor, a missionary of some dopey order. According to old Heinslater, the Japs have built good roads, made China safer, clamped down on Chinese bandits." He stopped and studied Leah. "Don't you believe it. Killed a lot of poor men for no good reason, more likely. How he squares this with his Christian soul, God knows."

"You're not in the God business?"

"Not yet. I'm a journalist."

"Oh."

"Don't say that. We're the truth squad as opposed to the salvation squad, and we get to look around." He pointed out the window as the train hissed to a stop at a station. An enormous pile of sandbags was stacked at the end of the platform. Parked on the siding was an automobile painted in green and grey camouflage with a machine gun mounted on the roof. A bored soldier, puffing on a cigarette, sat cross-legged behind it. Another soldier sat in the driver's seat hunched over the steering wheel. He peered into the windows of the train.

"Lots to see," said Eldersen. He smiled, showing his jumbled teeth. "Where are you off to?"

The waiter returned. "Whisky," said Eldersen and turned to Leah who asked for bottled water in Mandarin. Eldersen let out a small whistle of approval. "Languages are hard for me. Have a tin ear. The Mancunian accent." He eyed her. "That's the reason I'm here, really. Did well in the northern papers, not quite posh enough for London. Kept getting assigned to cover sport or," he paused, not wanting to overstep the boundaries of politeness, "adultery cases between Lord So-and-So and the Honourable Whatsit. It's your turn now." He liked her wry smile.

"My turn?"

"I'm interested. Young woman alone travelling *into* China, not out. Raises the old reporter hackles. Can't help myself."

"Not much of a story. I grew up in Hong Kong and was good at languages. A friend asked me to set up an academic study tour in Manchuria for some British entomologists. End of story. I'm sorry it's so boring."

"Interesting. I think you've edited out a lot." He wasn't about to ask too many questions, afraid his intrusiveness might frighten her off. Time to go slow, old chap, he cautioned himself.

They ordered dinner. Eldersen asked for the bottle of whisky to be brought to the table. He poured generous splashes into Leah's glass. It didn't help much. He found it difficult to break down her reserve, despite her willingness to converse.

A party of six Chinese public servants came in. The waiter kept bringing them more food. In fascinated horror, Leah and Eldersen watched as the men chewed their food with relish, then spat it out.

"Fear of poisoning," said Eldersen, "saw it in Shanghai. Strange race, the Chinese, very Byzantine. A certain weakness in the soul. They'll never beat the Japs."

Leah dismissed Eldersen as another hack writer, an unattached stringer. She knew the type. They breezed into Hong Kong, made snap judgments about the political situation or the Chinese way of life, then breezed out with a fistful of quaint photographs for the English picture newspapers.

"Everything good in Japanese culture has been taken from the Chinese," said Leah.

"A patriot, makes a change," said Eldersen.

"I have to go now. It's An-li's turn to eat. One of us must stay in the compartment. Thieves are rampant," said Leah.

"A sign of the times," said Eldersen. He rose with the linen napkin still tucked into his waistband and bowed his goodbye. He forced himself to sit back down, but his eyes followed Leah's body, which swayed in time with the rocking of the train. He was pleased that it was going to be a long journey.

OVER the next few days, Eldersen sought Leah out, bringing into their compartment a bottle of whisky and an accumulation of stories that Leah thought might be untrue.

"I thought you said you worked for Reuters," said Leah.

"Sometimes. It depends on who pays more. I've a nose for news." He tapped his nose and sipped the whisky. "Going to Manchukuo to see the Japs in action. I was just in Shanghai."

"I don't remember your byline."

"No," he said effortlessly. "The life of a stringer is never easy. They often just put 'Reuters Agency.' What can you do?"

It seemed to Leah that Eldersen made up stories to cover up things he didn't want to explain.

To while away the days of tedious travel, An-li and Leah taught mahjong to Eldersen and Sonia. Eldersen persisted, memorising the symbols and what they meant. He played to win. Sonia played half-heartedly. An-li often won.

"What did you expect? It's a stupid Chink game," said Sonia.

"Now, Sonia," said Eldersen, "play nicely. It's only a game."

"That's right," said An-li. "I make tea now." She pushed opened the compartment door and headed for the restaurant car to get hot water to brew one of her special teas. When she returned, she handed Sonia hers first and watched with satisfaction as the Russian woman drained the cup.

That night Sonia had to get up constantly to go to the toilet. Her banging around woke Leah. On Sonia's fourth foray, Leah snapped on the light and looked at An-li, fast asleep. "Stop pretending, An-li. I know what you did. It won't help matters."

An-li didn't move, adding a small snore.

"Please do something useful instead," said Leah and turned off the light. Sonia stumbled back into the compartment, cursing.

During the next day, An-li spent very little time in the compartment. When the other two left for lunch, she whispered to Leah, "On the surface everything is normal, but underneath . . . people are nervous. They believe no one. The Japanese are everywhere and nowhere."

The afternoon dragged on. Eldersen began to lose steadily to Leah despite his improved strategies. "It's a subtle game," said Leah.

"If you say so," said Eldersen.

A glum conductor knocked on the compartment door. He looked at his feet as he spoke. "By government order, this train is requisitioned by the Chinese Army. Passengers will disembark at Peking. For those continuing on, it may take several days to assemble a new train."

A soldier in an oversized uniform entered. An officer stood at the door and watched the raw recruit in his ill-fitting uniform silently tack down the window shades.

"They don't want us to see out. Maybe it's armament dumps, or maybe they are training along here," said Eldersen.

An-li hurried off to the kitchen car to pump the staff about what they knew and weren't telling.

Sonia uttered several Russian oaths and said, "Come, Benjamin, let's drown our sorrows at the bar."

With a slow smile, Eldersen said, "Not at the moment."

"Suit yourself," said Sonia, rising quickly, leaving the door open. Eldersen closed it firmly.

It was warm in the carriage, and the lowered blinds gave the compartment a strange nap-time feel. Leah shut her eyes, hoping Eldersen would take the hint and go away. But beneath her closed eyelids, she knew he was watching and weighing up something; quite what, she didn't know. He fiddled with the mahjong tiles, scooping them up in one hand—click— and letting them fall into a heap on the table between them—clack. He had no appreciation of the game's intricacies. Concealment gave the player greater manoeuvreability; one hid the state of one's hand from an opponent by using the *chow,* a run of three tiles of the same suit, or the *pung,* three identical tiles. It also increased the score. She opened her eyes. "Must you, Ben?"

"Your story is a front. Why are you going to Manchukuo?"

"Normal life does continue. People do mundane things. There is nothing sinister or below the surface. There is no angle."

"Let me tell you a story, Leah. Ever heard of Captain Amakasu?"

She shook her head.

"About seven years ago, Amakasu was convicted of murder—no, make that murders. He strangled an anarchist leader, Osugi Sakae, his wife, and their six year-old nephew during a Tokyo earthquake—a convenient time for getting rid of troublemakers. Amakasu was an officer in the military police. He was sentenced to ten years. Only, he was on the right side politically; his sentence kept being reduced. Now he is the Chief of Police in Hsingking. I'd say you'd want to watch your step around him. They are all thugs."

"It's a cautionary tale for anarchists," said Leah. "The Japanese Consul in Hong Kong approved of my trip. He'll vouch for me."

Eldersen gave her a searching look.

She felt her face growing red, but met his gaze. Let him think what he wanted.

Eldersen lit a cigarette and savoured its acrid taste. His smoke hung in the closed compartment. He slapped the table hard. Tiles fell off. "See, Leah, things fall apart."

12

THE BLUE
JAZZ CLUB,
PEKING

PEKING WAS MOBBED: people seeking sanctuary, others desperate to get out, waiting around for visas, tickets, cabled money. There were no rooms left in the Western hotels. Eldersen cadged a room with a journalist mate who was hanging around Peking waiting for something to happen. By the time the three women reached the Dynasty Deluxe Hotel, Sonia was willing to offer the concierge five times the going rate. An-li and Leah were adamantly opposed. Someone less favoured would have to be hustled out to make room for them. Leah pictured the strained, travel-weary faces of such a family being paraded under their noses to the utter disdain of the concierge, who would hurry them upstairs to the newly vacated room with its still-warm beds. The hotel manager laughed at their scruples, then proposed floor space at the end of the top-floor corridor. "Very private, and for you a special price," he said. It was twice the cost of a hotel room in normal times.

By evening, they had found a vacant room in a Chinese hotel. Leah tipped one of the workers to deliver two notes, one to Eldersen to tell him where they were staying, and the other one to the railroad office.

"My God, the room's a closet," said Sonia as she slammed the thin door closed. "Are we all meant to sleep on that thing, *together?*"

"It's a *kerang*. It's warm and comfortable. There's a brazier underneath to heat it, and the quilts," said Leah, examining them, "are clean."

"I'll sleep on the floor," volunteered An-li.

"I feel like a trapped rat," said Sonia.

"I'm ready to sleep anywhere," said Leah, and she began to undress where she stood.

Leah listened to Sonia's raspy snores and An-li's wispy sighs. She found the enforced intimacy suffocating. Their breathing clogged the airless room. She remembered tales of cats who sat on babies' chests and sucked out their breath so that their mothers found them in their cots, dead. She heard a different noise, a heavy slippered tread. It lingered outside her door. She eased out of bed, tiptoed around An-li, and crouched to pick up an envelope that had been shoved under the door. For several minutes, she debated where to read it. She trod on An-li's outstretched hand. An-li gave a small yelp and sat up.

"Sorry, sorry," said Leah. "I don't think the water agrees with me."

She fled down the hallway to the toilet. Inside the smelly cubicle, she examined the envelope. In brown ink, written in an old-fashioned hand, was her name, Miss L. Kolbe. She tore open the envelope and read:

Man is to be trusted and yet never to be trusted completely. If this is not understood, it is impossible to make use of the right people correctly. The Blue Jazz Club tomorrow night. Come alone.

Leah recognised the words of Emperor Yung Chen, who, in the sixteenth century, had unsuccessfully tried to bring order and accountability to the wayward rule of the three thousand eunuchs in the Forbidden City. The Blue Jazz Club she didn't know. She shredded the note and watched the pieces flutter and sink down the toilet. Slowly, she walked down the hall, determined not to look behind her.

ELDERSEN came around early in the evening. He was confident that a train would be cobbled together sometime the next day. He had made inquiries while he poked around Peking with an interpreter in tow. "Let's make a night of it," he said as if he had just thought of the idea and not spent the whole afternoon puzzling out what Leah was up to and how he could appeal to her.

Sonia jumped off the *kerang* and said, "I'd love to."

Leah massaged her temples. "Oh, Ben," she said, "it must be the Peking dust or a change in the weather, but I don't feel up to it." She saw the disappointment in his face. "But please, you, Sonia, and An-li go. It will be quiet here and do me good."

"I'll stay too," said An-li.

Leah rubbed her temples, saying, "No, please, I insist."

An-li studied Leah's face. It hadn't taken on that strange dead pallor and she wasn't shading her eyes from the electric light. There was no headache. Leah wanted her to keep an eye on the Russian and the reporter. She didn't trust them. Reporters were stupid, always writing about things they knew nothing about and adding up one and two to get five. "Thank you, Mr. Eldersen, I accept your generous invitation," said An-li.

Sonia rearranged her face and said dryly, "It should be quite an evening. Thank God, *now* we won't have to dress for dinner. We can go as we are."

As they left, Eldersen turned to look at Leah, who was wearing pleated trousers and a white silk blouse. She leaned against the door, languid, beautiful. He wished he were staying with her.

☉

THE Blue Jazz Club was having a slow night. Many tables stood empty. Three tables away from Leah sat a contented Chinese family taking in the show. They toned down the atmosphere of a home-grown nightclub pretending to be a Parisian dive, turning it instead into an oddly wholesome family affair, like a wedding with both drunken, lecherous guests and sleepy children. At the table, the two children jumped off their chairs and made a couple on the dance floor. In a tight embrace, they paced the floor. Their parents—the mother with marcelled hair and the father in a Western suit—laughed at their antics The female-for-hire taxi dancers, with their practised sang-froid, ignored them. This was business, after all.

Leah nursed her drink, pushing the lemon around in the glass. A waiter asked if she wanted another. Leah said no, afraid to consume too much. The music lulled her as she watched the dancers and their partners passing. It was all a show, the girls acting compliant, the men feigning desire. From nowhere, she felt an ache, a stab of loneliness. Cezar. Where would he be? At the casino, or in that same anonymous hotel room with another girl? His body would move so . . . so gracefully, his hand fitting into the small of her back, and the seductive pressure of his leg pressed against hers. She tapped a foot in time with the music.

The glances of the men lounging around the room flicked over her, to the taxi girls. Several girl couples were perfecting their tango steps. Their bodies dipped and slithered to the music of the Chinese band, whose members were in well-cut evening clothes and slicked-back hair. Leah was struck by the odd sweetness in the girls' movements, like schoolgirls at a cotillion whispering secrets behind their hands, concealing their cherry-red cupid's-bow lips. Their dancing was full of yearning for escape. On the sidelines, Leah saw the men silently calculating each dancer's worth. The music finished.

Several dancers returned to their tables; others joined the men slouched against the wall to hold inaudible conversations. The drummer beat the cymbals. The stage lights blinked and a spotlight hit the dance floor. Caught in its arc were four Russian acrobats. The three men, dressed in silky black Cossack trousers and red embroidered high-necked shirts, shouted "high ya" and "ups" to a woman in a thigh-slashed sparkling dress. They did leaps and shoulder stands as the woman twirled around, flashing her white thighs. For the finale, the woman did a series of cruel splits as the three Cossacks stood breathing heavily, their arms on their hips. In the hard yellow light, Leah saw the powder-caked creases of their lined faces, how the men's hair was dyed a fierce black, and the woman's dark roots showed through the blondness. Leah pictured Sonia on stage, wiggling her hips, her eyes thickly kohled. Yes, she'd smile that lupine smile and promise anything for an easy life. During the clapping, the Chinese family left in a noisy heap. For a moment, Leah wished she could run after them and invite them to return so she could watch them watch her pretend to enjoy herself. The club went dark.

A callused hand touched Leah's bare shoulder. Her skin tightened and crawled under its contact. Chang whispered into her ear, "Miss Kolbe, always a pleasure." The lights came back on, dim and moody.

She turned and said, "Mr. Chang, I do hope so. Please sit down."

"In a place like this," he said, "one must dance."

Tango music filled the room. Chang placed a firm hand under her elbow and steered her onto the dance floor. He gripped her hand, her fingers tight against each other. Her breasts grazed his suit. She wanted to lean away to study his face, but he pulled her against him until his thigh was between her legs and she was dizzy from following his expert twists.

"We dance well. Are you travelling well?" said Chang in a quiet voice.

"Do you come here often?" she said.

He loosened his grip and grimaced. "Clever, Miss Kolbe. Where you are going, such humour may not be understood. The Japs find cruelty amusing."

He pulled her close and executed a complicated back step. Leah moved her feet to avoid stumbling. "Miss Rubstov, she is behaving herself? Sometimes Miss Rubstov forgets what side she is on. The Russians have always wanted Manchuria. Parts of Manchuria, I am told, are very Russian, like the city of Harbin. Their heads are full of plots and counterplots. Trust only yourself."

"Perhaps, Mr. Chang, Miss Rubstov should be sent home. I don't need her."

He seemed to consider the suggestion as he twirled Leah out under his arm, his hand clasped tight around hers, and then pulled her back toward his chest. "Miss Rubstov is another pair of eyes and hands. A second pair is always useful in difficult times, don't you agree, Miss Kolbe?"

In the dim light, shadows played tricks. She couldn't read Chang's expression. Did he feel concern, or was he warning her? The music stopped. Chang let go of Leah's hand. They stood side by side.

The bandleader tapped his stick on the music stand and waved his arms. The music became syncopated, jazzy. Chang swayed to the music, his eyes closed. Uncertain, Leah watched until Chang's eyelids popped open and he said, dreamily, "You must contact Pu Yi's Chief Eunuch, Quan. To Quan you will say 'I wish you great happiness.' Quan will repeat these words and ask 'What country are you from?' You must say 'The Land of the Dragon.' You understand?"

She nodded as she smothered the urge to quip "Schoolboys at play." Already Chang had moved a few feet away. Out of nowhere, the floor was flooded with taxi dancers. Leah caught only Chang's parting nod in her general direction as a taxi girl with a pinched faced grabbed Leah's hand and began to dance. They improvised a two-step that made a joke out of an American blues number played by the band aping French nonchalance. At the end of the song, Leah attempted to pay for the dance. The dancer refused and led her away to join her fellow dancers at a corner table.

Leah ordered drinks for the five bob-haired women, who were all wearing revealing dresses. The women talked about the men hanging about and teased one another. Her dancing partner patted Leah's hand and said, in English, "Men are stupid." Leah shrugged her agreement and asked for another round of drinks. The women demanded champagne. The Russian acrobats pushed past their table. In their street clothes, they looked like drab middle-aged commissars. The taxi dancer said, "Bandits and whores. They go with anybody."

"Do you know—?" Leah began.

"No," said the taxi dancer. "We dance more now."

The noise rose, the club grew crowded and smoky. Leah ordered more drinks. Men came regularly to the table and hired the women. Her English-speaking partner smiled sadly, then put on a bright face as she went off clasping the hand of a man with wispy hair and a fat stomach. Leah felt like an unwanted child, left to gape at the bigger, more talented children at play. She rose unsteadily to her feet and made her way to the door to hail a rickshaw puller. By the glow of the oil lamp attached to the front of his cart, she watched his bare legs flicker through the quiet streets of Peking to her hotel.

13

MANCHUKUO

A COLD WIND whipped through Hsingking Station as Leah, Sonia, and An-li, seated on a hard bench, waited for the Japanese soldier to allow them to leave. The greying Chinese stationmaster was busy explaining for the third time to the soldier why the women's visas' dates and tickets didn't match. The soldier kept cocking his head at the stationmaster, looking stern. Eldersen waved his press card around. The soldier ignored him.

"I give up," said Eldersen. "I'll be at the Yamato Hotel Central. Eventually, the soldier will get tired of being officious and walk away." He waved brightly, bowed to the soldier and said, in a pleasant voice, "Bugger off."

The soldier returned the bow. Sonia choked on her cheroot. For the fourth time, the stationmaster said, in a patient voice, "There are unexpected delays. We cannot be held responsible."

The soldier managed "Wait here" in Chinese and hurried off. The seat got harder. Leah feared they would be sent back on the next train. Sonia whispered "Money," and rummaged through her handbag trying to determine how much one should offer as a bribe to a soldier.

"No," hissed Leah. "We'll end up in jail."

The soldier returned with his lieutenant. The lieutenant insisted they open their suitcases and handbags. The soldier dumped everything out onto the dirty floor, then shook the cases hard. The lieutenant stared impassively at the women. Finally, the lieutenant said, in broken English, "You can go now. But you must report to the Central Police Station in three days." He held up three fingers, then scribbled a note in Japanese. "You must give this to the Chief of Police. You understand?"

The three women nodded and bowed their heads. The soldier saluted the lieutenant and they marched away. "Let's get out of here," said Leah and began stuffing her clothes back into her suitcase, relieved the soldier hadn't found her little gun, but very worried about meeting the police chief, Amakasu.

Outside, the grim day had changed into wet, cold dusk. In the ageing taxi, Sonia strained to read the Cyrillic signs through the heavy rain. She ordered the taxi to stop in front of the Old Russian Hotel. Above the hotel doorway was a faded picture of onion-domed St. Basil's. The lobby smelled of cabbage and vodka. A Slavic woman with a broad forehead sat behind a battered desk displaying the hotel register. Sonia signed her name. The woman read the signature aloud, sounding out the name slowly, staring at Sonia as if trying to place her, then grunted hello.

"It's been a long time," said Sonia in Russian.

The woman shrugged in recognition and fiddled with her faded pale hair. She called, "Sasha."

A pimply-faced youth with a bad haircut appeared. "My son," said the woman. "Take the bags, Sasha." She handed him two keys.

"You don't mind sharing with An-li rather than with me, do you, Leah?" said Sonia.

"No," said Leah. "You smoke too much."

When they reached the room, Sasha placed the suitcase on the luggage rack and wandered around the room, flicking the lamps on and off to prove that they worked, and opened a window. He stuck his head out and inhaled deeply. To get rid of the boy, Leah tipped him generously. His pimples glowed fiercely.

"It's okay here, if you have money," he said and abruptly left.

An-li locked the door.

"Do you think it's safe?" said Leah.

An-li ripped off the tatty mustard-coloured bedspread. She studied the sheets, then ran her hands over them, sniffing at them. "No insects, no bedbugs. But it's an unhappy place."

Lying in the lumpy narrow bed, Leah thought about Sonia, about how Chang had lured her into working for him, and how she had ended up in the Old Russian with its air of defeat, like a tubercular old man. God, she'd give anything not to be here but back in Hong Kong in her own sunny hot room, clean and safe. . . Her mind drifted to Captain Amakasu. Eldersen was just showing off how much he knew about Manchukuo. Amakasu would be too busy to question them personally about what they were doing here. Their papers were watertight. Eldersen should write about Sonia. She'd spin him such tales from her past that Eldersen would lose interest in their dealings in Hsingking. He could entitle it "How I Travelled though China with the Last Remnant of Czarist Russia." Leah attempted to explain the joke to An-li who, in a sleepy, cross voice, said, "She's a whore."

"Sonia's meeting her contact, Vasiliev, tomorrow. I'm going to present my papers to Pu Yi's office. Wish me luck."

"I'm coming too."

"No, An-li. I need you to follow Sonia."

An-li sat up and peered through the dark. "Wear your black suit, no makeup, and don't smile."

"The Japanese respect official papers. Everything will be fine."

"If you say so," said An-li. In a Peking street in the middle of the day, she had seen white-gloved Japanese officers grope Chinese girls who submitted to their touch with anguished faces and tears. No one did anything to stop the soldiers, just ducked their heads and avoided the girls' pleading eyes. Ashamed, An-li had gone back to the hotel room and picked over Leah's clothes, throwing away those she considered immodest.

⌒

IN the uncertain winter light, shadows formed on the flaking walls of the Japanese offices of Hoshino Naoki, Director of General Affairs, and Chief Civilian Officer. In ancient days, such shadows inspired Chinese scholars to flights of imagination, but Leah saw only Japanese soldiers marching in formation or a soldier pointing a rifle. Finally, a real soldier entered the waiting room and bowed.

She followed him through a long corridor and up a wide staircase to a room in which groups of armchairs were scattered around. The soldier bowed deeply in front of a large gold-framed picture of Emperor Hirohito and stood at attention behind her chair. His breath fell on her neck. Every now and again, she heard a faint creak as he moved. She forced herself to sit naturally and studied a smaller, black-framed photograph of Pu Yi standing in a semicircle of Japanese dignitaries. Half the dignitaries wore full military dress; the rest, morning coats. Not one of the men smiled. Pu Yi looked numb, his eyes cast sideways onto General Hishikari Takashi, as if reassuring himself that he appeared sufficiently in charge.

A Japanese officer with a thin face dominated by thick eyebrows entered and inclined his head an inch as Leah rose to her feet. "Colonel Yoshioka, Attaché to the Imperial Household. I have been examining your papers, Miss Kolbe," he said in a high-pitched whine.

Leah raised her head. She was taller. She bent her knees and rushed into speech. "I am pleased and delighted you have taken your valuable time to consider my lowly request. I am privileged to be the humble representative of eminent British scholars. They are eager for me to speak of their studies to his Excellency Pu Yi."

Yoshioka prevaricated. His Excellency had a full schedule. His diary was booked months in advance. There were so many decisions regarding the building of a new country: banking arrangements, a new currency, customs duties, enforcing the land rights of Korean settlers, and establishing the monopoly board to control opium. His Excellency was also in charge of assisting the Japanese Imperial Army in explaining to the citizenry of Manchukuo what unity with Japan meant and the benefits that would accrue to all Asian people. He looked at her, hard-eyed. "Do you understand such unity, Miss Kolbe?"

"Not in depth, Attaché."

The attaché explained in detail the edicts Pu Yi had signed. Leah nodded and smiled in all the right places and managed not to look surprised when Yoshioka stated blandly that Japanese citizens had more rights than Manchukuo Chinese because the Japanese had brought peace and prosperity to the new country. Tea was brought in. The steward, dressed in a high-necked black jacket, poured green tea into sky-blue glazed cups. Leah restrained herself from placing the exquisite cup into her handbag as the attaché droned on in his waspish voice about forging new alliances. It dawned on Leah that Yoshioka thought she represented the first feeble attempt by the British to test a new relationship with the rogue state of Manchukuo. Yoshioka sent for a note-taker, who wrote at a furious pace. Leah played along, discreetly name-dropping, mentioning high-profile Hong Kong officials and Mr. Wang, the richest Chinese in the Colony.

Abruptly, the attaché tapped his watch and stood. With a bow six inches deep this time, he promised nothing, but said he would look into the matter.

Once outside, Leah walked aimlessly, wandering around the blunt new buildings of the Japanese. The buildings had been designed by a group of Germans. It was what she imagined Berlin might look like; full of concrete edifices with harsh lines like bunkers proclaiming a new authority. There was nothing Asian about them. She drifted into the older parts of the city. People gawked at her but kept their distance. She plastered a smile on her face and tried not to mind that she was the oddity here. One child looked at her and immediately started crying.

There were slogans and banners everywhere exhorting the Chinese to extend the hand of friendship to their glorious Japanese brothers and join in the new renaissance of the East. In Hong Kong streets the Chinese were loud and voluble, but here people spoke softly and their faces betrayed little emotion. They were like mulberry leaves devoured by silkworms. How many were informers and spies?

Footsore and cold, she took a taxi to the palace of Pu Yi. From the taxi window, she stared at glassy-eyed Japanese soldiers guarding the tall iron gates and the buildings beyond. In the middle of the compound was a plain square building, more a prison than a palace. Depressed and weary, she asked to be driven to her hotel. The driver kept checking his mirror as he took a circuitous route to the Russian quarter.

14

THE MAN OF A THOUSAND CONNECTIONS

LEAH LIMPED UP the stairs of the hotel and unlocked the door to her empty room. Exhausted, she kicked off her high heels and flung herself onto the bed. She closed her eyes, but sleep wouldn't come. Her feet were icy. She wriggled out of her skirt and pulled the rough blankets over her. The whine of the attaché's voice droned in her head. Had he believed her? Was an underling already busy investigating her bona fides or, God forbid, Sonia's? She could see the attaché handing a bulging folder with her name in large black letters to the Chief of Police. There was a loud knock at the door. She froze.

"Open up," said Sonia, rattling the doorknob.

In her petticoat, Leah opened the door to Sonia and a leering, short rotund man with blue circles under his eyes and spidery capillaries on his prominent nose.

"Meet Vasiliev," said Sonia.

Vasiliev grabbed Leah's hand and kissed it passionately. Slyly, Leah wiped her hand against her slip.

"I saw that," said Vasiliev. "She's cunning, Sonia."

"Oh," said Sonia, "she's good. She's been well trained. Her father—"

"Wait here. I have to get dressed."

"Vasiliev doesn't mind; he's seen it all before," said Sonia and barged past Leah into the room.

Vasiliev sat on Leah's bed. Like a valet, he handed Leah her skirt and blouse. He watched her fumble with the buttons. "You have Slavic eyes," said Vasiliev. "We will get along."

Leah smoothed down her skirt and gave him a stiff smile.

"Don't mind Vasiliev. He's had a hard life," said Sonia.

"Too true, my darling Sonia." Vasiliev fluffed up the bed pillows and lay back. Sonia sat next to him and started to stroke his hand. Vasiliev embraced Sonia in a brotherly hug. Over Sonia's head, he raised a mocking eyebrow. Leah ignored it.

"Have you been in Hsingking long, Mr. Vasiliev?" asked Leah.

"Let's not be so formal. It's just Vasiliev, makes things easier. Yes? And how are you finding our provincial city, Leah? Your servant An-li has been very busy sightseeing. We kept bumping into her today, didn't we, Sonia?"

"It's a small place," said Leah too quickly. "I poked around the palace today. It's a fortress."

"Our trumped-up little emperor, Pu Yi, is penned in well," Vasiliev said with glee in his voice. "None of the royal family can so much as stick their heads outside without a Jap in tow. I have it on good authority," he said pressing a podgy finger against his red nose and looking wise and crafty, "that Pu Yi can't even stroll around his own garden. Some garden: brown weeds. A dog wouldn't piss there. Once he tried to promenade around, but Jap soldiers ran out yelling and screaming and herded the mongrel back to his doghouse. He's on a very short leash."

"Does anyone see the emperor?"

"The eunuchs trot back and forth at will. They're the ones with power, besides the Japs. The Japs can't stand them; the idea revolts them." Vasiliev laughed and rubbed a hairy hand across his crotch.

"Vasiliev knows the important eunuchs," said Sonia. "He knows everyone."

Vasiliev licked his lips. "They like their entertainments; I do my best to keep the important ones like Quan amused. . ." He beamed at Leah.

"Do you see this Quan often?" said Leah in a casual voice, keeping her eyes on Vasiliev who slipped in a sideways gauging glance at Sonia.

Sonia looked pleased and self-congratulatory. And Leah realised that the two had joined forces. Where did that leave her?

"Sometimes we meet. Would you like to make Quan's acquaintance, Miss Kolbe?"

So formal, so cool, thought Leah and watched Vasiliev stretch and change position, to lie with his head at the foot of the bed. He propped his hand under his jowls and posed like an odalisque, his head twisted over his shoulder, his enormous backside confronting her like a haunch of meat.

"For a price, eh, Sonia?" said Vasiliev.

"As always, my dear Vasiliev. We must all live," said Sonia, lighting a cheroot as if it were agreed.

"Sonia, I haven't agreed," said Leah. "There are other interests to consider."

Sonia inhaled deeply on her cheroot. Then like a dragon whose smoky breath was escaping, she said, "Vasiliev already knows everything. He's been assisting Quan to smuggle out jewels and small precious objects. We arranged this in Macau."

Vasiliev said, modestly, "It's a delicate operation."

"But," said Sonia, "it has left a loose end."

"Me," said Vasiliev, fluttering his eyelashes.

Leah slumped into the rickety chair in front of the dressing table. If she looked into the mirror, she thought she would see the word *naïve* etched on her forehead. "I think you might have told me about this . . . arrangement earlier. . . . There is no point in working against one another."

"I'm telling you now," said Sonia, as if this would put things right. "Our Hong Kong partner would not understand the need for our strategic alliance." She flashed a conspirator's smile. "Vasiliev and I have devised a new twist. We're going to sell Quan to the Soviets—"

"It's a great plan," said Vasiliev hurriedly, ignoring Leah's look of distress. "Your client won't care, once he sees what Quan has collected. The eunuch is really worthless to him, but to the Soviets he is a prize. For them he has great propaganda value. He knows a great deal about the Japanese. And for the Soviets, Manchuria is important militarily. Besides," said Vasiliev speaking to the ceiling in a disinterested, distant voice, "these are dangerous times. Lots of dreadful deaths occur.

There is fighting everywhere. Quan will simply have died in one of these skirmishes. It's child's play, really."

Leah stared. In one swift move, Vasiliev had shifted the risk from himself to her. What about Chang's demand that Quan be brought to him? How would she explain this "twist" to him?

"It's a simple plan. Simple plans work best," said Sonia. "They've already wired a down-payment to my bank." She opened her black leather purse, pulled out a telegram and handed it to Leah.

It seemed genuine enough. It was from Mr. Charles Kirk, head of accounts of the Bank of Shanghai and Hong Kong. Ten thousand pounds sterling had been deposited to Sonia's account by a British bank. Then it said: "As per your instruction. Stop. Have contacted Mr. J. Hawatyne. Stop. Will arrange transfer of four thousand (4,000) pounds through him to Miss L. Kolbe. Stop." The telegram was dated the day of their departure from Hong Kong.

"Not quite a fifty-fifty split," said Leah sourly.

Sonia shrugged. "It took a lot of arranging. And there's a second payment due us when Quan is delivered."

Hard-eyed, Leah took in Vasiliev lolling on the bed and Sonia slouched beside him. He was a toad. Sonia must have warts all over her body. Methodically, Leah folded the telegram in half and began to tear it up. "We don't want to leave a paper trail, do we?" she said. Sonia and Vasiliev nodded wisely.

"Quan insists he meet with you two ladies to discuss travel arrangements." He heaved himself off the bed. From inside his breast pocket, he pulled out a small black diary. He thumbed the pages. Leah saw his tiny Cyrillic handwriting flash by—dates, names, codes. He was a man of a thousand connections. "We must go through with the charade," he said. "I'll contact you."

"I'll see you out, my old friend," said Sonia with an edgy, relieved laugh.

Vasiliev lunged at Leah and kissed her wetly on the forehead. Sonia linked arms with Vasiliev and escorted him down the hall. In the doorway, Leah watched them disappear. They made a strange couple, the tall angular woman with the short man who took two steps to Sonia's one. Theo, she wanted to scream, look what they have done to me. Double-crossing a man like Chang. What shall I do? It was like a terrible game of blind man's bluff, a game she had hated. The running, the screaming, the muffled giggles as girls were willingly groped. Once she had returned home crying. Theo had wiped her tears away with his thumbs and said, "Cheat when it's your turn. Rearrange the blindfold and hide when the other child is blindfolded." She hadn't minded playing after that.

15

SIGHTSEEING

"LEAH, WHAT POSSESSED you to book in here? It's a cross between a sleazy bordello and a Leeds boarding house," said Eldersen, watching Leah sip tea in the dining room that had been painted yellow but had sickened to bile.

"It's not that bad. A friend of a friend of Sonia's runs it. They are very accommodating."

Eldersen sat down in a battered chair. He motioned to Sasha to bring another cup.

"His cup going on your bill?" asked Sasha. "We don't serve nonguests."

Eldersen grinned. "Yes," he said, "very accommodating."

Sasha returned and set the cup down with a bang. Tea

splashed onto the table. He pulled out a dirty rag and pushed the damp mess around, then wandered off.

"So, what have you girls been up to?"

Leah drained her tea. "Not much. Waiting. Everything seems to take twice as long here."

"They make Whitehall look like amateurs," said Eldersen. "They have an endless supply of liaison officers. I think I've met all the slimy sycophants. One gave me a two-volume set of books explaining why Japan *had* to take over Manchuria. Lies, all lies. Last night I threw the damn thing in my waste bin. When I returned to my room, it had been taken out, dusted and put on my bedside table. I've taken to using my penknife to cut sections out to flush down the toilet. That should stuff up their sewage system right and proper. The Japs are—" His face froze; his eyes widened. "The Japanese are very correct," he added lamely as Leah turned to see a Japanese officer wearing snowy-white gloves and a blank face approaching.

The soldier bowed and said slowly, "Miss Kolbe?"

"Yes."

"For you, Miss Kolbe." He handed her a stiff white envelope with her name and the address of the hotel in beautiful calligraphy. The soldier bowed again, then straightened and marched out of the room.

Leah turned the envelope over to break the gold seal.

"You travel in elevated circles," said Eldersen. He watched Leah's face. An anxious smile played around her mouth. She looked relieved as she read the handwritten message on the linen-weave card:

His Excellency the Chief Executive Officer of Manchukuo
requests the pleasure of Miss Leah Kolbe's company,
Thursday the twenty-ninth at 4:00 P.M.
Cocktails to be served.

"Good news, Leah?"

"I've been granted an audience."

"Can a commoner see?"

Reluctantly, she handed him the invitation.

"Cocktails, in this god-forsaken place. How bizarre. Think you could get me in as your escort?"

"No," said Leah. "It's rude to turn up uninvited."

"How very proper you can be. At least it would be something to do. The waiting gets on one's nerves."

"Come sightseeing with us. We have to find accommodations for our English professors."

She looked so appealing when she invited him to accompany her. For a second, Eldersen almost believed that Leah was in Manchuria doing just what she said she was: paving the way for crazy British academics to come to this cruel, hard place and study bugs while the world prepared for war. "Thanks. I'd be delighted."

Like an ungainly school crocodile, the three women and Eldersen roamed the crowded city. In a dusty street, they watched a concrete mixer belch wet cement into buckets and labourers carry the buckets up rickety bamboo scaffolding to yet another depressing apartment block. This building would be like all the other recent constructions: institutional, lifeless, and somehow foreboding.

"Your professors will hate it here. Maybe they won't come," said Eldersen.

"Oh," said Leah, "they'll come all right. But how long they'll stay is another matter."

Eldersen grinned. She played the game well, never took the bait. She had a lot of patience. He admired patience. It meant you were willing to wait to get what you wanted. He'd gotten his best stories that way.

An-li led them to the old walled town of lanes and stall shops that sold fur, grain, and alcohol. In a tiny alley, a young man stood smoking near a toothless street vendor cooking on an open brazier. The vendor tossed onion, shards of meat, and bean sprouts into the wok. The cooking attracted two Japanese soldiers, who demanded to be served. The young man intervened, saying in halting Japanese, "Few more minutes, few more minutes." The thickset soldier ripped the cigarette out of the young man's mouth and shoved him sprawling onto the road. The vendor shovelled the half-cooked food onto a plate. The soldier sniffed the food and dumped it on the ground. He shouted at the vendor who was cringing and apologising. The second soldier pulled his gun on the young man as he attempted to stand and aimed it at his head. The young man threw his hands high into the air.

"Stop," Leah cried out in English, "he's only—"

The thickset soldier jerked around with a hostile glare.

Alarmed, Eldersen slapped Leah's face, yelling "Bitch" in a booming voice, and harangued her for being a stupid woman. The soldier smirked and nodded, then turned back to land a brutal cuff on the vendor's terrified head. The two soldiers caught the young man under the armpits and frog-marched him away.

"How dare——," spluttered Leah, rubbing her bruised cheek.

"Please forgive me. Those young soldiers . . . they are capable of anything," said Eldersen.

Sonia clapped her hands. "I, for one, found it very impressive and gallant," she said, continuing to clap.

"Shut up, Sonia," said Leah.

"Please let me make it up to you. I'll take you all out for drinks and dinner. The best place in town," said Eldersen.

An-li scowled, but Leah thought it couldn't be worse than the Old Russian. "I'll have champagne," said Leah.

Eldersen winced and hoped he could claim it on expenses. "Sure, why not?" he said.

☺

THE Yamato Hotel bar was done up in bureaucratic green and shiny metal. The bar was a long polished sheet of steel and behind it, lit shelves of enormous bottles of whisky and saki were mirrored. Despite his smiles, the Chinese bartender looked nervous as Japanese businessmen with their Korean "wives" came in. They drank steadily. A "wife" dug her red nails into her husband's jacket in an effort to keep him from slipping under the table. Another draped her man's arms around her own thin shoulders and held him up, her knuckles whitening. Other Japanese officers sat at womanless tables. Their rough laughter permeated the bar. It made Leah edgy.

Four Japanese officers and an unaccompanied silver-haired businessman came over to Leah's table. They insisted on buying rounds of drinks and brought out their halting English in an attempt to make conversation. Sonia flirted with the men in an offhand manner. The businessman was the most aggressive. He was interested in Sonia: he lit her cheroots, made suggestive toasts, and eyed her breasts. An-li sat next to Leah and intercepted the drinks meant for her charge. They sat on the table, the ice melting. Leah, glad she had taken the seat furthest from the men, kept up a façade of polite smiles as she sipped Eldersen's champagne. It was real French champagne.

Eldersen had bravely said to the bartender, "Put it on my bill. I'm staying here." He'd signed the chit without looking. To recoup his losses he kept repeating the Japanese officers names, mangling them, hoping he'd remember a name in the morning to contact for an interview. He doubted the officers would remember him. They were getting very drunk, slurring their words. The youngest officer had spent time in the United States. He proved it by showing off his slang. "You some broad," he said to Leah, who smiled weakly.

Eldersen couldn't stomach any more. "The ladies need their dinner, officers," he announced and handed out his calling cards with his name printed in English and Japanese.

"Mr. Kenzo has invited me to dinner," said Sonia.

Mr. Kenzo stood and ceremoniously invited Eldersen, Leah, and An-li to join him as well. Unable to think of a plausible excuse, Eldersen and Leah agreed.

The bar was crowded and noisy as Eldersen snaked Mr. Kenzo and the women through the scrum. Leah glanced into the mirrored shelves behind the bar. There, with his head lowered, deep in conversation with a pot-bellied Japanese gentleman, was Cezar da Silva. Leah watched Cezar nurse his drink, his eyes trained on the other man, who was talking rapidly and insistently. Leah tugged on An-li's arm. An-li followed Leah's gaze. Leah nodded at Cezar's reflection.

"The Eurasian?" said An-li quietly.

Leah whispered, "Follow him."

When they emerged from the bar into the frosty night air, An-li said, "I don't feel so good. It's too much for me. I'll go back to the hotel now."

A taxi pulled up. "Take it," said Eldersen to An-li.

"No," said An-li. "I'll walk. The air will help me."

Before An-li had finished speaking, Mr. Kenzo barged ahead and seated himself in the passenger seat. The others followed. Leah looked through the rear window at An-li, who hugged her padded coat tightly about her as she walked to the corner. She was such a small figure, alone in the cold. Leah wished she had been a better, sweeter child. On the other hand, she had to learn why Cezar was here, and what he was up to. She didn't believe in coincidences.

AT dinner, Sonia was hard and glittering, keeping the conversation focused on Japanese successes: the improved hygiene, the clean streets, the orderliness of things in such a new country. Mr. Kenzo beamed self-congratulations, as if he had accomplished all these remarkable things himself. Eldersen attempted to pin Kenzo down to specific plans for the future of Manchukuo. But Kenzo uttered only platitudes while his hands strayed from Sonia's knee to Leah's thigh. Leah edged away.

"Now we go to a nightclub," Kenzo announced.

"Terribly sorry," said Eldersen, "I've an early start in the morning."

"Me too," said Leah.

"Don't worry," said Eldersen to a pleased Sonia, who was quite looking forward to the company of a rich man willing to spend a lot of money. "I'll see Leah safely back to her hotel."

16

BEAUTY

 IN THE TAXI, Eldersen said, "Have a nightcap with
me. I've got a flask of good whisky."

"An-li's asleep."

"Well, then, my hotel, my room. It's only a friendly drink,
Leah, I promise."

"All right."

A brass alarm clock and a black Remington typewriter with
a piece of paper in its carriage were the only personal items visible in Eldersen's room. Leah read the first few words: "Soviet
armament manufacturers—"

Eldersen came up behind her and said "It's not polite to
read unfinished work."

"Sorry."

He poured whisky into tooth-glasses from the bathroom.

They sat on his single bed, drinking. He leaned against the bedhead. "I did manage to meet General Hishikari."

"I hear he is the real power behind the throne. What's he like?"

"Ever see a picture of those Easter Island statues? Enormous heads that stand like sentries on a remote Pacific island. Hishikari has the same immobile face, only the statues are better conversationalists. The general resents having to open his mouth." Eldersen sat ramrod-straight and moved his jaw like a puppet.

Leah laughed.

Eldersen relaxed and became expansive under Leah's grey-eyed gaze. He said, "The only thing the general wanted to talk about was Japan's military tradition; safe ground, I guess. He explained *bushido:* the greatest honour a samurai warrior can achieve is to die in the service of one's lord. Then he bragged about the harshness of their military training and how it builds character." He took a slug of whisky. "All it does is brutalise men like those young toughs this afternoon. When I pressed him about Japan's future in China, he ranted about Japan extending the helping hand to their Asiatic brothers. The iron fist, more likely."

He drained his glass and set it down. He reached for Leah's hand and played with her soft fingers, admiring each pink manicured nail. "Pretty hands, delicate but strong." He looked into her eyes. "Don't you trust them, Leah. They're bastards."

Leah disentangled her fingers. "I expect you're right. I have to report to Amakasu tomorrow morning. I'm not looking forward to it. Any tips?" she said a bit too cheerily. She took a large swallow of whisky, appreciating its sour burn.

"I hope your papers are in order. Then again, to the Japanese all Westerners are inscrutable, so your bug-loving English professors might be able to take in Amakasu. Best to be humble and sincere and wear your hair scraped back." He pulled her hair away from her face. "No good, still beautiful."

She let his hands rest on her face. He moved closer and she smelled his whisky-laden breath. "Don't worry," he said and bent to kiss her.

"Don't!" She stood.

Eldersen stared in disappointed approval. "See, that's what I like about you. Always one step ahead. What do you want, Leah? Yeah, I know a home, a marriage, the pitter-patter of little feet."

"No, I don't want that kind of life," she said honestly. "My father was a dealer in antiquities. There is a special kind of power attached to owning beautiful things; the hunt is . . . is an indescribable pleasure. I want to do it too and to do it well, really well."

Her eyes had a special light and her face was dreamy, moody. He wanted to shake her. Instead, he said, "China is one of the poorest countries in the world. They sell their children, for God's sake. It's riddled with corruption and greed. Beauty affects nothing."

"How very modern you are," said Leah. "Do you quote Auden and Orwell too?"

He snorted with contempt. "Poverty is ugly. I grew up in a two-up, two-down rat's nest of a place, cold and damp in winter and summer. Going to the local art gallery didn't change anything. Take the French and their poncing around. Beauty can corrupt. Ask Marie Antoinette."

"And your life," she said, "has it been transformed by chasing after war and adventure? Getting a scoop? You're just collecting other people's experiences."

"Maybe," he said. "At least it's honest."

"What are you hinting, Ben?"

He topped up his glass with whisky. "Nothing, really. But if your story is straight, Sonia's isn't. Mr. Kenzo is not just any businessman. He's a munitions dealer, with fingers in lots of pies."

"They've just met. Sonia's all right. I've known her since I was a baby. She wouldn't—"

"If you say so."

Leah handed back her tooth mug.

He sat looking at her empty glass while he finished the rest of the whisky. Leah roamed around the small room trying to collect her thoughts.

He gave her a searching look as if he were a border guard who might arrest her, and said, "I'm leaving in a few days. The only story here is the plotting that goes on behind closed doors and everyone is too afraid to talk about it. I'm going to Nanking by train. The Japs are fomenting trouble there. Daily shelling. Anyway, I'll look around, then go on to Shanghai and from there by boat to Hong Kong. It's time to clear out of China and Manchukuo."

"Lucky you."

"I can get you a ticket too."

"I'm staying," she said a little too readily.

He gave a self-deprecating shrug, "I'll get you a taxi to your hotel, if that's what you want."

He hated the way she rewarded him with an easy dissembling smile and said, "Please."

Outside on the street, he hugged her tight, then watched her taxi fade from view. He swore at himself for handling it all wrong.

17

AMAKASU

AMAKASU'S OFFICE WAS glass on all sides. From his vantage point, he could see, if not hear, everything that happened in the police station. He was very correct, in a heavy blue serge uniform with gold piping and a rising sun embroidered in gold thread on his collar. Leah thought that without his costume, the Chief of Police could have been mistaken for a bank clerk. He spoke in a quiet voice. Through the glass walls, she saw his staff diligently at work. Not one of them dared to look up from his piles of paper to see what the boss was doing.

His assistant served green tea and collected their passports and papers. It was a silent operation, apart from "please, may I have" and "thank you." Amakasu opened each passport, beginning with An-li's, and compared the photograph with the face. Amakasu read the note from the Japanese Consul, Mr. Okari, three times. Without referring to his notes, the Police Chief recounted how Leah had spent the past three days and whom she had seen. The young interpreter repeated Amakasu's words as if they were a shopping list. He finished with: "Miss Kolbe returned to her hotel room alone by taxi at ten minutes to midnight."

Leah nodded.

There was a timid knock at the door. A man in a chauffeur's uniform handed a note to the assistant, who passed it to Amakasu. Amakasu waved the chauffeur away impatiently. The man eased the door closed. The police chief read the note. He bowed toward Sonia and handed the note to the interpreter, who read: "Mr. Kenzo has sent his car for Miss Rubstov." Sonia gave a tentative smile. The assistant handed back her papers. The interpreter bowed to Amakasu and added: "Please, Miss Rubstov, you are to leave now." He apologised in Japanese to Amakasu for speaking out of turn. Amakasu dismissed his look of consternation as a relieved Sonia, hugging her papers and her handbag close to her chest, opened the door as quietly as possible.

Amidst the sea of desks, Sonia clumsily stuffed the papers into her handbag. After several attempts, she managed to light a cheroot. She did not turn to look back at Leah and An-li, but made straight for the door.

"Are you enjoying your stay?" asked Amakasu through the interpreter.

"Manchukuo is a model state," said Leah.

Amakasu nodded sagely. "That is true. It is a laboratory of Pan-Asian majesty. We will teach the Manchu much. The world will beat a path to our door." He pointed to the picture of Emperor Hirohito that hung on the wall opposite his desk. "You could help us, Miss Kolbe."

The interpreter translated Amakasu's words and looked for a reply from Leah. Like a modest maiden, she clasped her hands together and bent her head. Through her eyelashes, she focused on her passport, which Amakasu flicked through, stopping at her Manchukuo visa.

"We have prepared a series of articles in English that would be suitable for publication in the Hong Kong press under your name. With your permission, we will place the first of the three articles through our Japanese Press Agency."

"I'm not newsworthy, Mr. Chief of Police, sir," she said.

Amakasu gave a glimmer of a smile. "It is just a human-interest piece, but we thought a picture of you would add to its appeal." The interpreter finished speaking just as Amakasu tapped on the window. A man with a flash attached to his camera rushed into the office. He bowed low and waited for instructions.

Amakasu said, "We will take the photographs at the War Memorial."

They drove there in Amakasu's black limousine. An-li sat next to the driver. Leah sat between the Chief of Police and the interpreter, the photographer on the jump seat. Leah attempted polite conversation about the scenery. But Amakasu said, "Japan is beautiful. Here it is all ugly," so she shut her mouth. The short drive ended in a newly planted park of sapling elms. It was bereft of leaves and people.

The interpreter translated the large billboard attached to the iron front gates of the park: "Japan's gift to the people of

Manchukuo to mark the valiant deaths of those Japanese soldiers who gave their lives to establish the Independent Empire
of Manchukuo."

The photographer arranged Leah in front of the gates with
her hands pointing to the sign. The photographer unbuttoned
her coat, motioned for her to put her hands in her coat pockets. The wind had a cutting edge and blew her hair around.
The sky was grey. She could see her breath hanging in the air.
The interpreter said "Smile." Leah saw yellow spots before her
eyes. The photographer took several more shots as she was
commanded to look this way and that. Amakasu grew impa-
tient. He walked briskly up to Leah and stood next to her.
The camera flashed again.

Back inside his office, Amakasu shoved a piece of paper in
Japanese at her. Leah signed her name. The white-gloved
assistant returned their passports and papers. The interpreter
said, "They'll send the articles and copies of the photographs
to your hotel, Miss Kolbe."

Leah, bowing and nodding, thanked them.

AN-li helped Leah through the door of their hotel room.
Leah collapsed onto the bed, shaking. An-li put a cold com-
press on Leah's head and kept repeating, in a soothing voice,
"No one will publish them." A cold gust of shame flooded
Leah.

18

PALACE INTRIGUES

LEAH DREAMT SHE was naked in a Macau casino before a faceless dealer who had the shape of a praying mantis. The dealer kept snatching her cards back before she had a chance to look at them. There was no one else at the table, but she felt a lurking foreboding that she would be unable to retain her place at the table as a rush of gamblers, just outside her line of vision, pressed in. She awoke in the dark to An-li's comforting hands, attempting to rearrange her blankets. The room was freezing.

"How long have I been asleep?" she asked.

"Long time," said An-li. "While you sleep and last night, I find out many things about the Macanese."

"Oh," said Leah, "he is from Macau?"

An-li pulled the hanging cord. The room was flooded in light. Leah blinked and sat up.

"Now," said An-li, "is not the time for lies between us." She sat down heavily on the bed and stroked Leah's tangled hair.

Leah gave a long sigh that ended, "You're right. Tell me what you found out."

"This Cezar da Silva, he works for the Japs. He lives in the house of Mr. Fukuda. Mr. Fukuda pretends to be a rich businessman importing farm equipment for dumb, uneducated Chinese who can't farm. Not so. I followed them all night. They go to prostitute houses, one after another. It makes no sense, one after another."

Leah stayed very still, wishing she could close her ears.

"They also go to fan-tan houses. Today, after you fell asleep, I go out again."

Leah's face was pinched and white.

"No, I made sure that no one followed me. Who notices an old woman with a willow broom stolen from hotel?" An-li got up and bent her back, limping slightly.

"Very clever," said Leah, clapping her hands.

"I go to Mr. Fukuda's house and pretend I'm looking for work as a cleaner. A woman tells me this Mr. Fukuda is in charge of Hsingking prostitutes and gambling, and that he sits on Manchukuo's Opium Board. He is very important man, big man. Very rich. The Macanese is his man. He runs Macau and maybe Hong Kong for him. He's not for you," An-li finished.

Leah sank back on to the bed and shut her eyes. "That's enough. I don't want to know any more." Under the covers, she touched her heart and felt it beat. There must be something wrong with her heart deep inside. Maybe it was misshapen or had an undetected flaw like those that develop in porcelain. On the surface, the glaze takes and the piece is remarkable, but over time a fault appears; the porcelain paste had not been properly washed or a stone chip had remained, and gradually the pot corrodes, breaks into worthless shards. If only it were sometime in the future. Desperately, she wished she were in a safe place and she had a new lover, so she could forget about the break in her heart and the need to get up tomorrow to face another terrible day. She feigned sleep.

An-li turned off the light, undressed in the dark, and climbed into bed.

A Japanese soldier escorted Leah through the palace grounds. It was a flyblown, makeshift compound. It had been the site of an industrial plant—for packaging salt, she thought—and contained a weary European house surrounded by tin sheds and workers' bungalows. They passed a disused tennis court. The sagging net was riddled with holes; the grey concrete swimming pool gaped, cracked and empty.

The soldier led her to the Emperor Pu Yi's office, grunted at a chair, and left. Almost no light entered the room; the smell of stale cigarette smoke choked her. On the desk were framed pictures of Pu Yi's investiture and of foreign dignitaries. In the investiture photograph, Pu Yi wore a comic opera uniform with gold epaulets that didn't sit square on his sloping shoulders. Amongst the photographs of foreign dignitaries, she recognised Mussolini. He had scrawled a personal message she couldn't read. They seemed to share the same tailor.

She tugged at her skirt, examining it for non-existent wrinkles, spots, or a pulled thread. Throughout the day, she had wallowed in doubt, exacerbated by imagining spying eyes whenever she ventured close to the hotel window.

Before she'd left Hong Kong, she had spent hours in the library of Jonathan's club researching old interviews with Pu Yi. From the yellowing newsprint, she had learned that despite the emperor's fluent English, journalists had been forced to go through the charade of using an interpreter. Would the interpreter be one of Amakasu's men? In all likelihood, he would speak stilted propaganda prose at her and then relay minute-by-minute breakdowns about this meeting to the Chief of Police.

Pu Yi was definitely a lower-case emperor, irrelevant to her mission except that it was through him that she would make contact with the eunuch Quan and obtain the jewels. All this planning, days and nights of anxiety, and still she was no closer to meeting Quan. She might have to endure endless imperial audiences, obliging her to bring a steady supply of tokens of esteem. Or, more likely and more worrisome, there would be no more audiences and no hope of meeting Quan. Then she would have to rely on the self-interested goodwill of Vasiliev and collude with Sonia in double-crossing Chang. She consulted her watch and made a mental note, "4:18, A frown passes over Miss Kolbe's face as she awaits His Excellency, Chief Executive Officer Pu Yi."

She shut her eyes and conjured up a vision of Theo sitting on the red lacquered chair in front of her. Theo had a benign air and radiated confidence. "Forget the twerp," he said, "it's the eunuch you need to impress." Yes, but how?

Leah opened her eyes to hear a clearing of the throat from a pretty pageboy dressed in a blue serge suit with too much wrist and ankle showing. She jumped to her feet and bent her head. Behind the page, in a hound's-tooth jacket and Oxford bags, was Pu Yi; at his elbow was a round-faced man with a tight-lipped dour face, dressed in the black silk gown of a mandarin, wearing a silken skullcap that bore a crimson button in its centre. The silk-gowned man looked into the middle distance.

"Miss Kolbe," said Pu Yi in English, "such a pleasure to see a new face."

Leah raised her head as Pu Yi seated himself in the red lacquer chair with carved dragons on the armrests. He was a thin, fragile man made smaller by enormous tortoise-shell glasses perched on a nondescript nose, his little head bobbing above a skinny neck. She had read that his favourite film star was Adolphe Menjou and that he, too, liked to dress up. He was Menjou without star quality or pencil moustache. There was no interpreter present. Grateful, Leah relaxed slightly but remained standing.

Pu Yi signalled to the pageboy, who kowtowed and laid a leather-bound album in Pu Yi's lap. The emperor opened the album and turned the pages slowly, humming tunelessly. He found the page he was searching for and motioned to the boy to take the album to Leah.

"Sit, please, Miss Kolbe," said Pu Yi.

Leah sat and stared at the indicated page. It bore a water-colour rendition of a queen ant followed by an amorphous mass of lower-ranked worker ants. Pu Yi's chop mark was affixed to the drawing.

"Wonderful detail," she said.

"Ants are such loyal followers," said Pu Yi.

Uncertain if his words were a coded message or a statement of fact, Leah looked interested and waited.

"Ants are social insects. An ant colony may have a dozen, hundreds, thousands, or millions of members. The colony may have one or many queens. A queen's job is to lay eggs. Most members of an ant colony are workers who, like the queen, are females. The workers build the nest, search for food, care for the young, and fight enemies. Males live in the nest only at certain times." He paused.

"I didn't know," said Leah.

"I've made the study of ants my life's work. Such an ingenious insect," said Pu Yi and continued, slightly irritated by Leah's interruption. "The male's job is to mate with young queens. After mating, the male soon dies. Ants have many different ways of life. Army ants live by hunting other insects. Slavemaker ants raid other ant nests and steal their young, which they raise as slaves. Harvester ants gather seeds and store them in their nests. Then there are dairying ants that keep insects that give off a sweet liquid when the ants milk them. Such a variety, so exquisite . . ."

"I have brought you a gift, Your Excellency." She withdrew from her handbag a black leather book with its title in faded gold-stamped letters: *The Study of Ants: An Elucidation of the Hymenopterous Insect,* published in 1740. The volume was tied with a red ribbon.

Pu Yi's eyes glowed with happiness. "So kind, and such a thoughtful gift. I shall treasure it. And now cocktails. We prefer sloe gin fizzes, but I know you ladies like Manhattans."

The pageboy opened the drinks cabinet, withdrawing a silver cocktail shaker, and set to work.

Leah's Manhattan was undrinkable, but she took appreciative sips as she led the conversation toward the English entomologists. Engrossed in the engraved plates of his present, Pu Yi inclined his head at the silent, silk-gowned man who held his tumbler of sloe gin, waiting for Pu Yi to drink.

A little louder, Leah said, "Professor Robins is especially interested in the ants plaguing the crops in your northern city of Harbin, Your Excellency. It will be the first academic study of its type."

Pu Yi raised his head, a slow smile spreading across his face. With childish delight, he clapped his hands. "Real Englishmen coming to study the insects of our kingdom. Wonderful. I must help them."

The page jumped forward to catch the book as Pu Yi leapt up and seated himself at his desk, picked up a gold pen and then stared off into space.

Awkwardly, Leah stood with an empty glass in one hand and the emperor's album in the other, not daring to break Pu Yi's concentration. The Chief Executive Officer began to write in Chinese. When he finished, he frowned at the black-gowned man who produced from the folds of his robe a jade chop case. Pu Yi stamped the paper. The cocktail party appeared to be over. The page relieved her of her glass and the ant album.

Regally, like a small, insignificant man impersonating Adolphe Menjou impersonating an English country gentleman, Pu Yi said, "Quan will see you out, Miss Kolbe," and handed her his handwritten document.

Leah half-kowtowed, half-curtseyed, and said, "It's been a pleasure, Your Excellency; thank you for the audience," and followed the eunuch out of the room. Quan closed the door behind him. In a whisper, Leah said, "I bring you great happiness."

"What country are you from?" hissed Quan.

"From the Land of the Dragon," Leah said.

In the gloom of the hallway, they studied each other.

"Give it to me," said Quan.

Pu Yi's letter disappeared up Quan's long sleeve as the attaché, Colonel Yoshioka, marched down the hall toward them. Quan managed a strangled, "I trust you, only *you*."

"A thousand apologies," said the attaché in his high-pitched bleat. He shot a poisonous glare at Quan. "There was some mixup with the time."

Quan cast his eyes down and looked momentarily sad. "I shall be severe with the page."

A smirk played at the edge of his lips. Leah wondered if Quan might not enjoy being severe with the page. One heard strange rumours about eunuchs.

Leah bowed deeply. "His Excellency has been too kind in expressing his interest in the English expedition. I found his ant—ah, depictions—impressive and humbling."

The attaché looked relieved as he dismissed Quan with a wave of his gloved hand. Quan kowtowed to them both, but rested his eyes for a second longer on Leah. When he lifted his head, he blinked hard as if to underscore his earlier words.

"It will be my pleasure to arrange for a driver and a car," said Yoshioka.

Outside in the windy compound, the attaché slammed the door of the army car behind her. He knocked on the closed window. Leah wound the window down. The attaché's head filled the empty space. "Miss Kolbe, when you finalise the arrangements for the scientific party, please file them with my office and the Chief of Police's, Mr. Amakasu. That way, nothing will go *wrong*."

Leah found her throat suddenly dry and croaked out a muted, "Yes, Attaché Colonel Yoshioka, sir."

Satisfied, he banged on the hood of the car. The driver engaged the engine. As they sped away, a spiral of dirt came through the open window and struck Leah's face.

19

QUAN'S JEWELS

LEAH, AN-LI, AND Sonia stood in a back alley, examining an abandoned two-story building. The door was slightly ajar. Leah volunteered to go first, and squeezed though the opening. Sonia was last and caught her skirt on a protruding nail. She spat out "Damn!" in a voice that sent the mice and rats scurrying. Inside, Leah lit a match. Bits of rusting metal and straw lay on the floor of what once must have been a factory of sorts. The match burnt her finger. She lit another and saw, at the end of the room, a staircase leading to the next level. The stairs ended at a wall with a door, just as Vasiliev had said. Leah pushed on the creaking door; a rush of cold night air hit her. The moon was up. They were on a square bit of roof from which rose another—secret—story. No doubt there was a second way into the building through a maze of other buildings that Vasiliev had no intention of revealing. He must have relished the idea of sending them out into the middle of the night to stumble around in a deserted building. On the other hand, it also meant Amakasu's men were likely to be safe at home tucked up in their beds.

"An-li," Leah whispered, "I think it's best for you to wait here by the door. Just in case."

"Just in case what?" said Sonia.

"Anything," said Leah.

"I'll stay," An-li agreed and hunkered down beside the secret door. Sonia passed her, nearly treading on An-li's foot. *Maybe it was time to fix Sonia more tea?* The thought amused An-li as she pushed her hands up into her sleeves in an effort to stay warm.

A light shone under a door midway down the hall. Casually, Leah patted the pocket of her coat. She felt the derringer's reassuring hardness. Sonia tapped lightly on the door—two short knocks and one long.

"Come," said Vasiliev.

Leah opened the door wide to see Quan reclining on a daybed. Beside him sat a pretty Chinese boy of ten or twelve and a girl who was the mirror image of the boy. Vasiliev sat sprawled in a chair and motioned toward two high-backed chairs.

Quan looked the women up and down, glancing at Leah without a flicker of recognition.

"Good choice?" said Vasiliev to Quan.

Quan returned to his toys—ran his fingers up the delicate arm of the boy, stroked the thigh of the girl.

"Quan steals—no," Vasiliev corrected himself, "Quan *liberates* valuable treasure from an illegal government for the greater good. Our greater good." His greedy face lit up.

"How is he able to steal?" asked Leah.

Vasiliev's eyes narrowed. "He hides things beneath the folds and inside the sleeves of his gown. It's good the exalted ones loved small things." He let out a lecherous giggle and remarked on the eunuch's envy of family jewels, amused by his unsubtle double entendre.

A deep scowl clouded Quan's face. It was clear he didn't like Vasiliev's mocking tone. Quan squeezed the boy's genitals until he cried out. The girl, too, had tears in her eyes.

Leah pressed her hands together to keep from slapping Quan. "Is this necessary—" she began.

Vasiliev cut in quickly: "It's a pity none of the furniture can be salvaged." There was genuine sadness in his voice.

Quan accepted the soothing sounds of Vasiliev's voice as an apology. He comforted the hurt boy and wiped the girl's tears away with his fingers. From inside his robe, he pulled out his purse, took out some coins and tucked them into the children's hands. They smiled tentatively.

"I didn't come here to see this . . . display," said Leah.

"Don't be so squeamish, Leah," said Sonia. "Sometimes one simply has to play along. It's a Chinese tradition. Quan's just excited."

Vasiliev nodded sagely. "Part of the culture," he said.

"Let the Soviets have the perverted bastard. They deserve one another," said Sonia, as if the matter was decided.

"I want to see the goods. I must see them," said Leah.

"It's good to have agreement," said Vasiliev smugly. He got down on his hands and knees, lifted the skirt of the daybed, and pulled out a large lacquered case with a brass clasp. He stood and blew the dust from the lid, then undid the clasp. The specimen box opened, revealing three drawers. Sitting with the case on his lap, he pulled out the first drawer. Underneath a thick shield of glass, beetles lay pinned. He stared at the glass for a moment, his face wreathed with self-satisfaction. "The perfect disguise. Try and find them," he said handing the case to Sonia.

Eager, Leah pulled her chair closer to Sonia's. Together they ran their fingers over and under the case, intent on finding the secret compartment. Nothing. Leah pulled out a specimen drawer. She stared at the twenty-five dead bugs pinned under glass to a white board. She studied a large beetle. Its round black shell was lustrous and shiny, its head tiny, the eyes hard dots. She slid off the glass and prised up the beetle. Underneath in a hollowed-out depression was an inch-high ivory box. She lifted it out and cupped it in the palm of her hand. She breathed slowly. The box had an open-weave floral design on top; on the underside was a carved dog, whose leash connected the lid to the bottom. The patina of the ivory had softened over the centuries to a delicate parchment.

"Nice, eh?" said Vasiliev.

Sonia started to unpin the next beetle, a dull grey one with a bigger head. Vasiliev caught hold of Sonia's hand. "No," he said. "It takes hours to arrange them. The more settled the bugs look, the less notice will be taken. I used ordinary insects. Who would look twice at such disgusting things?"

Sonia contented herself with crooning *"Krasivaya, krasivaya* (pretty, pretty) beetle."

With a proprietary air, Vasiliev painstakingly fiddled with the ivory box to reset it in its place, then repinned the beetle. "I'll have to clean the glass again," he said and snapped the drawer shut.

"Where are the larger pieces? I can't wait," said Leah.

With a flourish, Vasiliev tapped on the wall and lifted out a small plywood section painted to match the rest of the room. In the gap were three valises stacked one on top of another. From under his shirt, Vasiliev drew a gold chain with three brass keys. His showmanship was nauseating, but Leah watched, mesmerised, as he opened the first suitcase. Empty. Then he inserted a pocketknife and levered up its false bottom. There was nothing in the secret space.

"Where are they? What are you playing at, Vasiliev?" said Leah. "I've had enough of your—"

"Don't worry, Quan is busy getting them," said Vasiliev, patting the fine leather. "Always keep the luggage with you. Baggage cars are such a temptation for thieves." He laughed at his joke. Sonia smirked. Vasiliev's voice became serious and businesslike. "Quan must be discreet. The Japanese have asked for an inventory of Pu Yi's treasures. The eunuchs are scurrying around drawing up lists, subtracting from lists. It's a delicate operation."

Vasiliev translated what he had said to Quan. Quan looked grave and nodded, his eyes alert and knowing. His look unsettled Leah. Quan had devoted his life to manipulating people, alternately fawning and backstabbing. Compared to Quan,

Vasiliev was a rank amateur. For all she knew, the setup with the twin children was part of Quan's plan to outfox Vasiliev, conning and flattering Vasiliev into playing the pimp so he would lower his guard. How heartfelt was Quan's appeal to her at the palace? "I trust only you." Was it a stage-managed ploy to build trust between them and separate her from Vasiliev and Sonia?

"What about Quan? He can't pass for a normal person," said Sonia.

Vasiliev rubbed his hands together. "Wait, you'll see," he said gleefully and curled a stubby finger at Quan. Grudgingly, Quan rose and waddled out behind Vasiliev. The two children moved closer together. The boy put his arm around his sister's shoulders. They stared goggle-eyed at Leah and Sonia.

"Do you think all this drama is necessary, Sonia?"

"Be quiet, Leah; the children."

"For God's sake, they don't understand English." In Mandarin, she asked, "What are your names?"

The children continued to stare. Leah clapped her hands loudly. The children blinked but didn't startle. Leah tugged at her ears. The children nodded. "They're deaf, Sonia."

"See," said Sonia, "Vasiliev leaves nothing to chance."

The door opened on Quan, now wearing a Western suit, a silver toupee on his head, his smooth faced adorned with a wispy moustache and goatee.

"Meet Professor Wang, China's eminent scholar of insects. He's going to consult with the Colonial Government in Hong Kong about bugs, their effect on public health, infestations or whatever," said Vasiliev, waving his arms around like a maestro. His veined face flushed purple with pleasure. "Show 'em, Professor."

Quan walked awkwardly in his leather shoes, lifting his knees up smartly and then plonking his feet down as though he were marching.

"The Professor has to learn to walk," said Sonia.

Vasiliev translated Sonia's comments to an annoyed Quan. Vasiliev strode around the room and, puppet-like, Quan matched his gait. The light from the naked bulb cast shadows on the wall. The children made harsh gurgling sounds. Quan shot them a poisonous look. They lapsed into silence. My God, what a menagerie, thought Leah as she kept her eyes on Quan. Theo had always drilled into her that one could do business with any-one. She wondered if he would have changed his mind if he had met Vasiliev or Quan. Then again, Theo had known Chang.

"Satisfied, Sonia?" said Vasiliev.

"He's improving."

"Let's drink to it," said Vasiliev, extracting a bottle of vodka from his bulging briefcase. "No need for glasses, we're all friends here." He took a swig and passed the bottle to Sonia. When it was Quan's turn, he looked dubious and passed it to the boy to drink. Then he gave the bottle to the girl. Quan laughed as she spat it out. He cuffed her amicably and passed the bottle to Leah who returned the bottle to Vasiliev saying, "Not now."

"Very wise, Leah. The time for drinking is when the money is in the pocket," said Vasiliev with a slow wink at Sonia.

Like a snake with its tongue out, Quan observed Vasiliev's wink and Sonia's arch smile.

Oblivious, Vasiliev continued: "I've arranged rail tickets from Hsingking via Nanking to Shanghai, and a boat from there to Hong Kong. It's safe, I'm told. I'll bring the suitcases on the day. Mustn't arouse suspicion. Quan, for reasons only a Chinaman could understand, insists that he will bring his bugs to the train station and meet us there." Vasiliev frowned. "I know, Sonia; believe me, I'm not happy about it either, but Quan is very stubborn."

"Everything should be kept here," said Leah.

Vasiliev's face drooped. "Not possible. Quan has a number of safe houses. Not even I know them all. We have to trust each other." Then he brightened: "I've asked a few *friends* to see you off at the train station. It will work out. They are well trained." To Quan, he said innocently in Mandarin, "I'm just giving her some details about the trip."

"As we planned?" said Quan.

Vasiliev crossed his heart.

Seemingly satisfied, Quan walked to the daybed and set the boy on his knee. He patted the child's hair.

"Let's go now," said Leah, unable to watch Quan play with his pets any longer.

Vasiliev squeezed Leah's hand until it ached. As he bear-hugged Sonia, Vasiliev whispered something to her, but Leah couldn't make it out. For a moment, Quan's eyes met Leah's questioningly, then swiftly his expression changed, heavy-lidded, into desire as he placed his hand on the boy's genitals.

"Come on, Sonia," said Leah loudly.

"All right." Sonia trailed down the dark hall after Leah.

An-li rose from her haunches and gave Leah a searching look.

"It's all arranged," gloated Sonia.

20

CLEARING OUT

A PACKAGE ARRIVED, hand-delivered by a policeman. A note on Amakasu's personal letterhead was clipped to three large glossy photographs. The interpreter had very kindly translated the Japanese into English in precise brackets inscribed above the Japanese characters. The note said:

Dear Miss Kolbe,
    Please do not leave the beautiful country of Manchukuo without first contacting my office.
                    Yours in friendship,
                    Chief of Police Amakasu.

Also included was a one-page typewritten story concerning her trip at the invitation of the Manchukuo Government. She was quoted as saying

Manchukuo is a wonderful example of true Chinese and Japanese friendship. As a European, it is exciting to witness a new form of Asian society being built. I am humbled by ordinary people stopping me in the street to tell me about their newfound prosperity. Everyone is friendly and generous. I hope other Europeans will travel to Manchukuo and see this for themselves.

Leah studied the photographs. In the first one, she was grinning and pointing to the sign on the iron gates. She didn't remember the photographer taking the second one. She was biting her lip, somber, her eyes filled with tears from the cold. It must have been taken, she reasoned, just as she was walking away from the monument since she had worn her coat buttoned up to the collar. The third was the posed photograph with Amakasu. They stood next to each other. His leather-gloved hands were clasped in front of him and he gazed fixedly into the camera, not acknowledging her presence. She was looking out of the corner of her eyes at him, a nervous smile on her lips.

At various times during the day she took out the contents of the envelope to gaze at them in dismay. She lit a match and held it over Amakasu, but then she reasoned the photos might prove useful should they be stopped at the border. She tore up the note and burned that instead.

She fantasised constantly about leaving Hsingking and woke each morning hoping for Vasiliev's signal that it was arranged. Instead, she and An-li spent their time inspecting houses, engaging laboratory and office space, haggling for servants and assistants to help the nonexistent academics. They had their very own spy now. He stood across the street from the Old Russian in a brown overcoat with the collar turned up, and a fur hat with earflaps pulled low over his forehead. He followed them at a respectful distance. After Leah wrote an obsequious letter to the attaché listing the arrangements she had made for the English professors, the man only turned up occasionally.

Hsingking attracted a myriad of people. There were Mongol nomads, Koreans who had been promised land, Russians still trying to figure out how they could work with the Japanese, German engineers, and the Manchu, who didn't want to talk to anybody and kept their heads down. An-li, to Leah's dismay, had befriended a woebegone Mongol in a moulting horsehair cape and his young wife. An-li was convinced that the man was the best fortune-teller in Manchukuo. When Leah tried to pin An-li down as to why his prophecy skills were superior, An-li said, "Because he is."

The fortune-teller relied on a tray of sand over which he held a stick. His wife knelt at his feet in the dirt and burned incense. The man chanted and called up a spirit to come out of the mountains. The spirit caused the stick to move in the sand and made weird patterns and strange characters. It gave cryptic messages: "The day shakes loose" and "Eyes have meanings." After a few days, An-li asked Leah not to accompany her to the fortune-teller. Her presence was disturbing the spirit. An-li refused to tell Leah what the spirit said, but she set up a little altar in their room, offering the spirit wizened fruit from the market. Once Leah saw the fortune-teller's wife alone on the street. The girl ran off with a haunted look on her face.

Leah and An-li saw very little of Sonia. She had moved her belongings to Mr. Kenzo's. As the short winter days closed in, they retreated to their room earlier each night. An-li sewed. Leah turned pages of books without interest. An-li recounted stories of her childhood on Lantau Island, where she had lived until the age of ten. Leah was soothed by the First-Brother-This and Second-Sister-That stories. She pictured a fat dumpling An-li tottering around her bigger brothers and sisters, happy, giggling. She tried to imagine the sound of An-li's innocent happy laughter. "All dead now," said An-li, patting Leah's pale hair. Leah squeezed An-li's hand, hard. Leah didn't mention Cezar. What was the point? Leah knew that An-li could not hide her dislike of him. Her nerves were too fragile to deal with An-li's disapproval.

There was a knock on the door. Sonia sashayed in, wearing a backless midnight-blue evening dress, carrying a cardboard dress box and a leather hold-all. "Mr. Kenzo is having a party. He asked that you come, Leah."

"I can't. I haven't anything as elegant as that to wear."

"Oh, I've seen to that," said Sonia. She paused dramatically, her eyes glittering. In a triumphant voice, she said, "It's arranged! For tonight. We're leaving straight from Kenzo's house. Vasiliev will come here, pick up An-li, who will pack your clothes in Quan's suitcases; then we meet him at Kenzo's, where we will be whisked away to the train station. No one will miss us for hours. We'll be at the border by then."

"Won't Kenzo miss you?" said Leah.

"After a few drinks, dear Kenzo remembers nothing. He'll

have other friends to keep him amused. Vasiliev has seen to that, too."

"How will we change?' said Leah.

"In the car, outside in the night. Who cares?" said Sonia and held up the leather holdall. "My travelling clothes are in here."

Leah opened the bag. "Did something die in here?" asked Leah.

"Don't be such a little lady," said Sonia. "It's the perfect disguise." She held up a filthy quilted jacket and padded trousers. "Vasiliev leaves nothing to chance. You want to pass as a peasant, well, you must smell like one."

"Sonia, you can't possibly wear these rags on the trip. We'll fool no one, only be arrested before we board the train. We might as well carry signs, here comes the circus: European women pretending to be Chinese peasants and a court eunuch dressed as a professor."

"I am not an idiot," retorted Sonia. "It's an old refugee trick. We'll wear our regular clothes underneath. I chose a fine black wool dress. Elegant, and it won't show the dirt."

An-li untied the dress box, pawing through layers of tissue paper to remove a dress of antique red silk with a gold thread dragon running up the low-cut back.

An-li made a clucking sound and hissed in Cantonese, "You will be naked. Tell her no."

But already Leah was unbuttoning her blouse and deciding she would wear her hair parted in the middle and pulled back from her face, lots of kohl around her eyes and no lipstick.

When she was ready, she twirled around for effect, saying to An-li ,"How do I look?"

An-li tugged at the thin straps of the dress.

"Stop that," said Leah. "It's a good disguise. The Japs will see only what they want to see."

"Perhaps," said An-li, who leaned in close as if picking a stray thread off Leah's dress and whispered, "Watch the Russian, she'll betray us."

Vasiliev's driver rounded a sharp curve and deposited Leah and Sonia in front of a low-slung concrete house illuminated by giant lanterns of red, green, and blue. The house was decorated in the Japanese style with rice paper screens and tall flowers in somber pots. Mr. Kenzo, who spoke English, escorted Leah around as if she were a prize cow. The men gawked. She was grateful for the fact that she didn't understand what they were saying. Amakasu, in evening dress, entered with two uniformed policemen. Through Kenzo, Amakasu said, "The photographs turned out well."

"I'm honoured you took the time to send them," said Leah. For a second, she thought she caught a smirk.

Kenzo made her try the warm saki brought around by teenage girls in blue cotton kimonos. One of these girls made sure her little saki cup was never empty. Trapped by Amakasu, Leah spent her time trying not to drink and to look fascinated as the Chief of Police collected a coterie of men around them who hung on his every word, none of which she could understand. Leah focused on Amakasu's hands as he gestured. He used a stabbing motion to make a point.

Regularly Sonia swooped past on Kenzo's arm, laughing thickly or smoking a cheroot. Leah watched Kenzo for telltale signs of drunkenness. She couldn't spot any. Then Vasiliev swept in with ten Korean girls, laughing and giggling. The men's faces lit up as the girls made their rounds.

Sonia came up to Leah and said smoothly: "I'll show you the rest of the house."

Leah bowed from the waist to Amakasu and followed in Sonia's wake. Amakasu watched Leah's retreating back. The dragon swayed when she walked. He caught up with her just as Sonia said, "We must hurry."

In perfect English, Amakasu said, "Is anything wrong?"

"An-li is ill," said Leah. "I am concerned."

"Shall I fetch a doctor?"

"That's not necessary," said Sonia. "You know these old Chinese, they prefer their herbal remedies. It's all fakery."

"Just so, Miss Rubstov. So you will be leaving soon." He gave an imperceptible bow and added, as if he had just remembered it, "My men are patrolling the grounds. One can't be too careful these days."

"I expect you're right, Chief of Police, sir," said Leah. "We live in difficult times."

Amakasu examined Leah's face for hidden meaning and, finding none, gave another modest bow. He sauntered back into the room, to be greeted by Vasiliev and a vivacious young lady who captured the police chief's hand and wrapped it firmly around her small waist.

On tiptoe Sonia led Leah down the hallway. "Psst," said An-li, standing just inside a bedroom. Sonia held up a finger to her lips and half-pushed Leah into the room. The red dress slithered to the floor and Leah shivered, wondering how they would evade the guards. How disadvantaged she would feel, disguised in the peasant coat and skullcap, if she were caught and brought before Amakasu! He would dispense with the interpreter and question her mercilessly, all the time gesturing with his insistent stabbing finger. He would find her guilty of something. She pulled on the thick socks and the slippers An-li handed her. When she stood up, she patted the coat and felt the comforting hard bump of the gun.

The security guards were bunched together smoking cigarettes and cursing the cold. They didn't look twice at two tall Chinese men in padded coats and skullcaps who argued loudly with an old woman about kitchen scraps.

BALANCING two insect cases on his trousered knees, Quan sat in the train station on a wooden waiting-room bench and tried vainly to look inconspicuous as the milling crowd jostled around him. A pince-nez was perched on his broad flat nose. He squinted through the thick lenses, searching the crowd for the three women. Swirling clots of peasants charged from one platform to another as rumours circulated about an arriving train. Soldiers shoved at gaps in the crowd, while others hauled people off the tracks, urging them to use the stairs or they would be killed. Far off, a train whistle sounded. The crowd swarmed. Two sleek peasants hovered near Quan's bench. Instantly Leah knew that these were Vasiliev's hard men. She had to force herself to keep walking toward them naturally.

In her black dress, Sonia followed Vasiliev; then came Leah and An-li, lugging the heavy suitcases between them. Sonia had refused to carry hers. "It wouldn't look right," she'd said. "Besides, Vasiliev may need my help with Quan." She'd smiled conspiratorially.

Vasiliev pushed his way through the hordes of would-be train travellers. He spotted the seated Quan and waved. Quan dipped his head in recognition. The hard men inched closer.

Vasiliev stood in front of Quan, blocking the crowd's view. As Sonia grabbed the insect cases from Quan and handed them to Leah, Quan lunged. His knife slid deep into Sonia's stomach. Sonia collapsed sideways onto one of the sleek peasants who, in turn, fell backward onto his companion. Leah jumped away and stood, gaping and trembling. A terrible sound from deep within Sonia filled the air. A thick stain seeped down the front of her elegant black dress.

Frozen, Leah watched its progression with horror until Vasiliev shoved her brutally aside, as he leapt toward Quan. Quan was too quick. He kicked Vasiliev hard in the groin. Howling, Vasiliev sank to his knees in a pool of Sonia's blood. Sonia lay still on the ground, her thin legs splayed open.

Roused, Leah turned and bent to tug at Sonia's skirt, to close her legs.

Quan intercepted Leah's outstretched hand. He pulled Leah away as she yelled "No! No!," clutching the specimen cases to her chest. Vasiliev's men chased after them, screaming incoherently.

An-li slung Quan a suitcase and used the other two as weapons, hitting people on their shins, to clear a zigzag path through the crowd. The train screeched to a stop. Someone yanked a carriage door open. Leah, Quan, and An-li squeezed through it and were carried along the corridor with the sea of people. The train whistle hooted. A father with a child in his arms made a desperate grab for a handhold. Someone dragged them on board. Through a window, Leah caught sight of one of Vasiliev's men running along the platform. The train picked up speed. The man stopped running. Breathless, he bent double at the knees and gasped for air.

Burrowing deeper into the train, An-li called out "Found our compartment."

They stumbled in, struggling with the bug cases and their heavy luggage. At first, all Leah saw was a well-dressed Chinese family. A fat baby sat on the mother's knee while a boy of three or four squirmed on the seat poking his father. Clutching his fidgeting son, the father nodded, and said, "Mr. Wu."

"Miss Kolbe and party," replied Leah, faltering.

Across from them, ignoring the hubbub, sat Cezar da Silva in a camel-hair overcoat.

Leah gawked at him as if he were an apparition. The train lurched. Leah fell against Cezar, who reached out to steady her.

"My God, it's you," said Cezar. "Leah-for-now."

"Yes," she said in automatic response.

In the small space, An-li hoisted one of the suitcases into the air, attempting to fit it on top of the Chinese family's odd assortment of tied bundles.

Cezar rose and said, "Let me." He rearranged the bundles and hefted each of the heavy cases into the air, stacking them one on top of the other. "A long trip?" he said.

Leah set the specimen cases on the compartment floor. Quan swooped and hugged them to his chest.

"Long enough," said Leah, who paled as she saw blood-stains on Quan's Western suit that were not quite hidden by the cases. An-li tugged at his jacket and said, "Sit." Quan sat down hard, keeping a tight hold on the cases, which he propped on his knees like a travelling writing desk.

"It's Professor Wang's first trip travelling with a European," said Leah. "I make him nervous and, of course, he is unused to the crowds." She smiled at Quan and touched his shoulder. "This is Mr. da Silva, Professor." Quan bowed his head in a nervous greeting, avoiding Cezar's eyes.

"A pleasure, Professor. Travelling with a Western woman can be an agreeable experience. You have a charming companion," said Cezar in Mandarin. He remained standing, his eyes flitted from Quan to An-li and Leah. The bloodstains on the professor's jacket interested him, but what he noticed most was how naked Leah's face was. In the early morning light she looked shell-shocked. That night in Macau, he had thought she was quite the loveliest girl he had ever seen.

"It hasn't been easy persuading him to accompany us. The Professor does vital work on insect-borne diseases," said Leah. "He's needed in Hong Kong."

"Really, so that's your secret, just-Leah. You're a public health inspector. I will enjoy the journey. You can tell me all about fatal diseases."

Unwanted tears sprang to Leah's eyes.

"Leave her alone," said An-li.

"I haven't done anything," said Cezar, giving An-li a deferential smile as he sat down. He would wait. It would be a long train ride. There was no rush. He could study Leah and her situation—he was sure there was a situation—at his leisure. He could plan his campaign as he took little satisfying peeks at her. She occupied his thoughts. He replayed their lovemaking in the cheap Macau hotel, how her creamy body worked, their walk in the night, his first sighting of her. He was confident he would learn her secrets. He would have her again.

Leah closed her eyes. Behind them, she saw Sonia's face drained of colour and heard her sharp cry of bewildered pain.

It wasn't supposed to have been like this. Sonia, for all her faults, should have been allowed to grow old in Hong Kong, taking young lovers, amusing herself at the gambling table, retelling old stories no one wanted to hear. She wasn't a good woman. But certainly, she hadn't deserved to die on a cold concrete floor stained with spit, her chic black dress hiked up over her stocking tops. It was so cruel. Leah opened her eyes and focused on the contented Chinese family. They exchanged small smiles of goodwill. She looked at Quan. He had removed his blood-splattered coat and folded it to use as a pillow. A repellent creature, devious and shrewd. Already, he was asleep, or so it appeared. He had thwarted Vasiliev and Sonia's plan to betray him and because of Chang, she was responsible for him. She stared at Quan's face and imagined a bullet hole in his forehead.

The insect cases on Quan's lap grew heavy. Pins and needles shot through his legs. His feet didn't quite reach the floor. Opening his eyes, he glanced around furtively, then placed the specimen cases on the floor. Out of respect for their contents, he removed his shoes. His white silk socks rested on the lid. Leah couldn't keep her eyes off his feet. They were round, like oysters plopped on a black plate, and gave off a briny smell.

Barbed wire strung over the train tracks flashed by. The sun struggled through grey clouds.

The baby woke and began to cry. The mother unbuttoned her blouse, exposing her breast, and the baby latched on, making satisfied sucking noises. The restless boy clambered off his father's lap to sit at Leah's feet, not quite daring to touch her shoes.

Cezar leaned across Quan and said, "Can I help, Leah?"

The sun flicked over his face. For the first time, she noticed small lines around his eyes. A part of her wished she had never risen from their shared bed and tiptoed away.

"No," said Leah. "It's a complicated business."

The little boy reached for her trousered leg. She shifted away.

"The Professor, he cut himself shaving?" said Cezar.

Before Leah could open her mouth, An-li said, in a censorious tone, "A pregnant woman fell and hurt herself. The Professor helped her. She fell on something sharp. She bled a lot."

"A good Samaritan, is he? Doesn't look the type."

"Not Samaritan," said An-li. "He studies bugs."

"A Samaritan is someone who helps people in need without expecting a reward," said Leah.

"Oh," said An-li, "like you and Mr. Fukuda, Mr. da Silva?"

Cezar sat perfectly still, as if he were calculating the odds or waiting for the next card to be dealt. The Chinese couple stared. He had a sense that they felt they were watching an unintelligible play in English, but that at any moment they would grasp the gist and clap or laugh. The boy played with the cuff of Leah's trousers, turning it up, turning it down.

"You know," said Cezar, addressing Leah, "Sonia Rubstov told me Leah Kolbe was an unusual young woman. She wasn't wrong, though she didn't mention your interest in public health."

A sharp exhalation escaped Leah.

"Don't talk to him any more. He's a gangster," said An-li.

A grim smile spread across Cezar's handsome face.

The train shuddered and slowed as it entered a station. Nailed to the train overpass were five bamboo cages. Each cage contained a severed head with its eyes closed and its twisted open mouth caught in mid-scream. One head belonged to a boy who looked about twelve. Inside the train compartment, the Chinese father grabbed his son, lifted him from the floor, and held him against his chest. The mother gasped and covered her eyes with her free hand. Quan opened his eyes wide. He gazed at each head as if checking to see if the executioner had gotten the knife cuts right. The father said in Mandarin to Cezar: "Railway workers accused by the Japanese of trying to organise a union, or so they say." He shrugged his shoulders in sadness, then murmured to his son, "Bad men, bad men."

Cezar nodded. In English he said, to no one in particular, "People will believe anything if you repeat it often enough."

21

WAR

*S*LEAH KEPT GLANCING furtively at her watch, calculating how long it would take to get to the Chinese border. The train stopped and stood waiting outside some nameless station. She imagined that a telegraphed message had been sent to the engineer to halt the train. All she could do was sit, anticipating the arrival of Amakasu's helmeted policemen. Just as she had resigned herself to this fate, the train belched smoke and started up again. The baby wailed intermittently. The little boy whined and sometimes succeeded in pinching the baby, which made her wail louder. Leah tried to ignore their whines and cries as much as possible as she slumped down into her seat. She and Cezar icily manoeuvred around each other, taking it in turns to meander up and down the miserable packed train, which had begun to smell.

The train slowed at the border crossing. Two middle-aged guards knocked respectfully on the compartment door. The Chinese family fumbled for their papers. With a winning smile, Cezar handed his over. The guards flicked through the pages of his passport and returned it. Quan leaned forward in his seat, reached into his shirt pocket for his papers, his feet firmly resting on the insect cases, his blood stained coat under his broad buttocks. He wiped his pince-nez on a white hand-kerchief as the guards conferred. Finally, they made Quan open his insect cases. The guards jokingly asked if the bugs tasted good. Quan's face clouded.

Cezar said, "To the Professor, these insects are not playthings. They are his life."

Embarrassed, the guards nodded and merely went through the motions of being interested in the women's three leather valises and their papers. Leah kept her expression as neutral as possible.

When the guards left, Cezar said, "It's a difficult job, know-ing who to suspect."

"I've heard the Japanese load whole rail carriages with illicit goods, drugs or guns. They don't bother with bribes. Is that true?" She looked questioning at Cezar.

"There is always contraband in a war," he said mildly. "Our fellow passengers could be smugglers. Who would suspect them?"

"I wouldn't know," said Leah, regarding the round good-natured face of tired Mrs. Wu across from her. Mrs. Wu would gladly have exchanged her bundles for a necessary stamp on their travel documents. "You have a vivid imagina-tion. They are just happy to be out of Manchuria."

"And you, Leah, did you enjoy yourself in the new king-dom of Manchukuo?" He asked his question casually, his face bland, displaying only a twinge of interest.

"I did some sightseeing."

"Me, too," he said. "I shall go back in the summer when the weather is better."

"How nice for you," said Leah.

"Sonia told me she was going to Manchukuo, too. You haven't by any chance run into her?"

An-li broke in: "No."

"I guess I was wrong," said Cezar.

"Yes," said Leah, suddenly serious, "No one would go to Manchukuo voluntarily."

"I expect you're right," said Cezar. "Sonia would have more sense. There isn't really much to see."

Leah nodded and closed her eyes, hoping she wouldn't be haunted by a vision of the shocked disbelief on Sonia's face as Quan pushed the knife in. Vasiliev would make a poor mourner. And there was the murderer, Quan, sitting with his neat little round feet propped on the cases, snoring con-tentedly. If Sonia hadn't handed her the cases, would Quan just as readily have stabbed her? In her head, she heard Sonia's smoky voice echo, in her dramatic way, "Fate, it's all fate." Destiny was as good an explanation as any other.

$\backsim$

THE route to Nanking was clogged with defeated or desert-ing Chinese soldiers. When the train stopped at a station, crip-pled beggars appeared at the carriage windows. Cezar threw them a few coins. Quan called them dogs under his breath.

Leah signalled to various hawkers and paid extra for food to go to the sick soldiers.

"They won't feed them," said Cezar. "They'll keep the money."

"You're wrong," said Leah. "These men fought for them."

"And what good did it do? It has changed nothing." It was the same argument Mr. Fukuda had used on Cezar when he had been Fukuda's guest. Fukuda had many prosperous operations: Korean prostitutes, gambling, a new opium plant. Opium had built Hong Kong and Macau. Everyone got rich. Manchukuo was following in the grand colonial tradition. No one was forced to use the drugs. Fukuda had begun to grate on Cezar.

In Macau, Fukuda had been on his best behaviour. There he had needed him. But the endless weeks under Fukuda's roof tested the limits of Cezar's patience—the charade of needing to pay for exit permits for the opium and the increased Customs excise had begin to wear thin. Fukuda had become arrogant and stupidly patriotic, intoning platitudes that Cezar fumed over in private. These boiled down to how honoured and grateful Cezar—a person of less than perfect origins, a Eurasian— should be to work for a Japanese. In fact, it was another excuse to screw him out of his rightful profits. In Hsingking, Cezar had played along, but he wasn't so sure he would continue the arrangement. There were people in Macau or in Hong Kong who would pay him well for what he knew. There were ways to take care of the Fukudas of this world. In this world, it was often necessary to make adjustments to one's course.

The train wormed its way through the vacant landscape. Railway workers had cleared paths on either side of the track to prevent attacks by snipers. To escape the tedium, and her thoughts, Leah walked the length of the train again. She recognised the tired faces of strangers, worked out who belonged to whom, what they ate for lunch or dinner. Beyond the carriages were open boxcars, crammed with poor immigrant Chinese escaping to God knew where. She pushed through the heavy door of the last carriage and was blasted by stinging, smut-filled air on the little open platform. Two young Chinese soldiers amused themselves by throwing cigarette butts into the air and pretending to shoot them with their rifles. "Bang, bang," they gaily shouted.

"Bang, bang," Leah echoed. She looked at the miles of track and, despite the relief of leaving Manchukuo and passing out of the reach of Amakasu, she couldn't shake a certain dread. She tried to tell herself it was a reaction to Sonia's murder and then having to sit, calmly, next to Quan, her murderer. She hadn't known the cost of keeping secrets. Theo had never told her of the toll they took. Or that the dividing line between what is real and true, and what is fantasy and a lie, is so thin.

At school she had played the role of observer and kept to herself. As a spectator, she had watched the girls coalesce in and out of cliques, ending friendships, starting new ones. When she was twelve, Leah attempted to explain to Theo the murky world of schoolgirl crushes. Theo shook his head in disbelief when she told him Hope Cuthbert was the sun around which all the other girls orbited. He had stroked her sad face and said, "I will tell you a secret. Schoolgirl friendships count for nothing. When you grow up, you will be beautiful. It's the relationships with men that will count. Life will be very different then." She had kept this secret from the other girls.

She couldn't picture her future now. Cezar had known Sonia. Had Sonia arranged her meeting with Cezar in Macau? Why? Was Cezar linked to Chang? No. Chinese Nationalists would never trust a Eurasian. Nor would the Reds. That left only the secret societies, the Triads. Or had Cezar's acquaintance with Sonia been just a coincidence? Coincidence or conspiracy? "Conspiracies," Theo had said, "exist in small men's minds. People are more complex." But this was the time for small-minded men. Everyone was tense, frightened. And some coincidences were too hard to credit; that was what she knew.

There was a buzzing overhead. It grew louder. The boy soldiers craned their necks skyward. Their faces drained of colour. They pointed their rifles into the air. Leah fell to her knees. Through the platform's grill, she saw two planes near the horizon. They flew closer. She saw painted red suns under each wing before the planes veered off. The nervous boys fired. Casually, like an afterthought, the planes dipped back and raked the train with bullets. Then they climbed higher, disappearing into the clear, cloudless sky. Her ears rang from gunfire; the train shuddered. A spray of sparks flew up from the track as it jerked to a sudden halt.

Leah jumped onto the tracks. Images of damaged specimen cases spilling jewels and of a bleeding An-li made her run faster. From two carriages away, she made out Quan's face. He was vomiting out the window.

"An-li, An-li!" Leah shouted.

An-li's head appeared next to Quan's. "Good, good," said An-li, waving her arms.

Quan grudgingly handed the specimen cases through the window to Leah. Unable to take his eyes off her, he proceeded to wriggle through the window like a fat worm, huffing and puffing, to land sweaty and dirty on his knees. A patch of wetness around his fly was revealed as he got slowly to his feet.

Soldiers poured off the train. Behind them came An-li, lugging the three suitcases. Cezar supported Mrs. Wu, who had a deep gash in her head. Mr. Wu hugged the baby close to his chest and held the hand of his sobbing son.

They regrouped some distance from the train in a shorn field. Quan perched on one suitcase and held the bug cases against his trousers to hide the stain. An-li tore up one of Leah's petticoats to bandage Mrs. Wu's head. The howls of the baby intensified the boy's mounting hysteria. His cries mingled with the shrieks of the wounded and the screams of weeping relatives.

A man ran toward them. "I'm a doctor. You two come with me," he demanded, pointing at Leah and Cezar.

"My wife, my wife," said Mr. Wu, tugging at the doctor's coat. The doctor glanced at the bloody makeshift bandage. "She'll be all right. Others are dying."

Leah and Cezar followed the doctor down the line, past soldiers who had formed a scraggy picket the length of the train. The last few carriages were riddled with machine gun holes.

Inside the carriage, the doctor ordered: "Move the dead to the baggage car. The wounded need space. Start with these three." He pointed to an old man, a young boy whose head didn't sit right on his shoulders, and a little girl who lay in the aisle next to her barely conscious mother. An ashen-faced man, gripping his chest as blood covered his fingers, dragged himself toward the doctor's calm voice. The doctor gently helped the man to lie down.

Leah knelt to lift the little girl. At the door, a middle-aged man in faded blue held out his stringy arms to hold the child briefly so Leah could jump without hurting herself. Tenderly, the man handed down the dead child, making sure her head didn't bump against the side of the train.

Leah walked beside the tracks, crooning "It's all right. You're safe now," as she struggled under the weight of the child and the uneven ground. Trailing her was Cezar cradling the boy.

In the baggage car, a steward stared as Leah clambered in with the child still in her arms. She straightened the child's limbs, smoothed her hair.

"Get sheets to cover them. There are more," said Leah.

The man stood, gaping slack-jawed at the dead girl. Cezar climbed into the carriage with the boy. The steward retreated into the corner next to a row of large locked wicker baskets and hunkered down. Cezar pulled him out by his black collar and shook him hard. "Get sheets. And hurry." The steward scurried to the baggage car door, jumped, and ran up the line.

"Not a pretty sight," said Cezar.

"No," said Leah, "we have your friends the Japanese to thank for this."

"It's nothing to do with me. I didn't fly the planes," said Cezar.

Several other men joined in to help carry the dead. By the time Leah, Cezar, and the others finished, twenty-five bodies were stacked in two ragged rows under sheets.

A soldier stuck his head in. "The engine's okay. The first three carriages are for the wounded. People will have to sit wherever they can."

Leah raced back to her seat. Three labourers had pushed their way in, sitting on their haunches on the floor, but An-li was in control, soothing the Wu baby to sleep in her arms. The three suitcases nestled on the luggage rack once more. Mrs. Wu drooped against Mr. Wu, their sleeping son scrunched between them. Quan, his fat face pinched with strain and disgust, sat with his feet several inches above the insect cases staring with revulsion into the faces of the three labourers, who ignored him. He wore his leather shoes now, too afraid to take them off in case more bullets were fired or the train was bombed. Leah squeezed in to sit in the narrow space jealously guarded by An-li. Cezar did not return.

THE train crawled into the outskirts of Nanking through an unending tunnel of razor wire strung to protect the tracks from sabotage. Mr. Wu pointed to the sea of black-roofed houses. "Look," he murmured to his sleepy son or to himself, "once all these roofs were painted red or blue. Now they have been painted black to hide from the Japs." He sighed deeply. The train jerked and stopped in the station. The three labourers shoved and pushed at each other as they dashed for the door. Mr. Wu stood and began pulling his bundles down.

Leah said to An-li: "Let's wait for the crowd to clear. We've missed our connection anyway." Quan nodded.

The crackling public address system announced: "All train service has been cancelled. Tracks further up the line have been damaged."

The disembarking Nanking passengers waved their tickets. With rising hysteria beneath their threats, they demanded that the stationmaster, who stood with his head bowed and his anxious eyes darting around for an escape route, do something. He shook his head and stared at his feet. Railway workers pushed through the crowd to form a tight protective circle around him and led him into his office. Someone closed the office door firmly. Leah could see his outline behind the frosted glass. He slumped in his chair, his face covered with his hands.

Angry knots of passengers drifted away, staking out their territory on the station platform or trailing with their bundles out of the station. A man with a red armband was trying to organise the wounded who lay moaning quietly in the cold afternoon as their families huddled beside them.

Mr. Wu stood uncertainly on the platform, supporting his swaying wife, who was dizzy from the loss of blood. Their little boy sat in the sea of their belongings, the baby wedged between his dirty knees. A woman in white passed Mr. Wu. He tugged at her arm, "Please help my wife."

The woman said, "I'm doing my best. All the rich doctors fled months ago when the shelling started. The army has commandeered the civilian ambulances." She lifted Mrs. Wu's bandage and grunted at the bits of skin hanging off her forehead.

A blood-splattered Cezar walked toward them. "You okay?" he asked.

"Yes," said Leah, "but we can't stay in Nanking. I must get home."

Cezar nodded. He and an army officer had been having harried conversations as they assisted the doctor with the injured. The officer had told him Nanking wouldn't hold.

The army was frantic to leave, already abandoning outlying areas to the Japanese.

"Here," he said and handed her through the carriage window a scrap of paper with Chinese writing on it. "Go to this address. She's a friend of mine and may be able to help. I'll join you when I can. Take my valise."

The doctor from the train called "Mr. da Silva, please help me lift this man."

Cezar hurried back to him.

22

ESCAPE
FROM
NANKING

THE RICKSHAW DRIVER quoted An-li an exorbitant price.

"Too much, too much," said An-li.

"For God's sake, An-li, take the damn rickshaw before someone else does," said Leah.

An-li perched on Leah's lap clasping Cezar's valise. The three suitcases were jammed in and tied onto the rickshaw's canopy while Quan, defiantly balanced on top of the insect cases, was in danger of falling off every time the rickshaw rolled over a bump or a pothole. The rickshaw puller groaned under the weight.

They passed through a neighbourhood of large houses, shuttered and closed. The streets were empty. Breathless, the puller said, "Anyone with money has left. Some Europeans stay. They say war is only for Asians. Do you think this is true?"

"No," said Leah. "Are you going to leave?"

The man thought about the barricaded shops and his wife who made brief forays from home during the strange daytime truces to scrounge for food, while at night Japanese guns boomed sporadically. Where could a poor man go? Who would take his family in? How would they eat? He didn't bother to answer.

He deposited them in front of a small crumbling house. Wispy lines of washing connected the brick house to a lean-to of bamboo with a tin roof. Children played in the dirt yard, chasing each other with sticks and squealing, "Gotcha."

"Wait here," said An-li to the rickshaw driver.

"Cost more money to wait," he said.

"Yes," said An-li.

Leah knocked on the brick house door. The children stopped running and gazed in solemn wonder. A young woman with a broad face and pigtails answered.

"Cezar da Silva sent us," said Leah and handed the woman the crumpled note.

Quan whispered, "Don't touch anything; disease," as the woman invited them in.

An-li and Leah sat on a low bench. Quan patrolled the perimeter of the room. His breath was rapid and his eyes flitted from a large cooking pot to the blankets on the *kerang,* as if looking for a place to hide, while he fiddled with the clasp of one of the specimen cases. The girl made tea. Leah gave Quan a severe look as she handed him his tea. Grudgingly, he put the cases on the floor. An-li placed them tidily with the other luggage.

"Mr. da Silva said you could help us find transport to Hong Kong," said Leah.

"The trains aren't running."

"Perhaps by boat down the Yangtze River, then to the China Sea."

The girl shook her head. "There is not even a sampan left. The wharves have been stripped bare."

Leah sipped her tea and smiled benignly. "How do you know Mr. da Silva?"

The girl shrugged as though she didn't understand the question and stared at Quan, who sniffed at the tea without drinking it.

Leah scanned the girl's earnest face. "Do you work for Mr. Fukuda?"

The girl bristled. "I don't know a Mr. Fukuda. Last week, my mother was killed by Japanese artillery. It's not safe here."

"I am so sorry," began Leah. "I know what it's like to lose—"

"Let's go," cut in Quan. "This girl can't help anyone. Look how she lives."

"Leave," the girl said to Quan.

"I'll wait outside," Quan said, as if he had decided this before the girl spoke. He cast a longing glance at his specimen cases neatly stacked by An-li's leg, but with an attempt at dignity walked out the door empty-handed. Through the walls of the house, they heard him yelling "Go home" at the children.

"We've had a difficult journey," said Leah. "The Professor must be excused for his rudeness. Fear does that to some people. It is important that we leave Nanking. The Japanese mustn't find us."

The girl looked from Leah to An-li, wavering. "It would have to be a small boat to travel down the Yangtze unnoticed. But a small boat is risky this time of year in the China Sea. It is rumoured that the Japs have mined the waters all along the coast. If you hide amongst the other Europeans in Nanking, it is, I think, safer for you."

Slowly Leah shook her head. "Cezar would not be safe."

The girl considered this for a moment.

To clinch the deal, Leah added, "You could come too."

"No," said the girl, flushing either from the tension of having to contact people she would rather not, or at Leah's insinuation linking her with Cezar. The girl refilled their teacups. The room was very quiet. Leah couldn't read her face. Finally the girl said, "Go to the European quarter. Stay at the Pacific Oxford. I'll see what can be done."

Leah leaned forward and touched the girl's shoulder. The girl flinched. Leah withdrew her hand.

"How can I thank you?" said Leah, reaching into her handbag.

"No," said the girl. "The time to pay is when it's arranged. Cezar will see to that."

THE city was fortified. Trenches lined the major roads and barbed wire arched over intersections. What Leah noticed most was that a street or two would look totally normal, buildings, signs, people going about their business. Then suddenly there would be a chasm and huge mounds of rubble, some still smoking, and children playing with shards of pots and families scrambling to find the artefacts of their former lives. As they approached the European quarter, the drone of airplanes grew louder. Leah stared as their rickshaw passed a Western movie house. A glass-framed poster of Norma

Shearer in a romantic frilly ball gown promised her the time of her life.

"Out," shouted the rickshaw puller and threw their cases at them.

Panicked, the three of them ran, clutching their baggage, and huddled by the entrance to the Pacific Oxford. Three workmen clung to harnesses slung over the flat roof, caught in mid-brush stroke as they painted the hotel black. They began to yell and scream as they were hoisted onto the flat roof. The hotel's front garden had been dug up and replanted with large shrubs behind which stood an empty machine gun emplacement and a row of foxholes. Hanging onto his bug cases, Quan dashed to a hole and rolled himself into an insignificant ball. Leah and An-li stood transfixed under the hotel portico. From the sky came sheets of paper, cascading down like wounded birds. One landed at Quan's foot. He picked up the flimsy paper and read aloud: "Capitulate. Save the lives of innocents and cultural relics. Japan will be kind and fair to the Chinese." His hands trembled. A gust of wind caught the paper. It sailed away to join the others in the gutter, where they lay with the dog droppings. He said, to no one in particular, "Lying bastards."

In the hotel room, Quan paced, babbling piteously about how he would be caught and tortured. He knew a multitude of ways.

"What about poor Sonia?" said Leah. "She never had a chance."

"That stupid woman was a pawn of Vasiliev. She was going to betray me. She deserved death."

"Maybe the Japanese think *you* deserve death," said Leah.

Quan charged, but Leah was too quick. He banged into the

heavy wardrobe. He scowled and rubbed at his shoulder. "You, Miss Kolbe, will be raped, probably to death." He smiled at his retort.

"Change your stinking trousers, Mr. Quan," said An-li.

He pretended he hadn't heard and mimicked pelvic thrusts simulating sex.

"You turtle dung," said An-li.

Longing for escape, Leah opened the window. Down below, a street sweeper raked up leaves and the Japanese leaflets. The tines of the rake scratched and echoed like finger-nails on a blackboard. A stout European woman wrapped in a black belted coat with a hat pulled well down over her eyes led a group of Chinese girls in spotless navy skirts and white blouses along the street. The schoolgirls were very erect, rigid, not a hair out of place. What would happen to these girls who placed each foot so carefully in front of the other? A man was industriously nailing plywood over his shop windows. The hammer blows thudded dully.

"I'm going to eat now," said Quan.

"You go with him, An-li. He shouldn't be left on his own," said Leah. "Leave the bug cases. They're safer here." In English she added, "He's a monster."

An-li nodded. "But he is *our* monster now."

"True," said Leah grimly.

Quan banged the door closed. Leah realised that it had been days since she had been alone. She wanted to shut her eyes and sleep for a very long time, cocooned like one of the beetles inside the trays. She opened her eyes and focused on the insect cases. It would be just like that shifty shit of a eunuch to con them. Display a few exquisite items to win their trust and then

hide the rest away in the seams of his clothes, sewn into his
toupee, down his underpants. She suppressed an out-of-con-
trol giggle. She owed it to herself, to An-li—yes, even to
Chang. If she was risking her life, she had an obligation to verify, to view the treasure. Theo would have done it. His motto
was "Know your stock, know your price."

She sat on the floor and slid the first drawer out. She peered
at the insects' blue-black shells, lustrous as South Sea pearls. Her
hollow-eyed image that reflected back from the glass cover was
a shock. Her skin was pockmarked with dead beetles, gnawing
away at her perfect skin. With a handkerchief to conceal her
fingerprints, she lifted the protective glass. Long drawing pins
pierced the area between each insect's head and thorax. The first
beetle was small, about the size of her thumb. Its bullet-shaped
body was covered with white specks and it had white lines on
its thready horned antennae. Its ugliness filled her with disgust.
She had to force herself to unpin it. Swallowing her antipathy,
she laid the leprous beetle on her lap so as not to damage its brit-
tle carapace. In the depression underneath, wound in a tight
ball, was a court necklace of lapis lazuli beads interspersed with
tiny white jade balls strung on gold thread.

She held it up to the light, watched the blues deepen, and
stroked its worked surface. From the floor, she could see her
face in the dressing-table mirror. Her eyes were wide, and a
glimmer of saliva hung from the corner of her mouth.

There was a knock at the door. She froze. There was another
sharp rap. She threw her coat over the insect cases and said,
"An-li?"

"It's Cezar. Open up."

She opened the door. He looked pleased with himself.

"I've arranged a boat, a junk. We have to leave immediately. Where are the others?" He looked anxiously around the room, then focused on her discarded coat on the floor.

"At dinner."

"Go get them."

"They'll be back soon. They've been gone nearly an hour."

"Then they should have eaten. They can skip dessert."

"You go. I've got to repack a few things."

He sat on the bed. "A few minutes won't matter. We can wait together."

She gave a quizzical smile and bent to her coat, tucking it around the open case as best she could. Standing, she saw the lapis lazuli necklace lying exposed on the floor. Cezar picked it up.

"Very pretty," he said, twirling the necklace in his fingers. "Are there more to pack? I can help," he said and tugged at her coat.

"Stop it."

"Brought the necklace all the way from Hong Kong, did you? I always travel light. It's safer. So many thieves."

"A girl gets attached to her jewelry."

"Don't play games, Leah. Let me—"

Quan opened the door and saw the necklace dangling from Cezar's hand. With a low growl, he rushed Cezar. Cezar stuck his foot out. Quan tripped and fell. On the floor, gasping with fury and pain, he rolled around screaming inarticulate curses.

"Someone else seems attached to the necklace. It doesn't suit him, though. Show me what else is under your coat."

"No. Why should I?" said Leah.

"Because," said Cezar quietly, "I can get you out of Nanking."

"Show him," said An-li as she entered the room and closed the door. "The waiter said our army has moved out. General Tang left last night."

Leah lifted the coat.

"Cunning. Very good, Professor," said Cezar to Quan, who sat, dejected, with his hands on his knees and a murderous scowl on his face.

"They don't belong to him. We're delivering—"

Cezar wasn't listening; already he was ripping a beetle from the board and throwing it to the floor to poke out an incised jade archer's ring from the cavity underneath.

"Beautiful," said Cezar. "We'll dispense with the specimen cases. We'll be travelling light."

The jewels made a dazzling heap: exquisite jade, a ruby that must have been plucked out of the headdress of a Manchu wife, pearls—some as large as Leah's thumbnail, others small and perfect. The pearl peeler who worked on the small ones must have realised that their rosy incandescent glow was worth shaving off several layers of nacre to make them flawless. Just to look at the pearls made Leah's eyes water. It was bizarre to see things of such singular beauty in the dull hotel room. Quan's threats trailed off, replaced by Cezar's exclamations of approval as he greedily uncovered one pearl after another.

"The pearls are part of a collection established early in the Ming Dynasty, late fourteenth century," said Quan mournfully. "The Emperor was particularly fond of pearls. I'm not sure why. His wife hated them."

But it was the jade Leah coveted. She wished Theo could see, caress, and later have been interred with such a piece, like the jade that aristocrats had used to seal a corpse's orifices and preserve it in its coffin, staving off putrefaction for all time. It hurt to see Cezar tearing at *her jade,* watch his hands fly over these pieces and add them to his growing pile.

"I want them back when we get to Hong Kong," said Leah.

There was a huge bang outside, not far away. The room shook slightly.

"They've started shelling again. Dress warmly," said Cezar. He stood and unlocked his suitcase. Underneath the lawn shirts and cashmere sweaters, wrapped in tissue paper, was a large piece of worn cotton and a set of clothes only a coolie would wear. He turned his back and began to discard his bloodstained suit. Leah, too, turned away and changed.

With a speed that surprised An-li, Quan snaked his hand into the unwatched pile of jewels and extracted a brooch with beaten gold links fashioned into the suggestion of a dragon breathing a spray of rubies. In disbelief, An-li watched Quan swallow the brooch. His eyes bulged in pain.

The shelling intensified. A bit of plaster fell. Calmly, Cezar rolled and tied the jewels in the cloth and slid the bundle inside his thick shirt. Leah was the last to leave. She stood in the doorway with her suitcase in one hand and regarded the room with its pulverised beetle shells and discarded clothing. It reminded her of Pu Yi's ant pictures, but should the caption read "Soldier ants on the march" or "Slave ants on the run"?

The plain girl from the brick house met them at the bottom of the back stairs. "You are late. We must hurry," she said.

The girl kept up a cracking pace. Leah's suitcase was heavy. She switched hands as first one arm, then the other ached, but always she was just a footfall away from Cezar. Cezar didn't know about the treasures in the suitcases. She forgot about the ache in her arms.

They neared the high walls of old Nanking. Leah saw shadowy outlines on the ramparts. The little band stopped. The girl put her hands together, silently imitating the rat-a-tat of machine gun fire. They zigzagged their way to the *Ichang,* the Water Gate Exit. As they neared the gate, the cold mud smell of the Yangtze River grew stronger. One at a time, they tiptoed through the gate and stood in the black shadows staring at the mouldering wharfs. There were no boats, not even the usual decrepit sampan hulks with their roofs caved in. They moved further up the river in a ragged line, watching the dark water. The mud sucked at their shoes and made walking difficult.

At last, the girl said, "We wait here."

"Will the boat come soon?" asked Leah.

"Soon," said the girl and held a warning finger to her lips.

Cezar and the girl moved a little away to stand by themselves. Leah could hear their faint murmurings. She saw the girl shrug and Cezar reach inside his shirt.

"Don't," Leah blurted and ran toward them, followed by a panting Quan. Cezar ignored Leah and handed the plain girl something, which the girl stuffed into her jacket pocket. Quan grabbed at the girl. Cezar hit Quan hard. Quan fell into the mud and struggled to sit up.

Small waves could be heard spashing against the riverbank. The dark sails of a fishing junk appeared. The girl motioned for them to remove their shoes and roll up their trousers. The mud was icy between Leah's bare toes. As the river slime rose higher, to his knees, Quan panicked. He couldn't swim. The weary girl placed Quan's suitcase on her head and towed him to the boat. Two fishermen hauled them in like large carp. The girl kow-towed to Cezar, then climbed out of the boat and waded to shore.

Later, much later, when Leah sat in a darkened cinema watching newsreels, she thought she caught a glimpse of a broad-faced, plain girl leading a battalion to oblivion. But she was never sure and comforted herself that it was not this girl, but another young woman who believed in slogans and a better way.

23

THE
JAPANESE
CAPTAIN

LEAH'S TROUSER CUFFS were stiff with mud. From the deck of the junk, she could see only a blank dark shore. How would they look from there—like dots? Or a few shadowy figures floundering around, caught up in someone else's bigger plan? Her feet were icy cold. She sat on the deck and rubbed them to get the blood circulating. Now and then, the sky lit up from an explosion. Everyone jumped and looked startled, their eyes large in their faces. Theo had always counselled caution. Smugly, he had patted his large belly and surveyed the safe surroundings of his imposing Victoria Peak house. He was dug in, protected. He always said, "Danger is for other people. We are middlemen. What other people do is nothing to us." Right, and look what had happened to him.

An-li put out a tentative hand and helped Leah to stand. "In the morning," An-li said. Leah nodded. Clasping their suitcases, they crossed the sloping deck to the tiny hatch and cautiously balanced as they descended the handmade ladder to an airless crude cabin containing two sets of bunk beds and more shelves. Leah stretched out on the worn top plank and pulled up a stale blanket. The sound of shelling increased, but she was so tired.

LEAH awoke, freezing and damp, in the blind-dark cabin that smelled of rotting timber, fish, and sweat. Water slapped against the groaning hull. Asleep below her, An-li shifted her weight and grunted softly. An arm's length away, Quan snored, and under him must be Cezar. Leah peered into the inky black. Was Cezar there? Maybe he was on deck with the two fishermen who sailed the ship. She should check on Cezar, see where he and his cloth bag had gotten to. But the effort involved in kicking off the blanket and groping her way up onto the deck was too great. She let herself drift back into sleep. In her dream, she heard the sound of Theo's heavy footsteps echoing down an endless corridor, one that she knew for obscure reasons she was not allowed to enter. Jonathan appeared. He was sitting at his desk. A smile played around his mouth. He pointed to the densely filled pages of a huge ledger. She couldn't see the names or the amounts. Then he changed into the dead little girl on the train. She struggled to wake up.

The morning was foggy, the Yangtze brown and turgid. In daylight, the junk looked as if it had weathered every storm in the China Sea. Its black sails were patched and patched again. An-li was talking to Pao, one of the sailors, who was bent over the brazier, cooking fish. Thin, wiry, and missing a few teeth, Pao groaned when An-li asked about his family. He was very worried but he and round-headed, leathery-skinned Hu had been paid in advance to sail to Hong Kong. They had used the money to send their families to a village in the country. "They are safe now, I think," he said, looking for confirmation from Hu.

The older man nodded, wanting to believe. Hu joked: "My sons look after your daughters."

Pao turned away. He had only five daughters but Hu had three clever sons.

"Maybe one of Hu's sons will get lonely in the country," teased An-li.

"I hope so," said Pao earnestly. "If not the first one, then the second, though now is not an auspicious time for marriage." He sighed wistfully.

Cezar stretched out his arms, patting his coat to keep warm. He looked pleased with himself. What Leah noticed most was that his shirt no longer bulged from the cloth bag.

Boom. The firing of the big guns rocked them. Flashes of bright light erupted in the monochrome sky. Hu turned the rudder hard, and the junk's sails picked up wind as it shuddered toward the middle of the river. Quan poked his ashen face out of the hatch and half crawled onto the deck, clutching his stomach. He vomited bile by An-li's feet.

"You have to clean that up," said An-li.

Pao handed Quan a sloshing bucket of river water and a rag. Quan dumped the water in the general direction of his mess. The vomit leaked toward the cabin.

"You fool," said Cezar and pushed Quan onto his knees to rub at the spreading stain. Quan curled his fingers into fists, then began to slap at the mess.

An-li looked at Quan's bent back. The brooch was poisoning him. Even if he lived, she doubted he would survive for long in Hong Kong. Chang would see to that. Or he'd end up begging in the streets, paraded around the back alleys like a bear, and people would pay to see him shamed when he pulled his pants down.

"What about mines?" asked Leah, attempting to be rational and sensible as the guns cracked. She gazed over the side, inspecting the water. Could she recognise a mine? Were they silver-grey, camouflaged to look like fish? Did they float like a jellyfish, opaque and amorphous, until they exploded?

Cezar walked over to Leah's side. He, too, scanned the water. "It's all propaganda," said Cezar, as if he knew what he was talking about.

It doesn't matter anyway, Leah decided. The junk could not manoeuvre swiftly enough to get out of the way. Maybe bits of jade would rain down during the explosion. She might be lucky and swallow a piece along with seawater as she drowned, becoming immortal like the emperors in Theo's stories of long ago. She considered telling Cezar her grim fantasy. Instead, she looked up from the murky waters and said, "Cezar, how are my belongings? Still dry and safe?"

He said, "Surely you don't want them to fall into the wrong hands. I've hidden them where no one will think to look. The Japanese are quite thorough in their searches. If they found something they weren't expecting—well, they can be very unforgiving. I would think about that if I were you. It could put us all in danger." He stared at Leah as if waiting for her to tell him more, to confess.

She looked out over the grey water, the dreary day. One part of her wanted to whisper, confidentially, "Cezar, there's a lot more. Help me to hide it away, too. We can be partners, we can be lovers." But curling more strongly into her ear was her father's voice: "Leah, darling. Keep your secrets, trust no one. Remember your training. Rely only on yourself. Secrets are always useful."

"Don't look at me like that, Cezar. You have everything," she told him.

Pounding artillery fire made them jump and hold their hands over their ears. When the noise faded, Cezar said, without irony, "The treasure may not matter if we are dead. But if we survive, who knows what will happen?" He looked at Leah with a mixture of shrewdness and longing.

Leah met his eyes. "If we survive, I want them back. I must have them. They don't belong to me."

"Whose are they?"

"I can't tell you that."

"Well, then I'm not going to tell you where they are," he said and walked away. He stopped to contemplate Quan, who crouched, damp and ill. "You should lie down, Professor. You don't look well."

"You mongrel whore," muttered Quan under cover of the next loud blast.

"I heard that, Professor," said Cezar. With his elbow, he knocked Quan's pince-nez to the ground where the lenses shattered, then jerked hard on Quan's goatee. Wisps of grey hair filled Cezar's hands. "Professor, the glue on the goatee softens in the sea air," Cezar said. "Your disguise wouldn't fool a child. You'd better hide if the Japs come around."

"We eat now," said An-li, holding up a charred fish.

⌒

THE war dogged them. The fog increased, carrying a miasma of desperate sounds and smells as the junk sailed into the South China Sea. All Leah could be sure of was that war was somewhere out there. On the junk, people's faces would suddenly appear, looking slightly smudged around the edges. Hu repeatedly sank a lead to decipher the muddy channels, as if he were reading entrails. Leah spent most of the day in the bow, her knees drawn up to her chest, watching Hu take the soundings and call to Pao.

No one wanted to go down to the airless cabin where Quan, moaning, huddled on the lower bunk. Leah heard Quan come up the ladder for the fourth time and shuffle off to the makeshift latrine, a rope attached to a bucket that was then dumped over the side. Quan sat with his trousers down around his ankles and gingerly massaged his stomach. His groans increased.

Pao called out "Shitter." "Dung-face," Hu responded. Pao sung out "Turd man."

Quan passed the brooch in a mound of excrement and blood. He forced himself to reach into the bucket and retrieve it. He flung the bucket far out over the side and let it drag in the water. The bucket filled with seawater. He poured the cold water down his stinging backside and threw the bucket out again. This time he washed his hands and the brooch. He pinned the brooch to the inside of his trouser pocket. Ignoring

Pao and Hu's hoots of derisive laughter, he half crawled back down the ladder.

Cezar asked Hu, "When will the fog lift?"

Hu shrugged and said "At least the Japanese can't see us in this."

"They'll hear him," said Cezar, pointing to the cabin.

"Maybe they'll think it's the wind," said Hu hopefully.

"Or maybe not," said Cezar. He wandered over to sit beside Leah.

"You okay?" he said.

"Do you care?"

"Yes," he said.

She didn't say anything for a while. Finally, she offered: "My father taught me that a bargain between two people is never equal. One person always wants more."

Cezar stood up. "My father also taught me a valuable lesson. He sent my mother, his Chinese concubine—whore—back to Manchuria when she grew old. It taught me to hold on to what I had."

Leah looked at his disappearing back. What had happened to the man in the Macau hotel room? He seemed to have disappeared.

⤚

By the end of the fourth day, Quan was delirious. An-li made him special teas, but they dribbled out as quickly as Quan swallowed them. Leah closed the hatch as much as she dared. Quan's shouting carried on the wind; he ranted about the old empress and her poisonous ways or about Pu Yi as a small imperious boy monarch, stupid to the core. Other times, he demanded to be fed the delicacies he had feasted on in the Forbidden City even as he clutched his belly and howled at the pain in his bowels. He had no idea where he was. He had forgotten entirely about the jewels in the specimen cases and the looted artefacts in their luggage.

Pao's and Hu's faces clouded with terror whenever Quan let lose a bellow of pain or cursed in rage at a nonexistent underling.

"Hear that?" said An-li in the falling dusk.

Quan was quiet for a moment. Leah heard the noise of a powerful engine.

"Jap navy," said Pao, ashen and pleading.

"They'll board, attracted by the noise," said Cezar, already climbing down the ladder. "Someone on board will speak a bit of Chinese. Quick, rope."

At first Quan fought, arching his back and twisting around as Leah and Cezar bound and gagged him. They wrestled Quan onto the floor. His face turned purple. The noise of the engine increased. Leah and Cezar exchanged looks over Quan's body. Leah nodded in assent. Pao came to the hatch, looked into the gloom. He returned with a bit of torn sail. Heaving and tugging, the three of them manoeuvred Quan through the ladder opening and onto the deck. There was a last feeble jerk from Quan, who opened his eyes wide, terrified, as they dragged him on the sail to the gunnels of the boat.

"Now," said Cezar.

They rolled Quan off. As he fell, the sail billowed out like an albatross wing. There was a loud splash. Pao slouched back to the helm. Leah and Cezar hung over the stern and saw Quan's body for a few seconds riding on the crest of a wave. Then he was gone.

Cezar and Leah turned away from each other. Leah looked down at her hands. They were shaking. She clasped them tightly together. She said, "I wish it were over," and lurched toward the cabin. Cezar watched her face, small and sad, her hair encrusted with salt water, disappear down the ladder. She said, as if in some measure of justification, "He killed Sonia."

His words floated down: "Ah, well, then."

Not much of an epitaph for Quan—or for poor Sonia. Perhaps it was the best Cezar could do under the circumstances. Below deck, she was hit by the stench of Quan. The smell oozed from the rank bunk.

"The cabin reeks," she called.

"Use my lime scent. It's in my suitcase," Cezar replied.

Her hands seemed to belong to someone else as she rifled through Cezar's clothes: silk ties, shirts with pearl buttons, a cashmere sweater. The jewels weren't there. She thumped on the bottom, empty. Running out of time, she picked up the cut-crystal atomiser and squirted it furiously around the cabin. Above, there was the sound of a large ship cutting its engines and then excited shouts in Japanese. She messed up her hair, smeared dirt from the floor on her face and pulled Quan's disgusting blanket around her. If she looked sick enough, she prayed the Japanese would leave her alone. She longed to be a sea-going animal and slip over the side of the junk, to disappear forever. But maybe, just maybe, she could also manage to float away with a suitcase full of artefacts, to set up house in a coral sea. She huddled under the vile blanket.

A Japanese sailor used a loud-hailer. His bad Chinese assaulted their ears. The sailor was dwarfed by the enormous conning tower, from which sprouted a massive gun barrel.

"An-li, go below," said Cezar.

An-li hurried down the ladder.

The Japanese captain was hauled onto the junk by two of his men.

Cezar blurted out: "We're fishermen, making our way down the coast to visit relatives, sir."

"Seen any ships? These are dangerous waters."

Cezar bowed his head and spoke looking at his feet. "No, Captain, sir. Not anything, sir."

Below, Leah and An-li heard the Japanese sailors stomping about and a number of staccato commands. Leah saw the sole of a boot, then a uniformed leg in blue. A sailor descended the ladder. His loud "Eh!" brought the others clamouring down.

Fawning, feigning chagrin, Cezar said, in a stuttering voice, "We have passengers, a European woman and her servant. The European is ill."

The captain glared.

Cezar, looking at his shoes, said, "These worthless women, they aren't at war with anyone."

The captain climbed down the ladder.

An-li stood in front of Leah with a basin. Leah coughed. A sailor looked away in disgust. Leah clutched An-li, a child seeking comfort in her nurse.

The captain studied the women. The young one might have once have been pretty; now she looked like a sick white dog. The smell of sickness overlaid with the sweet scent of lime was gut-wrenching. He kept his distance. He registered the suitcases stacked under the bunk. "Out," said the captain, making shoving motions.

Woozy, Leah had to be helped up the ladder. She dry-retched

over the side of the boat. A Japanese sailor stood next to her. He said something low and dirty. Another sailor swallowed a nasty laugh. Near the cabin opening, Leah sank to the deck, her head between her knees. An-li knelt and rubbed her back.

The captain directed one of his men to insert his bayonet into the suitcase lock. The case sprang open and he tossed the clothes out. He threw the empty case onto the floor. It thudded dully. The Captain picked up the case. It was abnormally heavy. Under the glare of a flashlight, he slipped the sailor's knife around the false bottom. A variety of jade and ivory objects peeped through the straw. He rifled though them quickly. From above, Leah stared down at objects that were no longer hers. The captain resettled the contents, tucking the straw around them delicately like a curator, then replaced the false bottom. He shouted an order. Two sailors carried the bags up the ladder, stomping deliberately as they went, on Leah's silk underwear littering the floor.

On deck, the captain shook his head at Cezar. "Stupid man," he said, and gave a contemptuous grunt. "Even as the slut escapes, she steals." A sailor directed the flashlight at Cezar's face. The captain put his thumb under Cezar's chin and lifted it into the white glare. "Mongrel, Eurasian. Mixed blood makes you weak, dumb." Then he repeated it in Japanese. His men nodded in agreement and puffed out their chests.

Cezar blinked in the light, unable to see, his loss of face complete.

"We go now," said the captain.

The patrol boat thundered north toward Shanghai. Its running lights left behind pools of gold flecks on the night sea, the rising sun flag waving brightly from the stern of the ship.

24

ON THE OCCASION OF HIS DEATH

CEZAR CAME UP behind Leah, pulled her hair, and yanked her around to face him. "You god-damn whore, you slut," he said. Then he hit her hard across the mouth, drawing blood. "I trusted you!"

She lunged and head-butted him in the chest. A clump of her hair came away in Cezar's hand as he sprung back. Dazed, he stood looking at the pale strands, white in the moonlight.

"Get away from me, Cezar. What trust? You stole from me. You still have the jewels."

With a balled-up fist, Cezar came at Leah again. An-li jumped between them. Cezar pushed her away. She tripped and fell, letting out a scream of pain. He bent down to help her up. Leah rushed him. He pulled at Leah's coat, ripped at her pocket, and the derringer rolled onto the deck. There was a mad scramble for the gun between Leah and Cezar as they stumbled over An-li. Leah grabbed it and attempted to stand. Cezar covered her hands and tugged. The gun went off, a flash, a bang. Cezar crumpled to his knees, swaying. The gun fell in a slow arc to the deck. Leah kicked it away and reached for Cezar. She laid him down gently. Hu brought a lantern and held it high. Cezar's face was waxy. An-li burrowed in and unbuttoned Cezar's bloodstained shirt. She mopped at the blood until she saw a small red hole surrounded by a larger black circle above his left nipple. She eased her hand around his back, searching for an exit wound.

"He's not bleeding much. The bullet is still inside him," said An-li.

She bandaged the wound using the clean side of Leah's camisole, the side the Japanese sailor hadn't touched when he had thrown underwear around like paper streamers before treading on it.

Leah watched the sweat collecting on Cezar's face. His eyes were half-closed and his breathing shallow. "Will he be all right? He's so cold," said Leah, squeezing Cezar's hand. She took off her coat and tucked it around him. "More blankets."

Cezar moaned softly.

An-li and Leah made a bed on deck for Cezar. They dragged the brazier closer to keep him warmer. Leah knelt over Cezar, dabbing drops of clean water onto his lips. Finally, Leah said, "Get some sleep, An-li. I'll watch him."

"He's young, Leah. He may live," said An-li, limping off toward the hatch. At the hatch, she turned and said, "He brought it on himself."

Hu and Pao stole frightened glances at Cezar and Leah and

mumbled quiet words of reassurance to each other. Hu said "The Macanese is slippery as an eel. He'll escape death."

Cold and miserable, Leah saw Hu's words form into various shapes, colours, mostly black and purple, but she could not place them into any order, filled as she was with a gun flash, a splash, the feel of Cezar's sweaty skin. Lost in these sensations, she rested her head on her knees. She thought about the what-ifs: *if* she hadn't gone to Macau, *if* she hadn't tiptoed away in the early morning, *if* she hadn't felt menaced by the Japs, or shocked and numbed by her own willingness to throw treacherous Quan overboard. She shook her head. What did it matter? She couldn't even recall what had been going through her mind when he had hit her and they'd wrestled for the gun.

She stretched out beside Cezar. His breathing sounded okay, a bit weak maybe. She draped her arm around him and whispered, "Don't die." He mumbled something. She leaned in closer. He was asleep. She snuggled into the curve of his back, touched his thick black hair. He was so beautiful. She was certain that he would relent and tell her where he had hidden the jewels. All she had to do was coax him a little. The fight had really been his fault. No, the bastard of a Jap captain. Cezar was really hitting out at *him*, not her. She was certain Cezar's fingers had pressed the trigger—hers were on top of his. She was only trying to protect herself and An-li. In the morning, he would realise this. He might be weak, but they would get to Hong Kong and a doctor would remove the bullet. It was only a small wound. The bullet must have lodged in soft tissue or a rib. Already his strong body must be forming a callus around the bullet, the nacre around a grain of sand. The derringer was really no more than a toy. She would tell Chang that Cezar had helped her. Cezar could have Sonia's portion. She imagined waking up in her own bed with Cezar by her side. They would be lovers forever. It was as if it had already happened—a long love affair—and she was remembering and savouring the affair's peculiar charms during a family evening out under the stars. She whispered "Love me" into his ear and kissed his lips. "Don't leave." The question she couldn't face was: Can I exist after this, if he dies? She wanted to watch over Cezar, catch his breath, will him to live should he falter during the night, but eventually she fell asleep and didn't dream.

LEAH woke in the warmth of the sun. Her mouth was dry and her back ached from the hard boards. She opened her eyes to An-li who cast a shadow over her.

"Cezar's dead," said An-li.

"No!" said Leah, turning to stare at Cezar. She held her hand over his nose, waited patiently for a faint breath to fill it. She tugged the blankets and her coat off him and laid her head against his bandaged chest. Nothing moved; the texture of his skin had changed, no longer butter-soft but hard and dry.

Long ago, sitting with Theo in a restaurant, she recalled tearing pages from her school prize book of Victorian poetry. One page had a black curlicue border and a heading in thick elaborate letters, "On the Occasion of his Death." What followed? What words would help: regret, love, in the fullness of time, sorrow, heartfelt, grief, pity, shock, sadness, sleep well my love, please don't haunt me, it's not my fault, please don't hate me, it's up to me now, or how long after the pain can I begin to forget him?

Leah asked Pao for a bucket. Pao ducked his head and silently gave it to her. Refusing all help, she swung the bucket out on a rope and hauled it in, staggering under its weight and sloshing water until the deck became slippery. She rinsed out the bandages, watching the slatey water turn pink, then washed Cezar's face. She stripped his corpse. Using the cloth, she worked her way down over his chest, stopped at the wound and began again at the fingers of his right hand, then the left. In one swift motion, she swept the cloth over his groin and finished with his legs and toes. She sat back on her heels and surveyed her handiwork. He smelled like the sea, salty and astringent. The seawater had left flicks of sand or salt on his eyelashes, gluing the lids together. She was glad of that.

Slitting the seams of one of Leah's petticoats, An-li made one continuous piece of silk. Together Leah and An-li placed the silk over Cezar's face, then tugged it down between his legs and, groaning under the body's weight, pulled the cloth up his back. An-li sewed up the sides of the makeshift shroud.

Unbidden, Hu and Pao helped to carry the body to the ship's side. Leah cradled the head. In unison, they swayed with the junk and on the count of three, heaved. He made a tremendous splash. The silk shroud loosened to float to the surface.

Leah watched the white silk bobbing until she supposed it wasn't a shroud at all, only one more whitecap amongst the rolling waves. Who was Cezar? How little she knew about him. She listed the facts she knew: His mother was Manchu, his father Macanese; he liked gambling; he liked expensive clothes and wore lime scent; he worked for a Japanese thug; he was good with women. Seven puny facts was not much to know about someone. She didn't even know how old he was.

She had stripped him down to his bare dead skin to find his soul. He had eluded her. She watched the ocean's endless horizon, transfixed.

Pao and Hu checked the currents and headed into the wind, the sails filling. The sooner they got to Hong Kong, the better. They would dump their passengers on the first remote island of Hong Kong they reached. Free of passengers, they fervently hoped their junk's good fortune would return. When they were nearer to Hong Kong, in safer waters, they decided to sail through the night, taking turns to spell each other.

An-li roamed around the junk, going down into the cabin, foraging amidst the abandoned relics of Cezar and Quan. She lugged up the cabin's blankets and tied them tightly to the ropes to get rid of the smell and odours that lingered, sick-making and malodorous. She brought up armfuls of clothes and dumped them overboard, cursing at their owners under her breath.

Leah caught sight of Cezar's cashmere coat riding a wave, one arm raised in a nonchalant salute before it became water-logged and disappeared. She turned to An-li, who held Cezar's cut-glass atomiser in her hand.

"No, I want that," cried Leah, running over. She squeezed the bulb; the scent of lime mixed with the sea spray. Tears welled in her eyes.

"I couldn't find the jewels," said An-li. "It is one thing to make sure the dead have their things. It is quite another for the living not to have what Mr. Chang so eagerly expects. We must look for them."

Leah wondered if Cezar would appreciate a treasure hunt on the occasion of his death. She rather thought he would.

There were the usual coils of rope, battened-down spare sails, kegs of fresh water, a bamboo bucket, and a fishing line strung up as a clothesline. Gravely, each woman took off in the opposite direction to circumnavigate the deck, knocking on the uneven boards and knotholes to find Cezar's hiding place. They took turns with the kerosene lantern, shining the light into crevices, inserting a fingernail between wobbly boards. By early evening, their hands were cut with splinters lodged in the fingers, but they had found nothing.

Leah questioned Hu and Pao. "What did you notice Mr. da Silva doing when he first arrived on board?"

Neither man wanted to talk about Cezar. Each felt they had witnessed so much misfortune, their luck might never come back. Their catch of fish would dwindle, Pao's daughters would remain unmarried, and Hu's sons would take to drink, gambling, and debauchery. Hu spoke for them both: "Please, lady, do not ask more. We are only fishermen. We want no more trouble." They looked haunted and uncertain. It was obvious that they knew nothing.

"Time to eat," said Pao, edging away toward the brazier and rice sacks.

Leah watched as Pao measured out the rice from a twenty-pound sack. Four full sacks stood next to it. They must have used part of their boat-hire to buy provisions. Probably they were going to take the rice back with them to their families in the country. It was odd, though. The stamped lettering on the sacks was red. And the opened bag and three of the full sacks were stitched with red thread. The fourth bag—a bit lumpier?—was stitched with black thread. Who would notice a bag of rice? The Japanese wouldn't. The sons of the rising sun were fed on superior Japanese rice and if that weren't available, well, they wouldn't touch these sweepings. Cezar must have crept up on deck the first night and stuffed the jewels in, then used fishing line to reseal the sack. What with the shelling and Pao and Hu having to navigate noiselessly down the Yangtze, no one had paid attention to Cezar, who had pretended to use the sacks as a makeshift bed, pushing and pulling at them to make himself more comfortable. It was an ingenious, simple subterfuge. She would wait until they got closer to Hong Kong. The jewels were safe where they were for now. She picked up the atomiser and sprayed a cloud of scent at the black-laced sack of rice, then threw the atomiser overboard, turning away before she heard it hit the water.

ANCHORED one day's sail from the outer island of Cheung Chau, Hu and Pao slept on deck, Leah and An-li below in the stifling cabin. Leah awoke with a start. She hadn't meant to fall asleep, had been certain she would spend the night wide-eyed, but tiredness had washed over her. She was grateful for the dreamless sleep. It was still night, maybe 2:00 A.M.

She crept up the ladder, pausing on each rung to make certain that neither An-li nor the men stirred. On deck she listened to the men snuffling and snoring. The moon hung pearl-white, glowing weakly. Timing her steps to match the small waves lapping against the hull, she glided over to sit beside the rice sacks. She unwound her peasant coat from her waist, slipped out a knife and a straightened fishhook from a pocket, then spread the coat flat. She cut the lining and made runnels up the seams. She sawed at the bag's black knot and then ladled rice from the full bag to the nearly empty one.

Her fingers touched something round and smooth, a pearl. She placed the pearl in the seam of her coat, then finger-sifted each handful of rice, finding wonderful prizes in each scoop. It became a meditative exercise—the reaching down; the feel of jade, of ivory, of lapis lazuli; the slipping of the treasure into the wadding. In the humid air she felt hot, then cold. Once or twice a gust of wind blew, rustling the rice like a sigh from Cezar. She paused and looked into the inky dark before the urge to search again overcame her.

Finally, she patted the remaining grains but found no more lumps. Hurrying now, she dumped fistfuls of rice back into the depleted black-stitched sack. The sky was softening into grey as she pierced the bag with the fishhook-become-needle and sewed it closed. Lastly, she ran tacking stitches up the wadding of her jacket to keep the jewels in place. She shrugged the jacket on, patting at various lumps in the wadding to smooth them out. She swept the rice litter away as she heard Pao stirring. She fell heavily against the open sack. Rice sprayed the deck. She called out "Damn," and knelt to clean up the spilt rice, cursing herself roundly for being clumsy, blaming the bobbing of the junk.

In the cabin, Leah made a great deal of noise, stuffing the few clothes she wanted into the centre of her coat, then tying the sleeves into a knot and tucking up the hem to make a crude bundle. An-li's eyes fluttered open. Even in the dim light, Leah was surprised at how frail An-li looked, shrivelled and careworn.

"I can't wait to be home," said Leah.

"It's not over yet," said An-li.

⌒

THE late afternoon drizzle carried the scent as they drew near to Cheung Chau. From far off, Leah caught sight of the fishing village, its haphazard wooden shacks perched precariously atop flimsy stilts stuck into the water.

They sailed past the village until they came to a deserted beach. Hu dipped a long pole into the water. He lodged the end of the pole between his face and shoulder, squeezed hard against it, and walked bent, almost horizontal, along the deck to guide the junk in. The underside of the junk scraped against the soft sand, then caught on a sandbar. Hu set the pole down.

"If you pay them, one of the villagers will take you to Hong Kong in a sampan," said Hu. "We go home now." He grinned, looked sheepish, and pulled out the derringer, barrel first, from his pants pocket. "I find this."

"Throw it away," said An-li.

But Leah shook her head and gravely held out her hand to Hu, who placed the gun in the centre of her palm. It was warm from Hu's pocket. The rain fell on it. She pushed it deep into her bundle. Maybe she would put it into a glass case with a plaque reading *On the Occasion of His Death*, like a Victorian memento.

She bowed to Hu in thanks and to Pao. "Safe journey," she said.

Awkwardly, Pao assisted Leah over the side of the junk into the warm water eddying around her knees, then handed down her bundled coat. She placed the coat on her head and waded to the shore. Hu lifted An-li into his arms and carried her to the dry beach. They waved to each other like old friends.

With a swaying gait, Leah and An-li, clasping their bundles to their chests, set off for the fishing village.

The last leg of their journey was spent squeezed into a sampan's covered sleeping quarters. The owner's wide-eyed children giggled at the dirty, stringy-haired European. It was late night when they slunk into the backwaters of Hong Kong Harbour. Leah gave the sampan owner enough money to make him forget his passengers.

PART III

HONG KONG,

SPRING 1938

25

THE
RETURN

WAKING, LEAH EXPECTED to find herself still lying on a plank in the airless cabin. Instead, her own bedroom had a surreal quality, as if she had dreamed it or conjured it out of the dank fog of the South China Sea. She gazed around the room like a visitor to a museum, noting the placement of objects, the relics of her former life: the bronze mirror, the scrolls, her baby jade. The sun flooded in. Really, what she wanted to do was turn over and sleep forever, delicious, clean, and warm. Even as she stretched out and wriggled her toes against the white sheets, twinges of sadness crept in. Cezar was dead, Sonia was dead, that shit of a eunuch was dead. How was she to live? Chang was alive. The jewels, she had the jewels.

She threw off the sheet and rushed to her coat bundle,

tossed so carelessly under her bed the night before. She dragged it out. It was heavier than she remembered. She untied the coat sleeves and with her teeth tore at the stitches, releasing the wadding and the jewels. They spilled onto the bedclothes. She sorted through them, touching and stroking the exquisite lapis lazuli like small chunks of sky, and rosy pearls, milky pearls, and ivory, but it was the jade that made her exclaim and her eyes water, the perfection of jade. Theo had waxed lyrical about jade during their dinner lessons, his face flushed and his long fingers punctuating the air to point and instruct. "Such perfection," he said, "you and I can only dream about. They say if you eat it, it confers immortality."

In ancient China, a newborn boy was laid on a bed and given jade while a girl was put on the floor and given a tile. Theo had loved to tell Leah how he had laid her, newborn and precious, on his wide rosewood bed and had given her jade, exquisite rare white jade. From the heap Leah extracted the pale white jade, the Altar of the Moon Jade, and licked it. It was cool and slightly salty.

She put on the archer's ring; it hung off her thumb. She imagined it on Chang's callused finger; now it would no longer be hers. What would he do with all this? Pull the graduated lapis lazuli off its golden cord, stone by stone? Trade these treasures to a feudal warlord for arms, or sell them in a job lot to a White Russian arms dealer? And what good would it do? The Chinese army she had seen was dispirited and disorganised. The Japanese would mow them down. Chinese lives would not be saved. Guerrilla bands roaming the countryside wouldn't last; a warlord would absorb them. She realised Chang had no idea what she had brought back.

Maybe she should sort through her trove and save the best for herself. Or better yet, why not say she had lost everything, blame it on the war. Pao and Hu hadn't seen her discover Cezar's hiding place. Even An-li didn't know. Chang would never find out. What an amazing secret she had. Her life to come would be full of powerful secrets and hiding places. She would secrete the jewels where no prying servants would go, in Theo's room.

Last night she had been so weary she hadn't even paused by Theo's bedroom door, or listened for his pneumatic breathing. Now she entered his shuttered room, dominated by the rosewood bed. The bare mattress was a shock. It drooped like a naked old man. She opened Theo's bedroom closet. His suits hung between camphor and cinnamon balls, the smells cancelling each other out. Tentative, she pulled at a sleeve, draped it around one shoulder then leant into the jacket. Nothing. No sudden solace, no reassuring hint from beyond the grave. She pushed the suits out of the way to reach the safe behind. Like an altar boy setting out the host, she grouped the treasures: necklaces in precise circles, rings next to them, pearls according to size, ivory amulets and carved trinkets, jewelled nail guards—and the jade. She cleared a space for the Altar of Moon Jade, put it down, picked it up, caressed it again. She couldn't bring herself to lock it away. Hiding it in the folds of her nightdress, she tiptoed to the study and taped it lovingly to the underside of the leather desk chair. Then she crept back to bed and slept until noon.

In the early evening, Jonathan knocked on the front door. "Is she in?" he asked An-li. He shifted from foot to foot. "I've come up here occasionally." He paused, trying to explain why he couldn't keep away, but An-li eyed him suspiciously as though he were a tax inspector or a spy. "That is for Leah, Miss Kolbe, well, it was the least I could do in the circumstances." He took a breath and asked the question that had been tormenting him for weeks: "Is everything all right?" He searched An-li's face for clues. She gave nothing away.

In the past, he had attempted to hold conversations with her during their long walks down the tiled hallway, but An-li would only say "yes" or "no" or "Miss Kolbe will be ready shortly," then would pour him a large shot of whisky that left a bitter taste in his mouth. He had waited in the living room contemplating Theo's treasures, scrounging for insightful comments about the curios. While Leah was away, he had read books about Chinese history and art. He found them boring and was only able to finish them if he sat very quietly and imagined Leah in his arms explaining the fine detail.

Leah came slowly down the hall. She peeked around the open door to see Jonathan sitting in a high-backed chair, examining a Ch'ing dynasty jar. He put it down hurriedly when he heard her footsteps and rushed toward her as she entered. He hugged her tight.

"You've come back," he said and kissed her hair.

She lingered against his lawn jacket and his freshly shaved face. He smelled clean and happy.

"Let me look at you," he said and held her at arm's length, trying to detect any change. He thought she looked thinner and she was tan, weatherbeaten, a flush of red on her sharp cheekbones. Her lips were chapped, and he longed to kiss them better.

She broke his hold, led him deeper into the drawing room, amongst the brocades and inlaid ivory screens, to sit on the couch. He held her hand and played with her fingers as he talked, serious and earnest. "I've been so worried. One hears such terrible things about the Japs, all that killing. And no word from you."

She smiled at him. He looked so young and carefree beneath his deep concern for her. And it dawned on her that she had a choice: to let him into her world or, at least for now, to keep him at bay, keep him safe. "Travelling was difficult at times. That's why I didn't cable. You can't rely on train schedules, what with troop movements—" She disentangled her hands. "Whisky?" she asked and walked to the liquor cabinet, stopping to snap on the radio, which, after it warmed up, blared out a foxtrot.

As she fiddled with the drinks, Jonathan said, "And the trip, it was worthwhile? Got what you wanted?"

She spilt a bit of the whisky and mopped it up. "Yes and no. I mean the academic aspect is set up, but the antiques, well, they weren't what I was led to believe."

Jonathan wished Leah would turn around. It was all a bit too offhand; he wanted to see her face and judge for himself. "And Manchukuo, what was that like?"

She walked back, swaying in time to the music, the whisky sloshing in the crystal glasses. "Grim. It was very grim, the food was horrid, and the people cowed. To better times," Leah said, and they clinked their glasses together.

They drank their whisky. In between sips, Leah hummed in time to the music. "Aren't you going to tell me anything, Leah?"

"Later, maybe. People aren't really interested in tales about other people's travels."

He so wanted to touch her, press against her rose silk dress, see her breasts, inhale her secret smells. "I've been reading up on Chinese art. That jar I was looking at, it's eighteenth century, Ch'ing dynasty. It's got dragons on it, so it could have been used by the imperial household." He cleared his throat and looked into her face, which, as he spoke, softened. "The curvature of the cover complements the jar's sloping shoulders and the graceful body, which narrows as it approaches the slender foot."

Leah clapped her hands. "Go to the head of the class. You have been busy."

He nodded self-consciously and added, "I've missed you."

She joked, "I've been in the wars."

Jonathan said, "I'm sorry. Is there anything I can do?"

"Let's dance."

Leah pulled him to his feet. Jonathan held her according to some half-forgotten schoolboy regulation, a length away.

"We're friends now," she said and readjusted his hands so her breasts brushed his body and he felt the curve of her back.

"Better?" she asked.

He nodded, brushing his lips against the side of her forehead.

Leah smiled encouragingly. It was so comforting to be in his arms, to be young, to know she was going to make someone happy and let the forgetting begin.

They seduced each other, laughing and talking and discarding clothes in a rush. Then they were naked on the oriental carpet. He smelled of soap and astringent hair oil. He was inside of her, rocking her hard against the worn carpet on the wooden floor. A flash of memory of the junk and Cezar hit Leah.

Jonathan felt the hesitation and looked questioning for a split second, not sure how long he could hold on.

Leah pushed the memory away and wound her legs tighter around him, saying, "Now."

He came quickly, shuddering and happy. He mumbled an apology while she licked at his shoulder, their bodies glistening with sweat.

"It's okay. We'll go to my room. I've never had a man in my room," she said.

Jonathan laughed and said, "Oh, Leah, I do love you so."

Leah slipped her dress on over her head, then stopped to pick up her underwear, saying "It's not necessary, Jonathan."

"But I want to." He scrambled into his trousers and followed her down the hall, beside himself with awe and disbelief.

26

INTERREGNUM

THREE WEEKS PASSED. Away from Leah, Jonathan daydreamed about her constantly, thinking of ways to be with her: long leisurely lunches, showing her off at his club, accepting dinner party invitations from matrons who understood that he would bring Leah as his guest, and finally returning to the Peak to spend the night.

An-li said little about the new arrangement, only noticed how watchful Leah had become, how she lingered in Theo's bedroom during the day with the door locked, how much whisky needed to be replenished and how Jonathan's hands were in constant motion as if he could contain Leah.

Lying in bed with Jonathan was like being under glass, shielded from life, from her secrets, an insect in its cocoon.

Innocently he asked: "How is Sonia? She hasn't been around."

"No," said Leah, stretching luxuriously, letting the strap of her nightgown fall down to reveal her breasts. "She met this Russian, something to do with the railway, an engineer, I think. Anyway, he was off to Korea or Tibet to design something there. He was very well off, and you know Sonia. It was a shock, though, her leaving just like that."

"Yes," murmured Jonathan, stroking Leah's breasts, forgetting to ask about Sonia's cabled money and the note he had written to himself to call on Sonia on her return and thank her for using the firm's services. He raised his head and said, "What an odd woman, to leave you in the lurch like that."

"Yes," said Leah, in between rewarding Jonathan with kisses, "but I can't blame Sonia. He was good-looking, in a distinguished older-man way. And then he was Russian too. He understood her, I think." Odd, the way the pain of Sonia's death had retreated and how easily the lie came to her. Sonia would have appreciated the irony of being thought to have ended her days with a perfect lover rather than with Quan's knife in her guts. "She was always on the lookout for the main chance. It's just the way she was . . . is, I mean."

"Well, then," said Jonathan, no longer caring where the hell Sonia ended up, "I'll see her on her return, bound to."

"Bound to," echoed Leah, reaching for his penis.

Leah allowed herself to drift with Jonathan. He lived a world away from secret organisations, spying Japs, and Chang.

An-li could find out nothing about Chang. He had gone away to join the guerrillas, one rumour had it; another was that he had been killed in Nanking; still another that he had become a spy for the Japanese, planning assassinations of Chinese officials who wouldn't cooperate with them.

Leah remained watchful. The longer Chang stayed away, the more she expected him. On the streets of Hong Kong, she scanned the faces of the people around her. Sometimes she had to will herself not to turn around and stare at an unknown man who stood on a street corner smoking a cigarette. Or she would catch sight of a *singsong* girl whose mouth turned down as she approached, who seemed to be signalling to a man in a black fedora. On one level, Leah knew she was being fanciful, while on another, she knew enough to keep up her guard. And the reality was that the jewels, her secrets, had taken on a life of their own. She spent hours in Theo's room on the unmade bed, examining the jewels, cataloguing them, putting them on, taking them off.

Almost daily, An-li suggested a visit to the herbalist in Tai Ping Shan, west of the city. An-li would shake her head gravely and say "Leah, you need balance," or "Your skin is sluggish."

"Not now," Leah would answer. Later, she would be surprised to find herself by the liquor cabinet pouring an early lunch or late nightcap whisky just to get through the day or to lighten her mood, or to sleep soundly.

An-li continued to harp about the need to visit the herbalist. Leah gave in with bad grace. She trailed along behind An-li in Tai Ping Shan. On the narrow cobbled streets, ragged refugees jostled them repeatedly. Leah pulled her hat down further over her face. An old Chinese man in a skullcap smiled and nodded. Leah felt his gaze on her back as An-li stopped and said, "Here."

The interior of the shop was cool. Filtered light played over the jars full of coloured powders and the dark wooden cabinets behind. The smells from the different teas loose in wooden barrels were comforting. A middle-aged woman with a delicately boned face and pencilled eyebrows leaned across the counter and welcomed An-li like an old friend. The woman had a soothing voice and made commiserating clicking noises each time An-li mentioned a different organ.

"Please stick out your tongue," said the woman.

Leah gave an irritated "okay" and stuck out her tongue. The woman studied it for a while, nodded to An-li, then examined each of Leah's wrists, feeling the six pulses in each that connected the vital organs.

The old man with the skullcap walked into the shop. Leah broke out in a creeping cold sweat. Her voice sounded different. She managed, "An-li, please get the teas and let's go."

The woman behind the counter sighed heavily and scurried around filling twists of paper with teas and talking of cold winds affecting Leah's spleen. The old man waited his turn patiently.

Outside the shop, Leah said in English, "I'll drink the teas, but it won't do any good."

"You are hiding something," said An-li.

"It's nothing to do with you," said Leah, prickly and defensive.

At home, in her study, Leah steadied her nerves with a glass of whisky. It tasted weak. She was certain An-li had watered it, but couldn't face confronting yet another look of concern and heartache.

She flipped through the post. It was mostly bills. The servants' wages were due. It took a lot of money to keep the house up to standard. The $4,000 (the first and only installment from Sonia) had gone on last quarter's bills, Theo's funeral, travel expenses. She had been away too long. She had yet to pick up the threads of Theo's antiquities business. Well, why not sell a few jewels? She was entitled to her five percent, according to her deal with Chang. And, if he never showed up . . . much more. But she had such chilling doubts. She agonised over how Chang might react to the loss of Quan and the priceless small objects the Japanese had confiscated. She pictured presenting Chang with a list of jewels sold and the price obtained and, at the bottom of the page, a thick line drawn and the notation, less five-percent commission to Miss L. Kolbe and a generous sum, $25,000 or $50,000, written out in full. And what would he do then? She imagined his dark pupils contracting to hard dots, then the sound of his callused fingers scrapping across the paper as he studied the list, the price obtained, her five-percent calculation. He would ask for the whole amount. No, he wouldn't even ask, only point to the total and extend his rough hands. If she argued, he would place a dollar amount on the loss of Quan and on the other treasures the Japanese had stolen. If she sold the jewels secretly could she manage to keep it all? Somehow, he would know what was missing.

Despite the war in China, museums were still collecting and funding a variety of archaeological digs in remote locations. Serious connoisseurs understood that certain treasures came to light during times of trouble, making their way to dealers who acted to preserve these treasures the best way they knew how. No one wanted to ask embarrassing questions. No one wanted to be labelled a war profiteer. She had a French contact,

Monsieur Frederic Martin. He was discreet and well connected. She didn't want any rumour about the jewels to
circulate in China or Hong Kong.

All afternoon, Leah worked on the letter. It shouldn't sound
desperate or fawning, more like an in-joke shared between
two fashionable people, a bit clandestine, and an opportunity
not to be missed. She settled on a phrase: "she had access"
(connoting something less than ownership) "to a few unique
treasures from China's noble past that had never been on the
market." It was a little push forward down her chosen path, a
stab at keeping afloat in dangerous times.

27

THE
COLLECTOR

FOR THE THIRD time, Leah read the letter from the diplomat/dealer Monsieur Martin.

Dear Leah,

I was saddened to learn about Theo's death. Your father was a true student of Chinese culture. I will miss his insightful comments and his enthusiasm for all things Oriental.

As to the other matter, France, nay, my child, all of Europe is holding its collective breath and unfortunately the market is sluggish. From every quarter one gets that most Gallic of shrugs and the words "liquid assets." Everyone craves cash money, not the treasures of the past.

In these times of uncertainty who can blame them? I haven't as yet written to American Chinese collectors, but these days many prefer more orthodox dealers in keeping with their bourgeois aspirations. I have contacted the well-known industrialist Monsieur DuChamps. He has a young and beautiful Chinese wife to keep amused. I will keep you informed and do my best.

As always, *ma chérie*,
Frederic

How could she have been so stupid? She should have told Martin that under no circumstances was he to consider Chinese collectors and hint or, perhaps, bluntly state, that the best prices were to be found amongst Europeans with a taste for luxury and history. It would have whetted Martin's appetite, and he might, she thought ruefully, have applied himself more diligently. He had let the proverbial cat out of the bag. Without exception, expatriate Chinese maintained family or business connections in Hong Kong and China. Eventually, the wrong people would be alerted. They would come sniffing around, poking their noses in, asking difficult, tricky questions. It was only a matter of time. Even if Chang were dead, he would have had accomplices. He had a secret society behind him, a whole tribe of people claiming to be from the Land of the Dragon with invisible links to the Triads or other gangs. Leah felt under the desk chair for the Altar of the Moon Jade. She touched its perfect cool surfaces, whispering, "Don't let them get me." She fought down the impulse to crawl under the chair.

Perhaps she should leave Hong Kong. Sail away with the jewels to Paris, London, or New York. Hong Kong was too small. It was suffocating her, causing her to jump at shadows, at the sight of harmless old men.

She asked An-li to get boat schedules and travel brochures for Europe and Australia. She whiled away a few days sipping An-li's teas and plotting her escape. "Everyone should travel," she told a dubious An-li. "We'll have a wonderful time." An-li nodded, unable to picture herself sitting in a foreign café, eating strange food. Leah, too, would hate it.

LEAH awoke in the dark to a quiet "Care for a drink?" from Chang, his face next to hers. She nodded, a cold lurch in her guts, as the whisky splashed into the glass by her bed.

"I'll drink from the bottle," said Chang.

The whisky hit the back of her throat. For a moment she was convinced she would vomit onto the sheet, but she managed to swallow and afterward to fake a welcoming smile.

He saw her white teeth flash and remained unmoved. "I see you are doing well. The Japanese have butchered thousands of Chinese. Who values these lives?" He shook his head slowly, as if all the lost lives were crowding in on his mind. He lifted the bottle of whisky and took a swig.

Leah's voice was thick and stuck in her throat as she said, "I was there. It was terrible."

"War cheapens life. Killing becomes accepted. We are all devalued. Don't you agree?"

"Yes," she murmured, at a loss as to what to say or do next.

She held the glass of whisky close to her breast and wondered if she was going to cry.

"Still," he said, peering at her face through the dark, "life goes on. We still want things. Even some we shouldn't have. The Chinese philosopher Lao-tse said 'There is no calamity greater than lavish desire. There is no greater guilt than discontentment. And there is no greater disaster than greed.' I am not a philosopher, but I have thought about these words during my travels. They can be applied to many people and situations. That is why we remember them." He turned on the bedside lamp.

She blinked in the light, pinned under his gaze. "But war and dying are final," she answered at last. "Everyone loses in war."

"And what have you lost, Miss Kolbe?"

"Everything—the eunuch, the curios, the jewels. Sonia is dead."

Chang patted her hand as if she had supplied the right answer, then he crushed it in his vise-like grip until she panted with pain. His fingers loosened; her breathing returned to normal. Chang smiled, sat down on the bed, placing an arm around Leah's shoulders, and drew her close. "Tell me what happened, how it all went wrong. I want to know the whole story. How the jewels were lost, how the curios—that is the word, isn't it?—were confiscated by the Japanese. And I want to hear from your own lips what happened to the eunuch."

"How did you know the Japanese stole the artefacts?" she asked, masking her terror, trying to sort out the tangles of her story, wondering if she could brazen her way through Chang's interrogation. She had nothing to lose. To Chang, she was a failure, a worthless accomplice. She had not delivered; their bargain was off. If she revealed the existence of the jewels, he would not be appeased, would understand that she had meant to deceive him. There would be no five-percent commission. He might even kill her. If she emptied her mind, kept to her story, he would have no alternative but to believe her. Lying well would save her life. "Who are your sources?"

Chang lit a clove cigarette. "Have you seen this, Miss Kolbe? It ran in the Tokyo press," he said, reaching into his breast pocket and pulling out a flimsy press clipping. "It's a good likeness, don't you think?"

He smoothed out the wrinkles and lifted his hand. She saw a girl in her black winter coat standing next to the iron gates of a soldiers' monument. "I can't read Japanese."

"I'll tell you the gist. It's about a Miss Kolbe's visit to Manchukuo and how she basked in the benevolence and good will of the Japanese. At first, we thought you had turned double agent, what with the death of Miss Rubstov. See," he said, pointing to the date of the article, "it ran after you had left Hsingking. But Miss Rubstov's good friend, Mr. Vasiliev, told us the true story. Unfortunately, we had to give him up to the Japanese. He was accused of black-marketeering and arms dealing. Both serious crimes in Manchukuo. I think they used Soviet machine guns to kill him. Sad, but fitting, or don't you agree?"

"It's a shock," she said. "It was all that damn eunuch's fault."

"Oh, Miss Kolbe, I'm so pleased to hear that. I knew there must be a simple explanation, because I never thought a young lady schooled so well by your esteemed father would betray us." He reached for the bottle and took another mouthful.

Leah picked her way through truth. Chang seemed to accept her version until she came to the bombing of the train outside of Nanking.

In any case, he listened politely, nodding his head, taking a few puffs of his clove cigarette, flicking the ashes onto the floor. "Tell me about this Mr. da Silva. How did you meet him?"

"In Macau, I met him in Macau."

"I had no idea you were a gambler. We Chinese are great believers in luck. Are you a believer, Miss Kolbe?"

She wanted to say "No, you're here"; instead, she offered, "Sometimes." She was grateful for the way the scent of his clove cigarette hung in the air. She had read that under great strain or fear, the body gave off an acrid odour. Her nightdress clung to her clammy skin.

He cleared his throat and spoke in Cantonese for the first time. "We have a great many friends. They tell us many things. Madame DuChamps, a great supporter of the free China movement, wires that her husband received an intriguing offer from a dealer in Hong Kong. No details, of course. Have you overlooked something in your account of how *all* the treasures of the great Manchu were lost?" His voice dropped to a whisper. "In English, the word you might be looking for is *access*."

He held her face in his hands and looked into her eyes.

"Stop it," Leah said, unhooking his fingers from her chin. "For weeks now, I've heard nothing from you. And then there were the rumours. Mostly that you were dead." She considered telling him about the double-agent gossip, but she didn't want to see his eyes narrow into hard black points. "And my debts are piling up. It was a costly business, Manchukuo. I need my commission."

Chang shook his head slowly. "Your commission for a task only half completed?" he whispered. "Just as I was saying, we return to lavish desire and greed, Miss Kolbe."

"Leah, you may call me Leah."

"Ah," said Chang, "I do like this European informality. Please continue, Leah." He refilled her whisky glass and took a few meditative sips from the bottle.

She wondered what she would say. She wished she were Scheherazade and could find a way into Chang's heart so she could escape her fate. She began in a small voice, but as she became engrossed in the story, her voice became matter-of-fact and her story-telling truthful. "I come from a country of two, my father and me. I suppose you could say it was a fortress, a walled city, full of beautiful possessions acquired through negotiation and treaty. Its charm, allure—call it what you will—was its neutrality. We formed an entrepôt of two: collecting treasures, researching and cataloguing them, trading them for others. The collection took on a life of its own." She thought of Pu Yi's worker ants toiling away for their queen, and Theo and his incessant need to acquire things; hers, too.

"We Chinese are always part of a group. A country of one is powerless. It cannot survive without alliances," he said, then added, "It certainly can't wage war or risk resorting to trickery or theft."

He spoke with intensity. She knew she was lost.

"I like to think, even if you had not turned up, I would have made a large cash donation to the Chinese war effort once the deal was done. *My* country can be benevolent," she said, giving a dry smile.

Chang pressed his fingers against the pulse in Leah's throat, toying with the pressure, hard then soft. Leah tried not to swallow; it hurt more to do so.

"Enough games," he said. "Get them. Stand up."

He pinned her left arm behind her back, yanking it higher until she gasped. Close together, they frog-marched to Theo's bedroom.

"In the closet, there's a safe," she gasped.

He let go of her arm. "Open it."

Leah twirled the dial, heard the tumblers click, then stepped back to swing the door wide. Over her shoulder, he peered in. "There should be more. The eunuch promised—"

"He lied. We had to leave suddenly. The Japanese were going to make an audit."

Chang picked up a hold-all lying on the closet floor. "Put them in here and don't be stupid enough to try to palm any. I'm watching."

Under his gaze, she began to lay each piece individually into the holdall, stuffing Theo's ties in to cushion them.

"Hurry up," he said.

"You have to take care with them. The pearls, especially, could be injured."

He shrugged with annoyance. "What is the punishment for treason in your country, Leah?"

She wished she had lived in a different kingdom. "That's all," she said, placing the last milky pearl into a snug nest. "One can always forgive oneself."

"Sit," said Chang, shoving Leah down onto a high-backed chair. From his pocket, he unwound a length of rope.

"Don't garrotte—"

"Of course not," said Chang, ignoring Leah's wild-eyed fright as he tied her wrists together and lashed her legs to the rungs of the chair.

How many people had he killed? She'd killed just one or two. She had learned to live with it. She guessed Chang had, too.

With a sad smile, Chang stuffed Theo's silk handkerchief into her mouth. At the door, he turned to study Leah as she sat immobile in the glare of the electric light, her eyes fierce and hard. "I'm leaving now. Remember, Leah, a country of one is always vulnerable." He shut the door with a firm click.

Leah strained to hear his footsteps echo down the hallway, but there was only silence.

28

A COUNTRY
OF ONE

LEAH STOPPED LISTENING for Chang's tread.
The merciless glare of the light revealed the bare-
ness of the closed room. She shut her eyes and
opened them quickly to blink away the persistent memory of
Chang's rough hands and his whisky breath hot on her cheek.
She pulled at her bonds and pushed with her tongue at the silk
shoved in her mouth. The chair rocked slightly. Afraid she
might tip it over, she sat unmoving as her panic ebbed. She was
alive, breathing, unharmed. But cheated.

Everything was finished, her sweet treasures gone. How she
would miss them. They had been hers for such a little time.
Crying in short heaves, she choked on the gag. Christ, what a
horrible death, killed by her own bodily fluids. Chang was a
sadistic bastard. She ran her tongue over the sodden silk and

realised that she could manoeuvre the gag by degrees. Spitting, tonguing, and, coughing, she expelled the gag. She took in lungfuls of air. It was a small victory. For a while, she was content to sit. She didn't want An-li or one of her servants to find her, tear-stained and bereft. She kept asking herself: Can I continue to exist like this? She thought she could; it wasn't as though she had a choice. The ledger was cleared; she could draw a double line at the end of the page and start afresh. She could walk the streets of Hong Kong without a hundred stray glances to contend with, or fearing, while she wandered through the Ladies' Market, to pass by an idling thug who would, as instructed, stick a knife in her ribs.

Her wrists tingled. The ropes bit into her skin. Leaning forward, she worried at the knot Chang had carelessly left between her wrists, so eager was he to possess her treasures. It took a long time. Finally she freed one wrist, then the other. She massaged her arms, watching the skin change to a healthy pink. She wriggled like a contortionist to untie her legs, but oh, so slowly, so as not to send the chair sprawling onto the floor.

She stood up, arching her sore back and flexing her hands. Slowly, she walked around the room reviewing its ravaged state: the open closet, Theo's clothes strewn on the floor, his Panama hat flattened and marred by Chang's dirty shoe print, the gaping maw of the empty safe, the chair where she had been imprisoned. She was an archaeologist studying a sacked city, all its treasures gone. She snapped off the light and shut the door.

Barefoot, Leah ran down the hall to An-li's room and knocked lightly on the door.

"It's me. . . May I come in?" cried Leah, not waiting for an answer.

An-li faced the wall, her body a white caterpillar underneath the sheet.

Poor thing, so exhausted she hadn't heard. Leah touched An-li's shoulder, shaking her gently. No response. With a mother's care, Leah lifted the sheet. She touched An-li's grey hair, sweeping it off her face, and stared at the cotton-clad body, so lonely. There were no signs of a struggle, no bruises or blood. Leah stroked An-li's cool skin. Her arms were so thin, her face careworn and wrinkled.

Leah crawled into bed, huddling close to An-li to breathe in her familiar smells—the coarse hair, the well-laundered shift, the witch hazel she used to lighten her skin. Curled against the familiar back, she wished she were a little girl again, that Theo had gone out for the evening and An-li had allowed her the privilege of sleeping in her bed. "Goodnight, sweet dreams," Leah whispered, planting a kiss on An-li's soft cheek, and laid her head against the pillow.

ONE of the servants found them. His howls of distress startled Leah out of her bottomless sleep. She sat bolt upright and screamed, "Be quiet." Then she realised where she was, what had happened. "It's all right. Calm down. Poor An-li died in her sleep."

The servant, a young boy, who had only been recently hired to do small jobs, nodded dumbly.

"I'll take care of this," she said.

The boy left. The nightmare of last night flooded back.

Tears welling, Leah pulled tentatively at An-li's stiff body until she was able to arrange her head facing southward, allowing An-li to begin her death journey. Kissing An-li tenderly on her rigid cheek, Leah said, in Cantonese, "Goodbye, First Mother." She felt so small, so abandoned, as she closed the door.

WITH a washcloth over her face, Leah rocked in the steamy bath like a wounded mermaid, scooping handfuls of water over her breasts, contemplating whether she had the courage to drown herself. She ducked her head under the water and willed her body to cease its need to breathe. Hopeless, spluttering and coughing, she resurfaced. A wave of nausea travelled through her as she recalled Chang's chilling words, "A country of one is always vulnerable."

Had she put the murderous idea into his mind? Had Chang gone straight from Theo's bedroom to An-li's? Or had he murdered poor darling An-li before he had crept into her own bedroom, plying her with whisky and late-night talk as if they were old friends? Deep in her soul, Leah knew *she* was guilty. Maybe she ought to walk through the crowded streets of Hong Kong ringing a bell like a leper, warning passers-by that she brought death and destruction to anyone dear to her. And what was she going to do with An-li's body? Could she coax a few of the servants to help bury An-li in the garden? Unlikely, and even if they did, one by one they would cease to turn up for work, too afraid of An-li's restless spirit. Reluctantly, she got out of the bath and resigned herself to asking Jonathan for his help.

"Jonathan?" said Leah wrapped in a towel, holding the telephone earpiece at an awkward angle, water from the bath dripping onto the floor.

"Leah, what's wrong? You sound terrible. Are you ill?"

"Jonathan, I need you. I can't explain over the telephone. Please come." She hung up the phone before he could reply.

JONATHAN knocked on the door. No answer. He rapped louder. Leah swung the door wide. He didn't know what he'd expected when she had called so urgently. He had run around the office issuing ridiculous orders and shoving papers at his clerk, then grabbed a hat and hailed a taxi. Leah was drawn and pale and her eyes had a startled look, but what alarmed him most was the thick band of red, raw skin around her wrists and yes, he shot a look at her legs, around her ankles.

"Are you all right? What's happened, Leah?" He caught her hands and examined her wrists. "What is all this?"

Leah disentangled her hands. "I don't want to go into that now." In a monotone, she said, "An-li is dead."

"Oh, Leah, I am so sorry," he said and hugged her tight.

Grateful that Jonathan had stopped asking questions, Leah allowed his soft neck kisses to turn into mouth kisses before chiding, "Not now." She led him down the long hall to the living room.

As they walked, Jonathan felt that in some obscure way Leah had changed. It nagged at him. It wasn't simply her grief. He watched her dress swish against her knees, her long legs take small steps, her arms close by her side. There was a containment he hadn't seen before, as if Leah were afraid to make a flamboyant movement that would draw attention, and instead had settled tentatively on the inhibitions of a Chinese woman. It worried at him, even as they sat on the sofa and his arm encircled her shoulders. "Leah," he asked quietly, "what are these marks, these abrasions? You must trust me."

She stared at her rope-burned wrists, then covered them with her hands, her face remote and uncommunicative. "Nothing, it doesn't matter now. An-li's death was so sudden. I need a doctor to certify that nothing . . . that she died of old age. Do you understand, Jonathan?"

"For God's sake, let me in, tell me. I would do anything to help you."

"I don't want an autopsy. It would upset her spirit."

"Why would she need an autopsy? She was old."

A look of sadness crossed Leah's face.

He retreated, stroked her hair. "Of course, I didn't mean to be unfeeling. I know a doctor, Clive Patterson. Have you met him?"

Leah shook her head.

"He's a good chap. He won't mind fudging a few details. People don't look too closely at a death of an old Chinese woman."

He saw Leah's look of distress return.

"I mean," he faltered, "he'll do the right thing. I'll call him now, if you like."

"Please," said Leah in a small voice, as if the asking hurt.

"Leah," he said, trying to be matter-of-fact and lawyer-like, "I think you had better change into a long-sleeved blouse and trousers. A doctor would notice your wrists and ankles."

"Yes, you're right," she said, kissing him lightly.

Defeated, he watched her walk away, overcome by her ability to shut him out.

CLIVE Patterson arrived just before lunch, having attended to his usual assortment of middle-aged female patients and their stomach complaints, which were a direct result of a life of ease and too much alcohol. He never censured their drinking, only warned them that too much alcohol could damage their complexions. The women always trilled appreciatively and invited him for cocktails—"That's all right, isn't it, doctor?"—they'd ask coquettishly. Most nights, he spent fulfilling these obligations, especially if their husbands were away. He had been in Hong Kong for nearly a year and was truly enjoying his Colonial experience. Patterson had heard rumours about the Kolbe girl and was intrigued by Hawatyne's hushed voice on the phone asking him for a favour.

Patterson settled into the chintz lounge chair, his legs extended, his hand around a welcomed G&T. "I need to ask a few questions, just to understand what occurred," he said.

"There's not much to tell," said Leah. "Everything was fine last night. We ate dinner . . ."

Patterson shot Leah a look of surprise as he pictured the two of them at the large rosewood table he had glimpsed as he came in, eating with chopsticks and talking in Chinese. It smacked of a certain exotic bohemianism. He gave an encouraging smile and hoped for a confidence.

"An-li," Leah continued, "complained that she felt tired, nothing more. I feel guilty that I didn't ask more questions and call a doctor, but she wasn't a believer in Western medicine. One of the servants found her in the morning. I . . . that is, she was a simple woman and I don't want to subject her to a lot of red tape. Jonathan," Leah reached out and held Jonathan's hand like a shy betrothed, "said you could help us."

"Well, why not?" said Patterson. "Why expose the poor old girl to the thrall of officialdom? We will list her as a refugee living in the Chinese quarter. No one here," he gestured around the room, "is going to query the death of another refugee. The place is bursting at the seams with them. Obviously she wasn't contagious, because she was living here and had not travelled to China recently."

"She hadn't been to China in years," said Leah.

Jonathan glanced quickly at Leah who increased the pressure on his hand. Patterson noticed the brief exchange. "If she didn't have any symptoms," he said smoothly, "it wasn't disease, more likely heart stoppage. These old Chinese just work till they drop, amazing really, probably was a lot older than she let on."

"No doubt you're right, Doctor," said Leah. "Heart stoppage. One doesn't think of the obvious in such situations."

"I'll need to make some telephone calls," Patterson said.

In the study, Patterson made a few phone calls, talking medically, colleague to colleague. He kept nodding benignly. Perched on the visitor's chair, Leah could detect no probing questions from the other end of the telephone.

An ambulance from the Chinese hospital arrived. Patterson said to Jonathan, "I'll sort this out. Take Miss Kolbe to the garden."

"It's for the best, Leah," said Jonathan. "It's out of our hands now."

Leah allowed herself to be led away to sit on a wicker chair and stare at the peonies. Several times Jonathan began sentences, only to be interrupted by Leah asking a servant to bring out sandwiches, fruit, tea, weak G&Ts.

"Stop it," he hissed. "Are you in danger? Is it over?"

She nodded and watched relief spread over his face as he leaned forward to kiss her.

"Ahem," said Patterson, strolling toward them, hands in his pockets. "I've filled out the death certificate. The Chinese hospital will dispose of the body."

"No," said Leah. "She can't go to a pauper's grave."

Patterson looked uncomfortable.

"Please, Jonathan. I want you to hire a mourner's hall, fill it with red and white banners. Red for happiness—she had lived a long time—and white for sorrow, my sorrow. I will get the Buddhists to arrange the rest."

Leah turned away from the two men and stared off into the middle distance. Already she could see herself, the lone mourner, on her hands and knees crawling toward An-li's coffin to show respect. Her heart felt very small. She rubbed at the cuffs of her white silk blouse. A hairline fleck of blood stained the silk.

"Do it," said Jonathan to a confused Patterson, who finally said, "I'll have the body released to me."

"Thank you," said Leah. "I am grateful to both of you. . . It was such a shock. You don't expect people to die just like that." She made an ineffectual finger snap.

"It happens," said Patterson. "I can prescribe something if you like, to ease your grief."

"No," she said dully.

"Quite right," said Patterson. "Something jolly then. Are you going to the Courtneys' party tonight? I'll get you an invite if you like. Mrs. Courtney is a particular friend of mine." His beefy, good-natured face lit up. What a coup, bringing the Kolbe girl, albeit with Hawatyne, to one of the best parties of the year. Mrs. Courtney—no, he corrected himself, Vanessa—would be impressed.

"I don't—" said Leah.

"Nonsense," said Patterson, "just what the doctor ordered," and he took a bite of the now-dry sandwich. Who cared what an old Chinese servant died of? Whatever it was, at least it wasn't contagious. Everybody knew servants led secret lives. He wasn't going to make a big hoo-ha. He had learned a great deal about discretion in a year. He was pleased he had become such a man of the world. His Harley Street practice, which he intended to set up when he returned to London, would benefit enormously from such a deft understanding of human nature. He accepted a G&T from the servant. "Chin-chin," he said.

Leah and Jonathan raised their glasses.

29

CELEBRATION

LEAH SAT ON her bed. She wished she hadn't said yes to the Courtneys' party. But if she didn't go, Jonathan would think she was brooding and hang around in his evening clothes trying to cheer her up or take her to bed. She caught a glimpse of her face in the bronze mirror. Her eyes looked different, cloudy or something. When she was nine, she regularly inspected her face in the mirror to see if her eyes had begun to slant, spending long minutes holding the skin corners of her eyes, stretching it to see if the world looked different. She watched herself walk to make certain she didn't imitate An-li's quick shuffle. Sometimes she had seen shadows hovering around the edge of the mirror, An-li's ghosts. She pulled at her eyelids. Nothing there, but it suited her; highlighted her cheekbones, hinted at the exotic.

Jonathan was surprised to see that Leah had chosen to wear a red silk cheongsam with a gold-threaded dragon running up the front of her dress. She had kohled her eyes in an upward slant. On each wrist she wore a thick gold bangle to camouflage the rope burns. "You look terrific," he said. "I'll have to keep my eye on you."

"Don't say that," said Leah.

"I meant it as a compliment," he said and kissed her cheek. "We don't have to go."

"No, you're right. Let's go and enjoy ourselves," said Leah.

JONATHAN watched Leah as she stood in the centre of a crush of people. She was smiling and exchanging pleasantries with Houghton, one of the colonial undersecretaries, in charge of what, he couldn't recall. Jonathan saw Houghton casting sly glances at Leah's thighs, clearly visible through the red cheongsam's skirt slits. My God, Leah looked stunning. He basked for a moment in the envy of the other men. Leah seemed all right, considering her shock at An-li's strange death. But the rope burns. What the devil had happened? She said she wasn't in any danger, but abrasions don't lie. He was certain that whatever had happened was related to the cursed Manchukuo trip. He should have insisted that she tell him the truth; instead, here they were at this stupid party. If only he could get her to leave Hong Kong. He had a plan for that. His mother had a cottage in the Cotswolds. He felt certain Leah would come to love the soft grey rain, the hills. After a while, they would marry, and then live in London. Well, maybe not right away. There should be a settling-in phase. His mother

would prefer that, and his sister, Cassandra, would enjoy helping Leah arrange a country wedding. No, Leah would hate
that. He tried to picture Cassandra and Leah together, sharing
confidences, talking about the latest fashions. Was a
cheongsam fashion? Maybe they should get married in Hong
Kong. A civil ceremony? Not ideal, but it would give Leah
stability and he'd ask to be given the Bombay office. They'd
start out someplace entirely new, together. No history for
either of them. India was full of art and antiquities. He'd let
her dabble in curios, if that's what she wanted. In time, Leah
would learn to love India and, he ardently hoped, himself.
Jonathan gave a shall-we-get-out-of-here look just as a strange
man in a rumpled lounge suit called "Leah" and waved. The
man pushed into the thick of the crush and deposited a kiss on
Leah's cheek.

"Benjamin, what on earth are you doing here?" said Leah.

"Wonderful to see you," said Eldersen, slipping an arm
around Leah's waist and skilfully extricating her from her
admirers. "I am so pleased you got out of Manchukuo safe and
well. I was on the USS *Panay*."

"You're all right?" said Leah, scanning for a limp or scars.

"Never better," said Eldersen. "I can't believe the stupidity
of those Jap aviators, firing on an American gunship. You
know the bastards even circled back to fire at us survivors in
the water. That didn't get reported. Hirohito and his cronies
said it was overzealousness. I believe everything the papers
said about Nanking." A haunted look flicked across his face.
"In fact, it was probably worse."

"Aren't you going to introduce us?" said Jonathan, pushing
forward to stand proprietarily at Leah's side.

"Jonathan Hawatyne, Benjamin Eldersen. Benjamin was in Manchukuo with us. He's a reporter," said Leah.

The two men shook hands, diffident, like new boys at school. Simultaneously they began to speak:

"How did you find Manchukuo?" said Jonathan.

"Have you known Leah long?" said Eldersen.

"Benjamin was fed a great deal of claptrap by blood-thirsty Japanese generals, and Jonathan is my lawyer. Jonathan disapproved of my going to Manchukuo," said Leah.

"He was right," said Benjamin.

"Yes," said Leah in a strained voice.

"How's your friend Sonia and An-li?" said Benjamin trying to steer the conversation his way.

"Sonia," said Jonathan, "went from Hsingking to—what was it, Leah? Tibet or Korea—with some Russian engineer?"

"Tibet. Sonia went to Tibet."

"Terrible woman." said Jonathan. "She didn't even return home with Leah to Hong Kong, left her in the lurch just like that." He snapped his fingers and looked severe. "A very strange sort of friend if you ask me, Leah."

Leah gave a hapless shrug. "Sonia was always enigmatic. It was part of her charm."

Eldersen gave Leah a cold stare.

"I mean, she's been gone for some time. I've begun to miss her," said Leah easily, daring Eldersen to ask any more questions.

"An-li is staunch," said Eldersen.

Leah nodded, turning her face away as if scanning the crowd for an old friend. Hope Cuthbert waved noncommittally. A waiter moved smoothly through the crowd collecting empty glasses. He took Leah's empty glass from her and replaced it with champagne.

Jonathan whispered into Eldersen's ear. "An-li died this morning. Heart attack."

Douglas Courtney, flushed from drink and still not used to the heat, even after three years in Hong Kong, stood in his immaculate dinner jacket with his wife, Vanessa, by his side. They had argued before their party over Vanessa's profligate spending. "Surely," Douglas had said, "even this crowd couldn't drink eight dozen bottles of French champagne at one party. It's a waste to give them the good stuff. People don't care what they drink after the first few." Vanessa had replied, acidly, "People expect us to entertain in a certain style. Even you should be able to understand that." They hadn't spoken since.

Douglas rapped on his champagne flute with a spoon and called everyone to attention. He said very nice things about Vanessa on the occasion of their tenth wedding anniversary. Vanessa smiled modestly like a good wife, pleased that she had arranged for Clive Patterson to come around the next morning when she knew Douglas would be sleeping off a very bad hangover. It seemed somehow fitting to begin a discreet affair after the first ten years of marriage. The timing was just right.

People clapped, drank, and toasted. Skilfully, Jonathan steered Leah into the centre of the well-wishers. Eldersen circled, determined to uncouple Leah from Jonathan's side, but he was defeated by the seating arrangements and the long dinner. As he passed Leah's chair, Eldersen leaned over and said into her ear, "I'll come to see you tomorrow," then walked hurriedly away before she could refuse.

When Jonathan took Leah home, he was overcome by how

tired and washed-out she looked. They sat in her living room drinking port. "I've gone off whisky. It upsets my stomach," she said.

"I'm sorry I made you go. It was a bad idea," said Jonathan.

"It doesn't matter. It was all right. It was odd celebrating an unhappy marriage."

"What?"

"The Courtneys don't like each other very much."

"You could have fooled me. Douglas said he would do it all again."

"People lie to themselves all the time."

"May I stay?" he said. "You shouldn't be by yourself, not after . . ."

He watched her face closing down, her mouth set in a straight line, her eyes veiled and determined.

"I'll be fine after a good night's sleep."

"Leah, we aren't the Courtneys."

"No, we're not. It might help if we were," she said, and kissed him lightly on the mouth. "Good night, Jonathan. See yourself out."

He watched her back, her high heels in her hand as she padded across the oriental carpet, the split skirt alternately flashing a delicious thigh, the silk wrinkling across her bottom. She tore at his heart: he wanted to plead "let me stay" and "let me in," even as he walked down the darkened hallway and out the door, closing it with a thud. Who the hell was Eldersen? What had really happened in Manchukuo? What about *their* future?

30

THE
ORIENTALIST

$\int$ LEAH RAN HER fingers over the photograph of
herself at age four or five, with An-li. It was a can-
did street shot, cardboard backed. A rickshaw, its
shadow almost touching An-li's feet, stood to one side. She was
in An-li's arms and was pointing at something. Theo, probably, who might have been aiming the camera, although there
was no hint of his silhouette on the road. She was dressed in a
smocked pinafore, white sun hat and leather sandals. An-li
wore her usual white tunic and black silk trousers. Her hair
had been vivid black, pulled back from her face to reveal a
high, unlined forehead. The photographer had focused on her
sunny blonde four-year-old face, well shaded by the hat. They
must have been staring into the sun, because the camera had
caught An-li with her eyes half closed. Leah attempted to

decipher An-li's expression. But An-li's face was indistinct. She couldn't tell if An-li was smiling or simply gazing, tight-lipped, straight ahead.

Leah rummaged around in the desk drawer and located the magnifying glass. Enlarged, An-li's face remained murky, her expression indecipherable. Leah searched her memory for that day, but its very ordinariness, an outing with her amah, left no trace.

The photograph was the only sentimental object Leah found amongst An-li's possessions: clothes, herbs, and iron teapot. She asked the houseboy to dispose of the clothes and to store the herbs and the teapot in the kitchen. The photograph she slipped into her skirt pocket.

She was aware of its presence throughout the day. Its hard edge bit into her thigh as she walked around the house with a pad of paper and a pen inventorying everything: the furniture, the scrolls, the porcelain, the bronzes. She wore a pair of white cotton gloves. The thought of Chang roaming freely, touching her things, filled her with a white anger that made her fingers itch to take the derringer from its secret place. To ward off her murderous rage, she inventoried.

Sprawled on the floor, she ran her hands over the dining-room table with its incised frieze and discovered a tiny flaw where someone had inexpertly glued a sliver of wood that had broken off. She wondered how Theo had missed it; he had always been meticulous, collecting only the most perfect pieces. The damage might have been caused by one of the ser-vants polishing it too vigorously; or might she as a child have run headlong into the table, chipping it? But she had never chased around the house because Theo disliked rambunctious play. He had been quite unable to run. Instead, he had taught her to step lightly through the house and to display a reverence toward his objects. She resented them at times, was jealous of the care and attention he lavished on them. It was like trying to live up to the perfections of an older brother or sister. Of course now, there was no competition. She had won.

To the casual observer, the damage to the table was imperceptible, but she wrote on the pad: *one quarter inch chip on left hand corner of the frieze reglued in modern times, unlikely to require refinishing, does not detract from value.* The pad of paper was full of similar notations.

The doorbell chimed. "An-li—" Leah began, then corrected herself, calling out in a thick voice, "I'll get it."

Dressed in baggy trousers and a bright green short-sleeved shirt, Eldersen grinned his jumbled-tooth smile. Leah stared at him blankly.

"Don't look like that. I said I wanted to come see you. You didn't say no."

"I'm sorry, I forgot," she said and let him in.

On the way to the study, he glanced into the living room and whistled, "You've got quite a museum here. All that's missing are hordes of school children in smelly blazers putting their sticky hands on glass cases and shrieking."

"There aren't any glass cases."

He stood in the entrance to the living room, entranced by an ancient celadon pot. "No, that's what makes it remarkable. Must be a small fortune in there."

Rattled, she said, "That's not the point. It's history and art of the ages."

He gave a good-natured shrug. Leah recalled his snide Marie Antoinette comment even as he answered, "Well, if you say so."

Leah directed Eldersen to the visitor's chair, but he politely remained standing waiting for her to sit. She masked her annoyance as she slid into the massive desk chair, into the welcoming space the imposing desk created between them. She took off her gloves, laying them on the polished blackwood. An-li's photograph cut into her leg. She repositioned it, her fingers fiddling against its firm surface. Fervently, she wished she could remember that day. She was surprised when Eldersen began to talk and had to remind herself to pay attention. Eldersen was an ambitious reporter. If he scented a story . . .

"Newspapermen are the biggest gossips in the world," Eldersen began. "I heard about An-li's death. I am so sorry. You must miss her terribly."

"It's kind of you to care. She was very special."

Eldersen nodded and ran an investigative eye over the antiquities on display. "That's nice," he said pointing to the *tsun*. "It's an owl, isn't it?"

Leah explained a little about the *tsun*, while fighting down a panicky fear that Eldersen, crazy as it seemed, was involved with Chang and that his interest in the *tsun* was a sign.

"You are an expert," said Eldersen. "The British Museum could use you."

She gave a deprecatory shrug. "It's a business. One has to know these things to understand an object's worth, its value." Interesting; despite everything, she could rise to the occasion. An-li had never liked the business. She had had a horror of dead things.

Eldersen got up to have a better look at the *tsun.* Then, non-chalantly, he reseated himself on a corner of the desk. He took Leah's hand in his and spoke quietly. "Information is my currency, the facts, what one knows is true. For example, a reporter friend of mine whom I met again in a Hong Kong bar told me about a Russian man in Hsingking who was executed for collaborating with the Soviets. Now what was his name?" Eldersen studied the ceiling as if the answer were written there.

Leah focused on the *tsun,* trying to determine if the blemish Chang had made with his fingers was visible from where they sat.

"Vasily, Vasilic, anyway something like that. But the really interesting bit was that this man was associated with a Russian woman found stabbed to death and *abandoned* in the main train station. The police, your friend Amakasu in fact, claimed it was a simple case of robbery gone wrong. Unfortunately, as we both know, nothing," said Eldersen, pausing to let the words sink in, "is simple in Manchukuo. It was Sonia, wasn't it?" He squeezed Leah's hand sympathetically, looking deep into her grey eyes.

There was a time, after she had finished school and before Theo died, that she had a recurring dream of standing in the wet sand of Deep Water Bay while an enormous wave surged, sucking the sand from beneath her feet and dragging her out to the vast ocean beyond. She could almost taste the salt water in her mouth.

"Then I heard a really bizarre story. One of those high-ranking eunuchs did a bunk with the puppet emperor's priceless jewels and collection of objets d'art. Someone claimed they saw him in fancy dress, in a Western suit and goatee, at the railway station about the time poor Sonia was murdered. Probably a wild rumour or a malicious lie."

She allowed one hand to remain in Eldersen's as she slowly drew out An-li's photograph from her pocket with the other. She placed it face-up on the desk. "That's me when I was little. Doesn't An-li look young? I think my father took the picture."

He examined the photograph, holding it up to the light. "You were a beautiful child."

"See how An-li's face is in shade. You can't tell what she is thinking. Theo isn't in the photograph, but you can feel his presence. A shadow over the proceedings."

"Yes," he said cautiously, waiting for her to drop more clues. "Tell me about Theo."

"Sonia is in Tibet. As I told you."

"You can talk to me. Tell me the truth. It won't go further than this room," said Eldersen, meaning every word. Distrust showed at the down-turned edges of her mouth, or was that fear? He stroked her soft cheek with the back of his hand. "It might help you to talk about it." He watched her grey eyes as they flitted over his face.

"Who do you take after, your mother or your father?" she asked.

He was taken aback. "Neither; I'm my own person."

"That's what we would all like to think. The truth is different."

"Oh well, truth. My mother, she did the best she could. She stood up for herself. And you, Leah?"

"My father was notorious. You can ask anybody in Hong Kong. They'll tell you. I'm just like him."

"I don't think that's true, Leah. . ."

"You don't know me." She stared into the picture of her younger self. "An-li knew me, maybe she even divined what would happen. There was a fortune teller in Manchukuo, an old man with a very young wife. She refused to tell me what she foresaw. If I had known, I would have sent her away." She brushed her fingers lightly across An-li's face.

"I'm sure you would have done anything to protect her."

"Yes, but I didn't." She sighed deeply and whispered, "That's the truth."

"What happened in Manchukuo?"

"If I tell you, will you promise not to write about it?"

Eldersen dropped his eyes. "Maybe."

"Not good enough, Ben. Are you a real journalist?"

"Mostly, but as I said that night in Manchukuo, people pay for information. They pay well."

"Now we're getting somewhere. Money. How do they know if what you tell them is true?"

"They trust me, I suppose. I've never lied to them."

Leah considered confiding in him. Maybe he could make sense of everything. He'd been around, seen people at their worst. Together they could sift through the wrong turns, make sense of the chaos, the deaths. But it was the people at the other end of the line that nagged. Who were the shadowy *them*? What would Eldersen do with the information? Would it be a hold over her?

"Sonia once told me trust is a very complicated thing."

"I expect you're right." His thick eyebrows knotted together as his expression became serious and urgent. "But sometimes you have to choose a side. The Japanese once tried to verify if a man they wanted was loyal to them or a double agent. Somehow they took a picture of him through the keyhole of his hotel room, the chair having been strategically placed beforehand."

"It must have been a small room," Leah said.

Eldersen smiled. "He was an unpaid spy and the room was tiny."

"Much more believable," said Leah, nodding her approval.

"Anyway, they showed the photograph to one man who said yes, he was the person who was consorting with the Chinese guerrilla movement. Then just to be sure, they sent it to another to verify the verifier. Guess who?"

"Ben, how on earth would I know?"

"Your mate Amakasu. He said it wasn't the chap. Adamant, he was. Later, and I don't want to dwell on this part, the Jap police caught a member of the guerrilla movement and he confessed with a bit of help that they used look-alikes. Look-alikes, imagine that."

"Amakasu is a monster. I hate your stories. No one ever turns out to be good in them."

"Me, too," said Eldersen sadly as he unfolded a Japanese press cutting. "You the original?" He pointed at her creased face as she stood next to Amakasu.

"I doubt there are two of me," she said dryly.

"You are an original, but one does like to check."

"I'm not going to tell you anything, Ben. I might have, but not now."

"I wasn't going to threaten to run it in the local press or anything nasty like that."

"I think you should leave now," said Leah, rising abruptly and striding to the door.

"Listen to me," he said, his hands waggling in frustration. "I wouldn't hurt you for the world. I . . ."

"Yes, but you've thought about it."

"What are you going to do, Leah?"

"Stay here. I trade. It's what Hong Kong is all about. It's what I do."

"People spend their time killing time here. The war is going to spread. The Japs want Hong Kong. It won't pass you by. Nanking is only the beginning of the murder, rape, slaughter. There's nothing here to hold you. The others are stupid enough to believe the British can't be beaten. They think that the good life of little work, lots of gin and parties, stale gossip, and trite affairs will go on forever." He put his arm around her and pulled her close. "Come with me. With your knowledge of the language, your contacts, we could work together. We'd be quite a team."

"No. I don't want to leave. Hong Kong is my home, my world. I don't want to trade in secrets, to spy. It is a kind of corruption; each step takes you further then you want to go."

"We all dabble in corruption sooner or later." He kissed her lightly, then let his arms drop to his side. "Do think about it. I'm staying at the Peninsular."

"Are *they* paying for it?" asked Leah, moving away.

He smiled sadly and shook his head. "If you change your mind . . . I'm sorry I showed you the clipping."

"I've seen it before. It doesn't matter."

Eldersen stared. "Ah, Leah, you have become such an Orientalist, caught up in your own history, your own intrigues." He took a last look at the room, taking in the ornate furniture, the *tsun,* and the display cabinet lined in silk, a pale backdrop against which delicate porcelain and animated ivory figurines nestled. "It suits you," he said. "But given time, you might become just another old Chinese woman with a white clay face, a cloisonné finger guard, and a slash of red on your once-enticing mouth."

"I'll take that chance. Age is venerated here. Take care of yourself," she said. She kissed him on the lips, then rested her head momentarily against his chest.

"I'll miss you," he said.

"Me, too. Goodbye."

Leah tucked her arm into his and walked him to the front door.

On the street, Eldersen turned to look back at the large domineering house. Leah was gone and the door was tightly shut. He had bungled things. If he had simply focused on recruiting her, hadn't brought up the intrigues in Manchukuo, kept his emotions out of it . . . With the right arguments, she would have come around. He made his way down the steep road to the Peak Tram Station, cursing himself and plotting his next strategic move. He ran over a number of plausible stories he could offer those in charge. He settled on: *Miss Kolbe is actively considering our offer.* It wasn't a total lie. He took his seat on the Peak Tram and waited for the doors to close.

LEAH retraced her steps to the study and sank heavily into the leather armchair. She stared at the photograph of An-li and herself. What was it about the photograph that drew her so? A day of innocence captured in black and white, a childhood Eden— her devoted amah and her loving father recording the event.

The *tsun* regarded her with its stony eyes. Once, she had caught Theo speaking to it, as if it were alive. The bird had remained silent, staring back at him in haughty disdain. She recalled how Chang had run his hand proprietarily over it. Perhaps that's when she had decided to deceive him, to change the terms of the deal. But she wasn't certain. Betrayal didn't exist until after the event, she thought. Until the moment when she said to Chang's face that she had had come away empty-handed, she was never certain that she would attempt it. The opportunity had presented itself and she had acted. It was a reflex action. It was all part of her training, her education. She shouldn't blame herself.

She drew on the cotton gloves, picked up the *tsun,* and set it gently down beside An-li's picture. Her gaze flicked from one to the other. "You understand," she told the owl, and rubbed at Chang's fingerprint on its wing. The spot remained. She pressed An-li's picture into the frame of Theo at fourteen. The photograph was only three quarters the size of Theo's portrait. His dark eyes peeped over the top of An-li's head, watchful and on guard. She lay her head down on the desk and let the misery wash over her.

When she raised her head, the study was in darkness. She switched on the desk lamp. The shadowy room comforted her. She was home. She reached underneath her chair and untaped the Altar of the Moon Jade. She caressed it in her hand. Theo would have been pleased. It was a matter of principle that one always took a commission. She had hers, and it filled her with hope.

SOURCES

I AM INDEBTED to numerous writers who helped me to understand the vibrant world of Leah Kolbe's Hong Kong, her appreciation of Chinese art, the political and military intrigues of Manchukuo, and the devastating effects of the Japanese war against China. Needless to say, any errors and misinterpretations are mine. In particular I would like to acknowledge the following works: Nigel Cameron, *Hong Kong: The Cultured Pearl*, 1978; Iris Chang, *The Rape of Nanking: The Forgotten Holocaust of World War II*, 1997; Caroline Courtauld and Mary Holdsworth, *The Hong Kong Story*, 1997; Yui Kong Chu, *The Triads as Business*, 2000; Frank Clune, *Sky High to Shanghai*, 1948; Geoffrey C. Gunn, *Encountering Macau: A Portuguese City–State on the Periphery of China, 1557–1999*, 1996; W. J. F. Jenner (trans.), *From Emperor to Citizen: The Autobiography of Aisin-Gioro Pu Yi*, 1987; Evan King, *Asia for the Asiatics*, 1945; Paul Kramer (ed.), *The Last Manchu: The Autobiography of Henry Pu Yi, Last Emperor of China*, 1967; Pan Ling, *Old Shanghai: Gangsters in Paradise*, 1983; National Palace Museum, *Masterpieces in the National Palace Museum (A series of catalogues on Bronze Mirrors, Chinese Jade, Writing Materials, Chinese Miniature Crafts)*, 1969–1971; Mary Gardner Neill, *The Communion of Scholars: Chinese Art at Yale*, 1982; Jonathan Porter, *Macau, the Imaginary City: Culture and*

Society, 1557 to the Present, 1996; Brian Powers, *The Puppet Emperor: The Life of Pu Yi, Last Emperor of China,* 1986; Han Suyin, *A Mortal Flower,* 1966; Leang-li T'ang, *The Puppet State of "Manchukuo,"* 1935; Weng Wango, *The Palace Museum, Peking: Treasures of the Forbidden City,* 1982; Barbara-Sue White (ed.), *Hong Kong: Somewhere Between Heaven and Earth,* 1996; Westel Woodberry Willoughby, *The Sino–Japanese Controversy and the League of Nations,* 1935; Frances Wood, *No Dogs and Not Many Chinese: Treaty Port Life in China 1843–1942,* 1998; Lin Yutang, *A Leaf in the Storm: A Novel of War-Swept China,* 1942.